Sapphires & Secrets

Book Two in The Magical Papillon Mystery Series

Sabine Frisch

Thinking Dog Publishing

Contents

Reviews for Other Books

Writing as Sabine Frisch:

<u>The Cannabis Preacher Series</u>

GoodReads Review: "The subject matter and title intrigued me having been around some of these sorts of dealings. From the beginning of this book had my attention; I picked it up to "just have a look" and suddenly found myself eight chapters into it. As the main characters were introduced, I started to feel that I had met all of these people before.Read on as Connor, the main protagonist, battles his demons up and down the shady side of Wall Street. There are just so many moving parts for any one control freak to manage. The greatest deal of all time starts to get out of control but every time he seems about to fall, he finds a way to land on his feet.We keep guessing:• Is he our hero or his own worst enemy?• Is this a runaway train or a slow-motion train wreck?• Will he end up in Financial Heaven, Regulatory Hell, or just a Fool's Paradise?Read to the end of this fun little tale and wait for the movie to come out."

Writing as Sabine Keevil

The SoundMaster Romance Series

<u>**Guitars & Cadillacs**</u> (Semi-finalist in the BookLife Fiction Prize Contest, 2023)

Editorial Reviews:

"Sabine Keevil has constructed the perfect fantasy romance in her novel Guitars & Cadillacs, the latest in the Soundmaster Romance Series... At the same time, she appeals to that part of us that longs to see the behind-the-scenes footage of celebrity lives."-Rachel Jagt, Rambles.net

"Ms. Keevil is a good storyteller, I'll say that right out. She has a good grasp of storyline, she's succinct and to the point, her characters are engaging, and she knows where she's taking them."-Laurie Joulie, Takecountryback.com

"Guitars & Cadillacs is the entertaining story of the fire and fury stirred up by the relationship between Reanne (Parker) and fictional country superstar Colton Wright...Offering surprise twists, intrigue and mystery...Keep turning the pages to see what happens next in the well-paced plot."- Pat Mandia, Country Weekly, the world's #1 Selling Country Music Magazine

<u>**Foolish Pride**</u>

Editorial Reviews:

"Keevil spins an engaging romantic tale and does a credible job of taking us backstage into the minds, lives and hearts of her characters."

-Pat Mandia, Country Weekly Magazine

"Canadian author Sabine Keevil (Guitars & Cadillacs) has done it again -- she revisits the world of SoundMaster with originality, humour and a large share of romantic spirit.

One of Keevil's strengths as a writer is her ability to create realistic characters, even in the midst of a story about the world of big money show business. She is unpretentious and honest and her characters are likeable from the beginning...Even in two nights, the characters became beloved -- a sure sign of a good story." -Rachel Jagt, Rambles - a cultural arts review magazine

Chapter One

"I 've been having nightmares about this opening for weeks," Matthew Turner confessed, draining his glass of punch. "Don't even ask."

Daniel Whitman, director of the Rosewood Hollow Museum, chuckled, shaking Matthew's hand as the last guests filed out, still buzzing with excitement. "As did we all."

Matthew blew a hard breath and rolled his tense shoulders as the last guests left the museum. Their fading chatter hung in the air, replaced now by an unsettling silence. He stole a glance at the Royal Veritas Sapphire, a legendary jewel recently found and the focus of this gala. Its brilliance now cast an eerie glow in the dimly lit hall.

"Katelyn, you can set the alarm now," Daniel called out. "I'll walk Dr. Turner out."

A nervous swallow escaped Katelyn as she surveyed the imposing chrome security panel. She'd only been on the job for a few weeks.

Katelyn's heart pounded in her chest, mimicking the countdown on the security panel. Her damp fingers fumbled on the keypad, each misplaced keystroke a hammer blow against her already frayed nerves. Ninety seconds to secure the museum, Daniel had emphasized, five times. Five times! It felt like a lifetime as she desperately punched in the code, praying for the satisfying beep of confirmation.

Silence. Relief flooded her. With a triumphant swing of her purse, Katelyn stepped out into the night, blissfully unaware of the single unlit panel on the massive shiny alarm board.

Hours later, when only the streetlights along the major thoroughfares remained lit, and most of the respectable citizens of Rosewood Hollow were safely in bed, a plain dark van pulled up in the alley behind the museum. Three figures quickly exited the van, their forms swallowed by the inky darkness of the alley. With practiced ease, they scaled a drainpipe, their movements silent and efficient. A stray sliver of moonlight glinted off their masks, briefly revealing a chilling glimpse of their determined eyes. These weren't amateurs; they moved with the practiced grace of seasoned professionals, their every step a testament to their years of honing their craft in the shadows.

The architect who designed the Rosewood Hollow Museum of Art and History insisted on a huge curved skylight to provide the artwork in the main gallery with the maximum amount of natural light. If anyone had been there, they would have heard the crash and tinkle of the skylight glass breaking and hushed clipped commands between the three figures.

They approached the museum's elaborate security systems, where Katelyn had stood only hours ago, arming a labyrinth of sensors and alarms designed to deter even the most daring of thieves. With a deftness born of countless rehearsals, the intruders circumvented each obstacle, never tripping a wire or activating a sensor. Their nimble fingers, encased in gloves designed to leave no fingerprints, danced gracefully over keypads and control panels.

Laser alarms crisscrossed their path, casting intricate webs of light that seemed impossible to traverse. However, to these intruders, they were little more than fragile threads. With a choreography of movement that resembled a delicate dance, they ducked, sidestepped, and weaved their way through the maze of lasers, the beams parting for them like parted curtains.

As they progressed deeper into the heart of the museum, the tension grew palpable, hanging in the air like an oppressive weight. The once-peaceful corridors, adorned with priceless artifacts and centuries-old paintings, now bore witness to the intrusion of shadowy figures, and the very walls seemed to whisper their silent disapproval.

Finally, they found the one object they were interested in - a raised glass case in the center of the main exhibit hall. Their leader, the tallest of the intruders, waited, then nodded at them briefly when they were all in position. Their communication needed no words. From here on in, speed would be of the essence. When each of them nodded in turn, he raised a small hammer and smashed the glass case. Within sat a dark blue sapphire, and even though the object lighting had been turned off for the night, it glowed with a deep inner fire.

When the sapphire left the weight-bearing sensor, the museum's security klaxons and horns began blaring at once, proclaiming the security breach for all to hear.

The leader of the group closed his gloved hand around the sapphire, shoved it into a velvet bag he carried, and nodded again to his comrades.

"Go now," he mouthed, and they sprinted down the halls, not caring about breaching the security lasers now, not worrying about anything except getting out of the museum, into the back alley where their van awaited, and off into the night.

$$\infty$$

Matthew woke with a start. What had disrupted his happy dream of a walk through the Rosewood Hollow Christmas market with his girlfriend Sarah, he didn't quite know, except... Except his phone was blaring with an obnoxious ringtone on the nightstand, and refused to stop.

Having experienced nocturnal prank calls on occasion — an occupational hazard for a history professor he had often jestingly informed Sarah – he was no stranger to unwelcome interruptions. The ringing persisted until Matthew, growing increasingly irritated, finally decided to answer it.

He responded with a choice expletive that most of his students might find comical, only to be met with eerie silence.

"What," he demanded impatiently, casting a weary glance at the bedside clock. *For heaven's sake, what could you possibly want at three-thirty in the morning?* he silently added.

"Matthew... Matthew? You have to get over here."

"Who is this – Daniel?" Matthew sat up, his curiosity piqued. "Daniel?"

"Yes," the museum director replied, his voice choking with anxiety. "Get over here. We've been robbed."

Chapter Two

Pixie zoomed around the backyard in a joyous game of chase with the children. Cory, the typically disinterested and nonchalant teenager, held a bright red tennis ball, intermittently teasing the tiny papillon while racing through the overgrown weeds of the wintry garden.

Sarah Anderson drew the kitchen curtains and brought her phone closer to her face.

"I love how they can just play and run with Pixie out here in the yard," she said to her friend Lily over the phone. "Michael is still trying to get Cory and Emma to Baltimore now and then, but even he's realizing he's fighting a losing battle."

"Tell me about it," Lily replied. She owned the local bookstore in Rosewood Hollow and had quickly become Sarah's closest friend during the few months Sarah had lived in the town. "Even his ex-girlfriend told him that Rosewood Hollow was a better place for those kids to live."

"Under the influence of ghosts," Sarah muttered, forcing the memory away. "What have you heard about Katelyn lately?"

"Still around," Lily said with a chuckle. "As you know, I couldn't offer her a job at the store here, but thanks to Michael, she landed at the museum, and from what I hear, she's loving it."

"Yeah, Matthew told me he put in a good word for her," Sarah said, her voice unconsciously brightening at the mention of the local history professor, which didn't escape Lily's notice.

"Sarah, I can practically hear you glowing over the phone, so spill the details – right now. How are things with the delicious, charming professor?"

Sarah's call waiting chimed insistently, something she didn't usually entertain, except for Matthew. Matthew had a standing invitation and permission to interrupt any call.

"I'd love to share, but it seems he's calling me right now."

"Sarah, don't you dare—"

"Sorry, Lily, gotta go."

Just as she was about to end her call, a text from Matthew came through. *Call me now – it's vitally important.*

Matthew wasn't one to toss around the phrase vitally important lightly.

Sarah raised her finger to dial, but the doggie door gently flapped at that moment, and Pixie gracefully hopped through it and sat before her.

There's trouble.

"Thank you, Pixie - I figured that."

It had taken her a while to admit to even her closest friends that she and Pixie had a unique form of communication.

Sarah could hear Pixie in her mind and vice versa. As far as they could discern, Pixie's previous owner had transferred, well, something or other, at the time of her death, granting Pixie the ability to communicate with other supernatural beings, ghosts, and select humans.

Sarah had adopted Pixie after her divorce when she moved to Rosewood Hollow. If she had to describe her relationship with the intelligent little Papillon, it would be, still figuring it out. But they shared an unbreakable bond, and a recent brush with the ever-present specter of death had taught Sarah just how deep that bond went.

"What's going on?" Sarah asked.

Katelyn – the museum – I think she's in trouble.

Sarah stopped, feeling Pixie's dark eyes on her.

"Alright, what's going on with Katelyn then?"

Just then, her phone rang again, and she picked it up.

"Matthew?"

"Thank God – where are you?"

No, how are you, what's going on, are you interruptible, is this a good time – this was serious.

"I was about to call you back. What's happening that has you so frazzled?"

"The museum was robbed last night."

"What? You were there – how..."?

"And there's only one thing that's been taken."

"Oh no, don't say it."

"The sapphire, Sarah, they took the sapphire."

Sarah's hand with the phone dropped into her lap. For months, there had been only one topic for Matthew – his role on the committee to bring the Royal Veritas Sapphire exhibit to Rosewood Hollow Museum. She and the children had endured countless lectures about the history and significance of the sapphire. She'd tuned out his voice so often as he went on about it.

"Pixie?"

The kitchen door slammed, and her son Cory came strolling in, the red ball still in his hand.

"What's the matter, you tired? You ran out on me. Worried about losing or what?'

Then he saw his mother at the kitchen table, her head in her hand, and he came to her.

"Mom – is something wrong?"

Sarah managed a thin smile.

"Looks like it, Cory. I'm talking to Matt. The museum's been broken into."

"Whoa. The museum? What about the sapphire? You know how he worries about it, how valuable that is. Is the sapphire...?"

Cory heard Matthew's voice through the phone and took it out of his mother's hand.

"Matthew? Is the sapphire...?"

Then he sat at the table across from Sarah and put the phone down between them slowly.

"They took it," he said softly. "And everybody's blaming Katelyn."

After the divorce, when Sarah had finally settled in Rosewood Hollow, and was still battling her own demons, along with the very real ghosts in her own house, her ex, Michael, had felt it necessary to visit, bringing along his latest girlfriend – Katelyn. Except raven-haired Katelyn, an avid gamer closer to Cory's age than Sarah's, had surprised them all by displaying a toughness even she didn't realize she had, helping to deal with kidnappers, ghosts, and a summoned dark energy that could destroy anything in its path.

"Nobody is as strong as Sarah," she had told Michael, "You'd be a fool to take those kids away."

Michael had acquiesced at that time, but their relationship was never the same, and Katelyn had decided to stay in Rosewood Hollow.

"What about Katelyn?" Sarah asked, raising the phone to her ear again.

"You know," Matthew said, the stress evident in his voice. "New in town, a carefree lifestyle, a new job, no money – they think she's good for it."

"Who is 'they'?" Sarah wanted to know.

"Museum management, and unfortunately, the police," Matthew said. "I gather there's some evidence—"

"I don't care about the evidence. Katelyn didn't do it, full stop."

"Don't be so—"

"And you should know better than even suggesting that, Matthew Turner. You were here when Katelyn – when she stood with us—"

"While Amelia turned into — whatever that was," Matthew finished. They'd all stood open-mouthed as their resident 'harmless' ghost turned into a deadly specter. "But beyond that, you really don't know anything about her."

"But she..."

"I don't want to believe it either."

Cory, who had heard the entire conversation through the speaker, shook his head. "She didn't do it," he said, with the absolute confidence only a sixteen-year-old could muster.

Sarah raised her hand and let it fall into her lap once more. While Cory, who had been difficult and withdrawn after his father's departure, had managed to shed the tough teenager shell he had retreated into, becoming a good student, an avid basketball captain, and a sought-after youth coach in Rosewood Hollow, he was still just sixteen.

"Cory - I know you like Katelyn..."

"I also know money doesn't mean much to her – how she ended up with Dad, I don't know. But stealing that sapphire for money – that's so not her."

Then maybe she didn't steal it for money, Sarah thought, looking down at Pixie. The papillon's dark gaze remained on hers, unwavering.

That sapphire has – abilities. Matthew knows that. And anyone doing half an hour of research would as well.

"That sapphire is more than just a pretty blue stone, isn't it," her son interrupted.

"Actually – you see..."

"Mom, you totally suck at lying. Any time I see you and Pixie stare at each other like that, I know that the two of you are having some sort of discussion."

"Technically, not a discussion," Sarah blew out a big breath that ballooned out her cheeks. "That sapphire is – exceptionally valuable."

"And so are the antique jewelry exhibit and the early gold coin exhibit. I've been helping Matthew catalog some of it. Besides, Matthew said, the sapphire got stolen—not, the sapphire and most of the gold coins. So?"

"Yes," Sarah finally acquiesced. "The sapphire has some – very unique properties..."

She was saved from finishing her sentence as the back door opened again, and Emma came breezing in. A few years Cory's junior, everyone, including Sarah, still thought of her as little Emma because she wore her heart on her sleeve and couldn't hide her emotions if she tried. And just now, her entire face glowed with a strange excitement.

"Lily just found out the museum was broken into." She saw her mother and brother and quirked her mouth, "You guys already know?"

"Matthew just told us." Sarah reached for her daughter and gave her a quick hug. "Good day?"

Helping Lily at the Rosewood Hollow bookstore was not a job for her little bookworm, it was more like a reward, one she even got paid for.

"Shelving, new shipments, customers - you know." Emma shrugged and tried unsuccessfully to hide the book bag with her own purchases behind her back. "So, what's this about the museum and Katelyn?"

Many people in Rosewood Hollow would repeat that question over the remainder of that cold and snowy February afternoon: What's this about Katelyn and the sapphire she stole?

Sarah's glance automatically drifted through the kitchen window to the abandoned neighboring house. The Jenkins, who had lived there, had been such a lovely, helpful older couple – right up to the moment they turned out to be ruthless treasure hunters.

"It's still innocent until proven guilty, right," Sarah said to Emma and Cory." I have to check into this Katelyn thing. Why is everyone instantly pointing fingers?".

A poor girl — a priceless gem — easy pickings. It made a quick, satisfying narrative. But Sarah knew more: she knew the truth behind the Royal Veritas Sapphire.

Bumping grocery bags on the street, two neighbors gossiped, eyes darting towards Sarah's house. A pointed finger confirmed it - Rosewood Hollow's rumor mill churned faster than a gossip rag, and with about as much truth.

Chapter Three

"She's an easy target," Sarah confided in Matthew later that evening. He'd just arrived after work, and they were enjoying the quiet routine of making dinner together, something they'd adopted in recent months.

"She showed up out of the blue last summer, with a wealthy Baltimore guy who got kidnapped for a day," Sarah continued. "Then she just... stayed. She hasn't held down a steady job, lives in a boarding house, and doesn't exactly live the settled life they'd prefer."

"Don't forget the motorcycle," Matthew added dryly and fed her a piece of cut bell pepper from the salad. "Apparently, a very large motorcycle is—"

"Scandalous,' Sarah finished, rolling her eyes. "Thank goodness for my trusty station wagon."

Matthew came around the solid wood counter in her old kitchen and put his arm around her shoulders.

"You are a part of Rosewood Hollow now, Sarah. People accept and love you just the way you are."

"Only because I'm not as different as Katelyn."

"Because you care. You volunteer at the historical society and the pound," he spared a quick glance at Pixie. "You help at the bookstore and the Fair Share food drives and you are an awesome mom. Your children are great human beings. You make an effort. Katelyn..."

"Katelyn is just different, Matt. Don't let Cory hear you talk about her like that."

"I'm not really sure why she chose to stay here."

"Maybe meeting a ghost will do that to you."

As if to answer her question, a door slammed somewhere upstairs, and Sarah could feel the vibrations through the floor into her feet.

"Pipe down, Amelia," she muttered and smiled at Matthew.

"Amelia still hangs around?"

Sarah shrugged. "Who understands ghosts? Sometimes I get the feeling she's around, and poking her pert 1899 nose into everything. Then I don't hear anything for a couple of weeks."

Matthew closed his eyes, and she could almost see him mentally sighing.

"The Royal Veritas Sapphire," Cory began, coming down the stairs and into the kitchen with his tablet in hand, oblivious to any potential interruption. "Are you ready?"

Matthew, who had been about to kiss Sarah, drew back, and Sarah grinned. "What 'cha got, sport?"

Since Matthew had become Cory's male role model, research, specifically historical research, had become one of Cory's passions. His classmates did not dare tease him about his newfound love of history, but they'd had a good chuckle when he corrected one of their teachers on some obscure historical fact and had been proven right.

"The Royal Veritas Sapphire," Cory began, and if he'd been old enough for reading glasses, he would have adjusted them on his face as he read off the screen. "The sapphire possesses a dual-edged enchantment, its origin shrouded in ancient royal lore. This extraordinary sapphire necklace, an ancient heirloom of unknown lineage, is renowned for its supposed mystical ability to make the wearer's words infallible and to shield them from the scrutiny of falsehood. However, its remarkable magic, like many powerful artifacts, is not limited to virtuous hands."

Cory looked up at Matthew and Sarah, and Matthew nodded in encouragement. "The Jewel of Truth," he said softly. "Continue."

"For centuries," Cory continued reading, "the necklace was a symbol of truth and justice, worn by wise and fair monarchs who upheld the kingdom's legacy of integrity. It ensured that justice was served without deceit, making the courtroom a haven of unwavering honesty. As a result, it became the ultimate emblem of a just and righteous rule. Yet, as the kingdom's fortunes dwindled, so did the necklace's prominence. Lost to the annals of history, it remained dormant until it emerged in a recent archaeological dig in Ireland. The Royal Veritas Sapphire" holds within its radiant blue depths the potential for both good and malevolence. It can elevate the truth and integrity of its wearer to celestial heights but it can also cloak sinister intentions in an aura of unassailable trustworthiness. As the forces of darkness and greed seek to harness its power for their own deceitful ends, a delicate balance between its beneficent and sinister forces hangs in the air, threatening to tip the scales of fate in a direction unknown."

For a moment, both Sarah and Matthew let the words Cory had read sink in. Finally, Matthew raised his head.

"Cite your sources," he said, as it was their custom, to verify the research, and Cory mentioned the scientific journal he was referencing. Matthew nodded gently.

"You do understand now why the sapphire has value beyond the plain monetary implications, don't you?"

Cory looked down at his tablet screen and then back at Matthew, and Sarah could practically see the thought process behind her son's eyes. "Because it makes you speak the truth," he ventured, and Matthew shook his head.

"That was its original purpose. But it can also make you appear to speak the truth," he said, allowing the words to sink in for a moment. "Meaning that no matter what you say at that moment, the people around you will believe it to be the truth."

Cory cocked his head and thought for a moment, looking between Matthew and his tablet.

"Even if you are lying," he finally asked.

"Especially if you are lying," Matthew confirmed, and Cory pressed his lips together.

"But that's..."

Matthew only nodded.

"Because when I coach basketball, and a kid tells me he couldn't make a shot because the sun was in his eyes, then sometimes – I know – it's just BS because he was not really trying."

Cory looked at his mother, but Sarah only smiled.

"But you're saying, with this sapphire..."

Matthew nodded.

"I wouldn't know," Cory continued.

"A pretty benign example, but yes, you wouldn't know," Matthew said softly, and upstairs, another door slammed. Sarah felt an energy humming through her floors and into her feet. She exchanged a glance with Pixie, and she knew they were all on the same page.

Cory set his tablet on the table, pulled out a chair, and sat, putting his hands together in front of him as if he were in school. For a moment, nobody spoke, and she could see the thoughts racing in her teen's mind:

An item that would blind the people around you to any and all lies. He was just beginning to grasp the concept, and a few times, he opened his mouth only to close it again.

"Oh man," he finally said, and Matthew peered at him over the rim of his reading glasses.

"So – now you know why the security around this sapphire was so tight. Very few people know about the secret of the jewel, but..."

Pixie chose this very moment to jump onto Sarah's lap gracefully and sat up straight.

Half an hour of internet research, Sarah heard in her mind, and she chuckled.

"Half an hour of internet research," she said with a shrug and put her hand on Cory's. "Not that you're not an exceptional researcher..."

"But the real point is, if I could find it – anybody could," Cory finished and shook his head. "Then I don't understand why they displayed it in the old museum and not a bank vault or something."

"Be that as it may, the national archive assessed our security and allowed us to host the traveling exhibit for several weeks – albeit in February when no other museum had requested time."

"How is Daniel," Sarah asked. She knew the museum director casually from volunteering on a few of the same boards and couldn't imagine the always prim and proper Daniel Whitman dealing with a burglary of these proportions.

"As can be expected," Matthew shrugged. "He feels guilty for not having supervised Katelyn locking up. So do I. After all, I recommended her for the job."

"For the museum gift shop," Sarah said pointedly. "The assistant post came up later."

"I still vouched for her."

"And she didn't do it." Cory slapped his hand onto the kitchen table, and Sarah automatically drew back from the sudden outburst. "Why are all of you so ready and convinced that Katy is guilty?"

"Katy?" Sarah asked, suddenly alarmed that her son was on a nickname basis with his father's former girlfriend. Don't go there, she admonished herself, almost at the same time as she heard Pixie in her head.

It's all quite harmless.

How do you know?

Pixie only winked.

"She didn't do it, I just know."

"Perhaps you don't know her all that well."

"She's different, that's all."

"Are you spending any time with Katelyn," Sarah asked, the alarm in her voice ratcheting up another notch.

"No – what?" Cory jumped up from the table. "No – of course not, that's disgusting. We played a few online games together, that's all."

A deep crimson blush crept up from under the neck of his sweatshirt, and Sarah looked away. He'd inherited that one from her.

At the same time, the lights above the counter flickered on and off briefly, and Cory rolled his eyes toward the ceiling.

"Thanks, Amelia. It's nice to know that I'm under constant surveillance between you, and..." He glared down at Pixie. "You."

"You're not under surveillance, Cory, cool it," Sarah said and nodded at the kitchen table again. Not looking at either of them, Cory pulled the chair back out and sat.

"Those things that happened last year — Amelia, the entity, and the Lumarians—"

"Obsidian order," Cory automatically corrected, and Sarah only nodded.

"It was a lot for you, and I worry sometimes..."

"It's fine, Mom."

"Don't let it make you grow up too fast."

As quickly as it had come, the moment passed as Emma came thundering down the stairs and pointed at the TV on the far wall.

"Turn it on," she said quickly. "It's all over the news. Hurry."

Cory, who'd been picking at his sleeve a moment ago, grabbed the TV remote before anyone else could and flicked it on to the local news station Sarah was fond of watching while doing kitchen chores.

On-screen, a young man in his twenties, with fashionably cut surfer blonde hair and a silver-grey suit, sat at a dark news desk.

"We are back, I'm Alexander Williams, and we're covering a stunning development in the heart of Rosewood Hollow," he said and looked straight into the camera for a beat.

"A daring heist at the Rosewood Hollow Museum has left the community in shock and awe. Let's go to our reporter Jason Rodriguez at the scene for the latest on this brazen robbery."

The scene changed to a shot outside the Rosewood Hollow Museum. There was the park where she and Matthew liked to go for a stroll when the weather allowed, Sarah thought with a pang. Now the park appeared packed with news vans, police cars, and a huge throng of onlookers who couldn't pass up the lure of a TV spectacle.

"Thank you, Alex," Jason said, holding his in-ear headset with one finger. "We are here at the Rosewood Hollow Museum, where earlier today, an audacious heist took place. The perpetrators, who remain unidentified, broke into the museum under the cover of darkness, making off with a priceless sapphire necklace."

Red and blue lights from the police cars drew eerie stripes across his handsome face and the museum's beautiful ancient brick facade.

"The scene earlier was nothing short of chaotic as alarms blared through the town in the early morning hours, drawing the attention of residents and law enforcement. The stolen sapphire necklace, known as The Royal Veritas Sapphire, is steeped in ancient magic, legends, and historical significance."

Sarah hadn't been able to get to the grand opening, so she hadn't seen the sapphire necklace yet, but when its image appeared on the screen, her breath caught in her throat. The piece was nothing short of stunning. A magnificent dark blue teardrop sapphire of dazzling color and clarity shone under the lights of the photographer. It was set in an intricately designed, antique-style pendant that only enhanced the stone's regal beauty. The fine, delicate links of the necklace chain would almost disappear when it was worn by a beautiful queen, allowing the sapphire to take center stage.

All too soon, the camera cut back to Jason Rodriguez's image, and even more people gathered outside the museum to discuss the heist.

"In a surprising twist," Jason continued, "A new employee at the museum, has been arrested in connection with the theft. Witnesses on the scene report that she was taken into custody earlier today amidst accusations of involvement in the robbery. Her exact role in the incident is still under investigation, and authorities have not yet released any further details."

"They arrested her," Cory cried out, watching footage of Katelyn being escorted by police. "No, they can't."

Cory's hands were flat on the table now, when Alexander Williams appeared again, smiling brightly.

"Thank you, Jason, for that update. It appears that Rosewood Hollow is in the midst of a gripping mystery, and we'll continue to follow this story closely as more information becomes available. Stay tuned for further developments on this daring heist. We'll be bringing you the latest as the story unfolds."

∞

Stunned silence filled the room as Matthew turned off the TV. He let the silence linger, then said, "I'm sorry, Cory. The police—"

"Are wrong again," Cory snapped. "They—"

Sarah silenced him with a gentle head shake. "I'm sure they are just questioning her. As they would question anyone who worked in the museum at that point."

"There must be more people then."

Matthew shook his head. "Most of the staff had already left that night. They were well into overtime anyway, because of the event. Realistically, it was Daniel, Katelyn, and me. I can still see it," Matthew narrowed his eyes. "I was going to the car, Daniel wanted to know something or other and followed me, leaving Katelyn to lock up. That was it." He raised his head with a wry smile and rubbed his hands. "She must have gone back inside and—"

"And stolen the sapphire? No way." Subconsciously, Cory had adopted the same posture as Matthew, sitting with his hands folded and his shoulders pulled up a little. But his eyes – his eyes glowed with irritation. "That would be dumb, and you know it," he finished.

"Besides," Emma threw in, looking up from her own tablet and the news site she had been looking at. "It says right here they most likely scaled the side of the building and broke through the glass dome."

"Yes, but she might have helped."

"And I'm telling you that is not like her. Katelyn would not..."

"Alright, everyone," Sarah interjected, hands up in surrender. Arguing won't help. Katelyn's with the police, cooperating, which is a good thing. She will likely be home for supper. Now, about that..."

"I'll set the table," Cory muttered, and Emma put aside her tablet to help without arguing this time. Only Matthew remained sitting at the kitchen table, staring at a point out in the garden.

∞

"I vouched for her," he said later, after the kids had gone to bed, and they were sitting in front of the old-fashioned fireplace with a glass of wine.

"I wouldn't worry about that right now.'

"I'm on the museum's board and many of its committees. I can't ignore that."

"You really don't think she did it, do you?" Sarah asked, sitting up a little straighter. Katelyn is so..."

"She is so - what, Sarah? She showed up on the arm of your ex-husband, a man almost twice her age and extremely wealthy. When Cory says money doesn't matter to her, he is not seeing the entire picture."

"I know." Sarah sighed and rested her hand on her chin. "So, what do we do?"

"You want my advice? Stay as far away as possible from this issue and let the police do their job. You do not want them in here again, asking questions, do you?"

"Not really." Sara involuntarily shuddered. She still remembered their local police officer, Penny Harding, coming to the house more than once, asking about the disappearance of her neighbors. None of her questions were easily answered without using the phrase, 'a ghost and I hit them with enough power to turn one of them into a pile of dust and ashes '

"I'll ask the kids to tone it down and not obsess over it, at least for now," she finally said, just as Pixie hopped up on the couch and snuggled up close to her.

He had it coming.

Who had what coming?

Jenkins. He tried to kill me. Of course, you would turn him into a pile of dust and ashes, completely understandable.

"That's good, thank you," Matthew said, oblivious to her exchange with Pixie. "If Katelyn is innocent, her name will be cleared soon enough, and the police can find the real burglar. No harm done, other than she may have to find a new job."

"You're right," Sarah said automatically because Matthew needed to hear it, but one look into Pixie's amused little face told her this was not the end of the story.

Chapter Four

"Rosewood Hollow is all abuzz suddenly. A juicy scandal, a newcomer at the heart of it—gossip at its finest." Lily glanced around her bookstore while chatting with Sarah, who had just dropped off Emma for her afternoon shift.

"And Matthew's worried about his own position now," Sarah said.

"Matthew," Lily laughed and raised her hands, making the dozen or so gold bangles on her wrists tinkle and chime. Lily had never met a vibrantly colored cloth she didn't want to turn into a flowing dress for herself, and today she was dressed in deep peacock blue and yellow. "Paraphrasing what Penny Harding said after interviewing him, it's that if there's one guy who would rather cut off his own nose than steal a historical artifact – it's Matthew Turner."

"That's reassuring, I'm sure," Sarah said.

"Although he is much better looking with a nose, I'm sure," Lily said, leaning in close, and the women laughed brightly.

"Daniel, on the other hand, will probably be reprimanded by the Board for leaving a new hire to lock up," Lily continued. "It was his responsibility. But why are you worried? I'm sure the museum is insured."

Sarah stood still for a moment. Could it be that Lily had not checked into the history or the significance of the Royal Veritas Sapphire, the Truth Stone? Could it be she didn't know anything about it?

"What? You're wondering if I know about that lame legend that's woven around it," Lily asked with her customary manner of seemingly reading Sarah's mind. "It's just a story somebody made up to make a good-sized stone more spectacular and valuable."

"Errm..."

"Sarah, not everything is supernatural or paranormal. This is just a gemstone and just a thief who wants to fence it. It wouldn't surprise me if they offered it back to the museum for a ransom."

Sarah looked down at her shoes – and over to where Emma was helping a customer.

"She's doing really well, isn't she?"

"Sarah."

"She enjoys the bookstore."

"Sarah. It's just an ordinary gemstone." Lily grabbed her by the upper arm just enough for Sarah to notice it and wince just a little. "Let it go."

Sarah nodded, grateful for the interruption, as Lily was called away to help a customer. "Easy for you to say," Sarah mumbled, knowing in her heart this particular gem held secrets beyond its beauty.

❧

She stepped outside, pulling her coat tight against the lingering chill of February. Historic buildings lined the street, their colonial facades adorned with steep roofs and dormer windows. Patches of snow remained, painting the sidewalk. A faint scent of wood smoke hung in the air as chimneys puffed white against the blue sky. Bundled figures, residents and visitors alike browsed the shops.

Further down, the village green lay blanketed in snow. A few figures dotted the space around the gazebo and twinkling evergreens. Scattered benches invited locals and visitors to soak in the winter scenery. Sarah's path led her directly to the old museum. This turn-of-the-century mansion, transformed by a visionary artist, stood proudly. The historic façade remained, while an angled glass gift shop and a light-flooding dome provided modern touches.

The dome was covered in a black construction tarp now, and that area of the museum was cordoned off with police tape. Three officers stood guard, and one of them cast suspicious glances her way after she'd been standing there for what she realized had been a good ten minutes.

"Hard to imagine someone scaling that wall, isn't it?"

Sarah turned around with a start, to find Matthew standing behind her.

"You gave me a fright! But yes." Sarah let her eyes slide up the side of the building, and the drainpipe where the police assumed the burglars had entered, and she felt her skin crawl.

"I – can't even imagine."

"Sarah," Matthew's voice held something cautious and downcast in it that made her look up immediately. "The... alarm was not set properly," Matthew continued. "The exact section of the building where they entered had not been alarmed, and Katelyn was the one who set the alarm."

Sarah said nothing, feeling the blood hammering in her ears. How could this be?

"I'm sorry," she heard Matthew say from a thousand miles away.

In her mind there was Katelyn coming to her house in tears when Michael had been abducted; Katelyn searching for the letter drop tree with the children, Katelyn pulling out a can of mace when they feared Michael's abductors were at the door.

It just couldn't be.

"Katelyn has officially been charged," Matthew said, his voice tight. "Aiding and abetting. Please, Sarah."

A war raged inside Sarah. The man she loved was relieved at the resolution, yet a single, unshakable truth echoed in her mind: Katelyn was innocent.

Sarah squeezed her eyes shut and inhaled deeply, but truth had a price. "They're wrong. Katelyn had nothing to do with the sapphire's theft. And I'll prove it, somehow."

"Matthew, please understand," Sarah pleaded.

"It's okay, I do," he murmured, voice strained. "Anyway, I just saw you through the window – gotta get back now. See you later."

Sarah adjusted her purse on her shoulder, watching Matthew disappear through the wide double doors into the museum, and then turned around. At this point, there was only one thing to do: buy a bottle of wine and strategize with Lily.

Chapter Five

By the time she got home, news of Katelyn's arrest and charges had spread like wildfire. Alexander Williams, the news anchor with the surfer look, had yet another update. Cory was buried in research and surrounded by stacks of paper, and his own, as well as Sarah's, tablet. Emma had come home early because customers only wanted to talk about the burglary, and Lily had promised to come by after she closed the store.

Sarah dropped into one of the soft chairs in their games room, wondering what to tell them. Cory believed in Katelyn's innocence, but he also adored Matthew. And Emma – Sarah closed her eyes and sank deeper into the chair.

Emma had a special relationship with Amelia, the ghost that haunted Thompson Hall. She didn't show often since they'd figured out the mystery around her death, mostly turning up in moments of distress or joy. Meaning... Sarah looked up, expecting to feel the cold draft that usually presaged Amelia's arrival. Instead, Emma walked in with two huge mugs of hot chocolate.

"Thanks, Em." She wrapped her fingers around the handmade pottery mug and leached all of the warmth from it. She and Matthew had bought those mugs at a local arts and crafts market, she remembered wistfully, and Matthew had said something incredibly romantic about sitting down to a quiet breakfast with her.

"She didn't do it," Emma said simply and sat in the chair beside Sarah.

"What?" Sarah did a little double-take. *She didn't do it* sounded so much like the voice she'd heard in her head all day long that it took her breath away. "What makes you say that?" she asked cautiously.

Emma only shrugged. "I just know."

"Yes," Sarah sighed. "Your brother is equally convinced of Katelyn's innocence."

"Not like that, Mom." Emma pulled back her blonde ponytail and looked straight into Sarah's eyes. Her bright blue eyes were so deep and open that it took Sarah's breath away. "I just know inside." She tapped the vicinity of her heart. "Just like I knew that Amelia would never hurt me if we could figure out what happened to her."

"Emma." Sarah put down the mug and pressed her lips together, trying to figure out what to say to her daughter. Just then, Pixie hopped up on the couch and kissed first Emma, then Sarah. Emma giggled and scratched the beautiful white and sable Papillon behind her pointy fringed ears. Pixie sighed with satisfaction.

"Don't look so satisfied," Emma grinned and proceeded to rub Pixie's little white tummy. "We know there are things you and I see that other people don't."

Pixie groaned out loud, and Sarah had to laugh. "You are positively shameless, little dog."

You are just jealous.

You don't communicate with Emma?

Not yet – in time.

"Girl time, ladies," Lily, who had a key to Sarah's house, wandered into the games room at that moment, waving a bottle of wine and two glasses.

"Sorry, Em, I don't think your mother…"

"I'm good, thanks," Emma giggled. "Did you hear anything new at the store?"

"Indeed, and none of it's good."

Lily opened the wine, handed Sarah a glass, and sat down with her own. "Police are convinced Katelyn was involved."

"But why?" Emma exclaimed, gesturing with her hands. "It doesn't make any sense!"

"Couldn't agree more," Cory chimed in from the doorway, grabbing a footstool. "Why would she do something like that?"

"Because of the stone's value, they assume," Lily said and took a sip of her wine. "And… she was also the one to set the alarm that night. All of the zones were armed correctly, with the exception of the one that allowed the thieves to remain undetected for so long."

"Might have been just a mistake," Cory muttered and looked down. "Besides, the alarm did go off."

"True, but far too late for security to do anything about the theft or, God forbid, stop the thieves. If it weren't for that alarm zone being off, they would have had to take a huge gamble on getting in and out fast enough without getting caught. From what I hear…," Lily stared down into her glass and swirled the wine around slowly. "It would have been nearly impossible to accomplish."

"Nearly, not entirely," Cory snapped.

"Cory, it's not Lily's fault," Sarah said, but Lily shook her head.

"That's OK. And their case would be shaky if that were all."

"There's more?"

"When they searched Katelyn's desk at the museum, they found a fat notebook full of research about the sapphire – and on how the different alarm zones work."

Lily swirled, then downed her wine in one frustrated gulp. "That's their story anyway. I tried reaching Katelyn through Penny, but they're keeping her isolated. Even my charm couldn't budge them."

"Thanks anyway, for trying." Sarah rose and contemplated setting a fire in the huge stone fireplace on the east wall of the room. Usually, Matthew was the one who dragged in logs and paper and lit the whole bit.

"Looks like I'm going to have to apologize to Matthew," she said. "He did ask me to let it go."

"You can – but I'm not," Cory said and looked at his sister. Emma smiled brightly at her older brother.

"Me neither Katelyn did not do it."

"Kids..."

This time Sarah did feel the cold draft sweep through the room and looked to see if she had opened the fireplace damper already. Something touched her hand, and just out of the corner of her eye, she saw the wispy white cloud that usually meant Amelia was manifesting in the room. She more felt than saw it, but Amelia didn't materialize entirely. As quickly as Sarah had seen anything, it was gone again.

They are right, Amelia whispered in Sarah's head. *It's the enchantment.*

Then the room returned to normal again. Sarah rubbed chilled fingers together.

"Amelia is getting weaker," Emma said sadly, looking at the same spot where Sarah thought she had seen Amelia's apparition. "Soon, she might not be able to visit anymore at all."

"She may be happier where she is now," Sarah muttered before the question she had been expecting came.

"Did Amelia say anything? I couldn't hear," Cory asked.

All eyes were on her now, and Sarah swallowed hard. She looked into her son's eyes and put out a hand to scratch Pixie's soft little head. She had raised her kids to always speak the truth, even if it was painful. Especially if it was painful.

"Amelia thinks you're right," Sarah said quickly, like ripping off a Band-Aid. "And – it's about the enchantment."

Cory lowered his head and looked at her from below long, dark lashes. To his credit, he did not gloat or brag. He didn't say, I told you so, merely nodded softly.

"So that's where we start," Emma said brightly, putting her hands together as if she were planning a fun outing.

"Katelyn was Dad's girlfriend, and that's wrong. I get that. But sitting in jail for something she didn't do, that's wrong too, right?"

"Yep," Sarah nodded for Cory and looked over at Lily for help. Lily still swirled her wine around in her glass and looked as if she were a thousand miles away.

"Can we sleep on it, Cory?" Sarah pleaded. He stiffened at the request.

"Every delay..." he started, but Sarah cut him off.

"I know Katelyn's in custody, but I need to consider everyone - you, Emma, and Matthew too."

At the mention of his mentor and friend Matthew Turner, Cory pressed his lips together and nodded.

"Fine, we won't do anything today. But tomorrow—"

"We will make a plan."

"Tomorrow we prove that Katelyn was innocent!"

Chapter Six

After the kids had gone off to their rooms, she and Lily sat with their wine in hand, staring into the fire.

"Help me fix this with Matthew?" Sarah asked softly, knowing that Lily was basically the person who had known him the longest and who had set the two of them up way back when. Lily only shook her head.

"Sarah," Lily refused to meet her eyes. "Matthew is a historian at heart. If he felt anything were threatening that..." Again, she shook her head. "I just don't know if he can get past that."

"Great." Sarah put her wine glass down harder than she had intended. "Another relationship wrecked by male pride and the inability to admit that maybe – just maybe – he might be wrong. And to top it off—"

"Sarah—"

"He blames me for—"

"Sarah!"

"What?" she snapped, picking up her glass, realizing it was empty.

"There's someone knocking at your door."

"Huh?"

Sarah put her glass back down and listened. Indeed, someone was knocking insistently at her front door.

The last time someone knocked at her door late at night—well, that had involved an entity, an enemy, and a pile of ashes.

"You want me to get it," Lily asked, putting down her glass.

The knocking would not stop; instead, it became more and more insistent. Lily finally threw up her hands and went out into the grand front hall. She touched her forefinger to her heart and the spot in the transom window where the famous Luminus crystal had once been, and she carefully opened the heavy oak front door just a gap.

"You know, this is not really the time to – oh, it's you." Lily hesitated for a moment and finally nodded toward the games room.

"Thanks, I couldn't find my key. "

Sarah had curled up in the corner of the couch, her legs curled under her, a blanket over her knees, and a glass of wine in hand when Lily came in again.

"Who - oh."

"I'll leave you alone," Lily said quickly and looked around. "Come on, Pixie, time to go outside."

I don't need to go outside. Tell her.

Sarah only waved her little dog off. *We'll be fine; by the time you chase a squirrel, this will be over.*

I don't chase squirrels. I terrify them.

"So," Sarah said and watched Matthew awkwardly trying to take a seat on one of the armchairs. "You've come to tell me I'm a nutcase for believing in Katelyn's innocence."

"Actually—"

"Because you can just come out and say it. If your job and your standing and reputation at the museum are so much more important than what you and I have been through..."

"Sarah—"

"And the fact that my boy up there in his bed idolizes you – if all of that doesn't count, then - well then…"

"You ready to listen now?" He sounded calm and reasonable, and Sarah nodded defiantly. "The thing is…"

Matthew fiddled uncomfortably with a black leather bracelet he wore. He and Sarah had bought matching bracelets just before Christmas last year. He wore a pair of black jeans that fit him to a T and a T-shirt that read, Don't argue with an idiot – he will beat you with experience. Cory would have loved that.

"The thing is – Penny Harding basically told me what the police had."

"A few notes Katelyn made and the fact that she was the one to set the alarm," Sarah spat, and Matthew nodded.

"About that," Matthew pressed his lips together. "I helped her with those notes."

"They mean nothing—You what?"

"She wanted to know what to say if visitors happened to ask her, so I helped her a bit."

"But that means…"

"That means nothing to the police at the moment, but I know she didn't write it down to steal the sapphire."

"And the alarm."

Matthew looked pained now. "I think she just couldn't remember the sequence. Against the rules, but she must have written it down to avoid having to keep asking."

Sarah could feel a smug triumphant look grow inside her now. "Then they have nothing."

"Not really." Matthew shook his head again and tried for a little smirk.

"Then they will let her go."

"Not - quite." Matthew put his hands together, resting his face on them for a moment, and closed his eyes. "They want a suspect. They have one. It will appease the visitors, the board, and the press. Nothing I could say or do would change their mind. Unless somebody else confesses. If that happens, they'll have to let her go – but that may take time."

Sarah felt that righteous anger growing inside her again, the one that had got her in trouble before, and struggled to take deep, even breaths. From somewhere in the distance, she could hear the doggie door flap, and a moment later, Pixie hopped up on her lap. The little dog put her paws on her chest and nuzzled her cheek softly.

Take it easy. You're about to summon a storm here.

I am angry. I should.

Take it down a notch. Nothing good comes from this.

With another deep breath, her hands buried in Pixie's soft fur, Sarah could finally feel her anger ebb again.

"Now what," she heard herself ask softly.

"You okay? You went white as a sheet there for a second," Matthew asked and furrowed his brow. He hadn't missed the brief interaction with Pixie. Sarah struggled to smile.

"It makes me angry when officials do things that make no sense to appease people who don't matter a lot."

"Don't I know it?"

"Katelyn—"

Matthew raised his hands. "She is odd; she was your exes girlfriend, and she has an unorthodox lifestyle – and that doesn't make her guilty, I know. I just hope you don't lump me in with those officials."

"Well..." Sarah dragged out that last word, but one look at Matthew's crestfallen face convinced her to change her mind. "I was pretty mad at you."

"I am sorry."

"Does that mean we're going to help Katelyn find out who really stole the sapphire?"

Sarah looked up to find Emma in her pink princess pajamas standing in the doorway to the games room, a white teddy bear clutched in her arms. Lily came in through the back door and stopped.

"We're helping Katelyn? Cool."

"Whoa – wait." Sarah raised her hands. "Where did all of this come from? All I said was I don't blame Matthew."

"You kind of did say they didn't have any solid evidence."

This from Cory, who also strolled in dressed in his pajamas.

"About the eavesdropping going on in this house," Sarah admonished and got to her feet. "Could we please respect people's privacy? I taught you better than that."

"And you're also hedging," Lily said, winked, and looked around for her wine glass and the bottle. "So, what's it going to be."

Sarah loosened her blonde hair from its ponytail and retied it again, just to gain a precious few minutes while all eyes were on her.

"We're not investigators."

"You figured out who stole the Luminus crystal," Cory said, dropping onto the couch beside Matthew. "Besides, it would be cool to work together on something exciting again." He elbowed Matthew in the side and winked.

"Kids, this is an actual crime. People with weapons – most likely guns – who break into a museum in the dead of night to steal stuff. I don't think this is a case for Nancy Drew and Co to do a bit of fun sleuthing."

Pixie nuzzled Sarah's cheek again and positioned her tiny body so the white tummy was over Sarah's fingers, convenient for tummy rubs.

But we are the ones who believe in her.

I'm not putting this family in danger.

And I am still here.

Time seemed to slow down for a moment. Sarah thought she felt that ice-cold draft again, and her eyes refused to focus for a moment. The air became heavy around her; then, with a little pop of her ears, everything returned to normal.

Lily suddenly put her wine glass down and rubbed her arms.

"Is your furnace okay?"

Matthew took the hint and built a fire in the fireplace.

Sarah went to the kitchen to make two mugs of cocoa for Emma and Cory and found Pixie had followed her.

What just happened? Pixie wanted to know.

I'm not sure, Pix. Everything became – unreal all of a sudden. I thought Amelia was trying to come through, but she didn't.

When you solved the mystery of her death, you opened the door for her to go home.

She can visit.

Yes, but I am thinking that takes a lot of energy.

Pixie? Sarah put down the two mugs of cocoa and picked up her little Papillon dog. The long ear fringe tickled her nose, and a quick swipe from Pixie's tongue made her laugh.

Do you think this is a bad idea?

Pixie squirmed in her arms a bit and locked her dark little eyes on Sarah's. Her tiny black nose touched Sarah's chin, and she heard the little dog in her head again.

The truth is never a bad idea, Sarah.

∾

Sarah sent the kids to bed with their cocoa and returned to the games room, where Lily and Matthew talked in hushed voices. Silence spread as she walked in.

"Seems like we just got over a crisis with ghosts and criminals in the house? Well – didn't we?" Sarah asked.

Lily twirled her wine glass in her hands.

"Honestly? I think it's kinda fun, Sarah. It's you who has kids and responsibilities. And an ex who might threaten to take your kids again."

Sarah smiled, remembering Michael and his massive SUV at the door. "I'm sure he won't want to set foot in Rosewood Hollow anytime soon. And you?" She pointed her chin at Matthew. "Nothing to say to all of it?"

"I'm a history professor, not a PI. But it doesn't surprise me that the museum board would decide to think, here's a convenient suspect. Everybody likes to follow the party line. So—"

"So, you really want to find out more, don't you?" Sarah cut him off, and Matthew nodded.

"When you put it like that - yes. See what's really going on. Because if it was not Katelyn..."

Sarah nodded. "Then who?"

Lily held out her hand for a high five and her glass for more wine, and Sarah allowed herself to exhale.

"Besides," Matthew said with a wink. "I've seen you when Amelia got you mad, I get the feeling you have – abilities up your sleeve we haven't seen yet."

Sarah chuckled and quickly held out her glass as well, avoiding an answer. She still remembered the anger and Pixie's warning.

Chapter Seven

The next morning dawned a bright and clear February day that was cold enough to turn the path to their door and the sidewalks into a glistening expanse of ice, and Cory was probably the most excited of them all.

Normally, he would have been out there, Sarah thought, mercilessly teasing his little sister. Today he sat indoors at the kitchen table with his tablet, a big mug of hot cocoa in front of him, and his and Matthew's favorite research portal open.

"He grinned at her and pointed at the screen with the toast and jam he held in one hand.

"There isn't much on this so-called enchantment, but trust me, I will find more."

"Good morning, Cory," Sarah shook her head. The kid who wouldn't roll out of bed for school was up early, had made his own breakfast, and already was doing what amounted to homework.

"Shouldn't you..." Then she wisely shut her mouth. Suggesting he should be playing outside would not earn her much but one of his now famous eye rolls.

"What have you got," she asked instead and leaned over his shoulder. "An essay on ancient enchanted artifacts. Geez, even I would have trouble with that."

"It's – hard," he admitted. "Not as hard as sitting in jail."

"Custody," Sarah corrected. "It's a long way yet to jail."

"Still..." Cory frowned at the text again. "Maybe Matthew can help me with this later."

"Where's Emma?"

"Somewhere," Cory said waving his sandwich vaguely at the entrance hall and the grand double staircase "I think she's looking for Amelia."

Sarah's heart sank a bit. Emma's *friend*, Amelia, the ghost who once filled the house, seemed to be dwindling with each passing month. Figuring out that her own father had accidentally killed her and covered it up had freed Amelia and soon she might vanish entirely. Sarah feared the day Emma's ghostly confidante would leave only a broken heart.

"Oh, and Aunt Lily wants to go to the museum with you," Cory continued. "She'll be here soon."

"Is the museum even open again?"

Cory only shrugged.

"Go try. I think she said if Matt and I wanted to be bookworms, you all would do something more fun."

∞

Not an hour later, Lily showed up with three Discover Rosewood Hollow Tickets, passes that were sold at all the local retailers, including her own store, and allowed entry into all of the Rosewood Hollow museums and historical sites.

"Really?" Sarah eyed the passes. "Discover Rosewood."

"Yup. City council decided they had to honor those for entry into the museum for all pass holders, so that is how we will get in."

"They'll know you took them out of your own store."

"And they'll know about you and Matthew. But being polite and all that, nobody is going to say anything. We'll take Emma."

The ticket booth attendant looked at their passes, then at them, and back down at their passes. She opened her mouth and closed it again.

"Everybody else is getting in, you might as well. Go on. But it is self-guided today."

Lily took charge and set off down the corridor.

"This old mansion, now Rosewood Hollow Museum, is quite a bit older even than your own Thompson Hall. It was originally built by one of the railroad barons." Lily stopped and looked up. A dark shadow spread uncharacteristically across the center of the main atrium. There, high above them, a section of the beautiful glass dome that usually lit up the museum had been replaced by crude plywood panels until the broken sections of panzer glass could be replaced.

"This is where they got in?" Sarah whispered the question barely a tremor above the hushed murmurs. Her heart hammered against her ribs, mimicking the frantic rhythm of her racing thoughts. They'd infiltrated the supposedly impenetrable dome, leaving behind an unsettling silence that echoed with the weight of the crime.

A hand squeezed hers. It was Emma, her grip firm and grounding.

"Feels heavy in here, doesn't it?" Emma whispered, her voice barely above a breath.

The adult within Sarah wanted to brush it off as nerves, but the chilling energy of the atrium silenced her retort. Instead, she nodded.

"It's more than that. It's like the air itself is thick with what happened, the walls holding onto secrets they can't quite keep."

"The main exhibit hall where the sapphire was taken is up ahead," Emma said and pointed. Not surprisingly, most of the other visitors also drifted past ancient paintings and tapestries, giving them only half a glance on their way to the main exhibit hall and the empty glass display.

Most of the display was now gone, save for the solid stone base it had rested on. The glass case, the lights, and the descriptive panels had all been taken down, and a simple sign stood in their place: Another Display Coming Soon.

"Disappointing," a couple behind them whispered, and moved on quickly, giving the gold necklaces, crowns, and jeweled tiaras in the remaining displays around the hall barely a glance.

But not Sarah. She stood staring at the sign and fought to catch her breath. Her mind effortlessly conjured up visions of the thieves as they ducked, rolled, and double-stepped around and over security laser beams until they stood right where Sarah was.

In her mind's eye, she could almost see them: Three of them, clad in black, communicating without speaking. A reverence followed, the leader claiming the sapphire with a touch more gentle than expected. Then, the piercing wail of the alarm, belated and ignored. The night swallowed them whole, leaving behind a chilling echo—memories of a crime witnessed in solitude.

"Sarah?"

She swayed now, stumbling once or twice, and would have fallen if Lily had not supported her.

"I'm fine."

Sarah hung on to Lily's shoulder and met Emma's brilliant blue eyes. Emma smiled and held up her hand, showing three fingers.

"I'm taking you out of here and to the café."

Lily took charge again and guided Sarah and Emma out of the museum, and into the gift shop and café next door. Emma didn't say much, but her eyes were on her mother's, and a serene little smile played on her lips.

"I told you, I'm fine." Sarah never took her eyes off her daughter. "I just skipped breakfast, that's all."

"Yeah, another reason for you to sit down and have something decadent. Follow me now, there's nothing more to see here anyway."

In the exhibit hall, a wiry man in his forties, dressed in a dark simple suit, and wearing shades, stayed behind, his head cocked as he watched Lily, Sarah, and Emma leave the room. Emma turned around at the door, and he quickly looked at one of the other displays, as if he were immersed in the history of a hatpin.

❧

Emma chattered on through lunch, about her shifts at the bookstore, the latest releases, the icy weather, and the benefits of small-town living. Sarah tuned most of it out while one question nagged at her again and again: How did she know how the thieves had entered and left? How many there had been? And more to the point, how much more did she know without being able to put her finger on it?

"Feeling better," Lily finally asked, and Sarah forced a laugh.

"Absolutely. I told you it was nothing."

"You looked beat."

Sarah waved the comment away. "No worries. But let's hope Cory has found something that could help us because, in the museum, there was nothing really helpful to see."

"Literally nothing." Lily speared a piece of cake. "Yet they took only that sapphire. Hundreds of other pieces just as valuable, left untouched. Makes you wonder, doesn't it?" Her voice dropped to a whisper, sending shivers down Sarah's spine.

"It was about the enchantment," Emma said, nonchalantly as if discussing the weather. It was about power, not value."

Lily scoffed, red curls bouncing as she tucked a strand behind her ear, her bangles clinking like rogue bells. "That story about the truth stone? Sounds more like a glorified mood ring. Not exactly worth risking your neck for, right?"

A beat of silence hung heavy between them, pregnant with unspoken curiosity.

"What if it's true?" Sarah suddenly thought. She didn't realize she had spoken out loud until she saw Lily give the look, the one that meant, My friend, you are crazy coo-coo bananas.

"Think about it. What if there is something to this enchantment, and the thief, or thieves, want to use it for their own purposes?"

"Uh..." Lily rested her chin on her hand and squeezed her eyes shut dramatically. Her bright mauve and purple dress, deep purple scarf, and yellow reading glasses had already drawn a few stares in the Museum Café.

"No," she finally pronounced. "What was it again? You're able to tell the truth with the sapphire? No, honey, we have polygraphs for that nowadays. And I know you have – um – special abilities, but this is a little nuttier even than talking with your dog."

Sarah flicked her eyes left and right, but no one was even looking their way, other than a man in a dark suit and sunglasses who quickly looked away when she spotted him. No wonder. With her brightly colored clothes and shock of red hair, Lily might as well have been a bird of paradise in a mundane, drab landscape.

"You saw Amelia, right," Emma said, still smiling serenely, taking another delicate bite of her scone, and this time it was Lily looking left and right. "So, you know there's more between heaven and earth than what you can see and touch, and it is just as real."

"I guess."

"So just wait to see what Cory has found, and we'll take it from there. Right, Mom?"

Sarah only nodded. *There's more between heaven and earth.* She'd have to have a serious talk with her daughter, and birds and bees had nothing to do with this one.

               ॐ

Cory, it turned out, had not only jumped but dived headfirst into his research. All surfaces around him held notes, printouts, and what appeared to be drawings. Drawings?

Sarah picked up one of them and traced the gentle blue lines of a multi-faceted gemstone with her finger.

"Nice work, Cory, did you do this?"

"Huh? Yes, just a quick sketch when I saw it on the screen."

Pixie bounced happily around the little group, but Cory looked back down at the screen and shook his head. "Something about this thing is weird."

"Weird how," Sarah asked, pulling up a chair beside her son.

"Weird because there's a ton of internet chatter about the theft of the sapphire – that's normal. What isn't normal is all these people chiming in debunking the legend as just a cute story."

"You see," Lily raised her hands, again making her bangles jingle.

"Aunt Lily," Cory invited Pixie onto his lap and hugged the little papillon, still looking at his tablet. "Discussion and a few arguments are normal. This – this looks like somebody is trying to flood the online chatrooms with one opinion: The sapphire is not real."

"Why?" Lily reached out and tapped Pixie on the tiny black nose. "And to what end? It sounds like a lot of work, and I don't imagine that sort of thing would be cheap to do."

"Which only means one thing," Cory said, holding Pixie a bit tighter. "The sapphire and its power are real, and somebody is trying to hide that fact."

Sarah sat – hard. She'd been about to make some of Matthew's tea for them all, and the finality of that statement out of her sixteen-year-old son's mouth buckled her knees. Her beautiful old Victorian home and kitchen suddenly felt dark and heavy. Across from her at the kitchen table Lily opened her mouth and closed it again, and Emma stared at the drawing Cory had made.

Her teakettle whistled, startling them all, and Sarah had just turned to it when she heard Pixie in her mind.

He's right, you know?

Why, and what do you know about it?

Amelia insisted it was the enchantment. Nobody knows more about that than a ghost.

"Say you're right," she said to her son and mechanically poured tea for them. "Say you're right, and somebody is trying to make sure everybody believes the sapphire is just a pretty blue stone that happened to get stolen. Is there any way we could find out more about it? See what's really going on."

Lily sat back and wrapped her hands around her tea mug. "I can't believe I'm saying this," she said so softly Sarah almost missed it. "But there's a guy in town..."

"A guy in town...yes?" Sarah spread her arms and put down a large mug in front of Lily. "Tell us more."

Chapter Eight

A guy in town turned out to be the owner of a tiny little antique store in a building so old it made Thompson Hall and the rest of Rosewood Hollow look like a recent subdivision. The little clapboard building sat on a tiny lot, squished against a condo building next door as if it were cold and leaning in for comfort.

The once-white exterior boards had faded to a comfortable muted putty color, the shutters, doors, and roof shingles a bright red, and an ancient hand-painted sign proclaimed in large letters, Murtaugh Antiques – Welcome.

Sarah, Lily, the kids, and, of course, Pixie stood on the sidewalk for a moment, wavering between wanting to storm right in and ask about enchanted objects and wondering if all of them, in fact, would find room in the tiny store.

Robert Murtaugh, the owner, had been an award-winning magician at one point. Footnote, Sarah thought, what exactly is a prize-winning magician? Who gives these prizes anyway?

Robert Murtaugh—or Robbie, as he was known then—had a headlining show in Las Vegas, so the story went, until the night one of his magic acts went tragically wrong. Rumor had it an audience volunteer passed away, and while no one could prove the accident was Robbie's fault, he closed the show and came back home to Rosewood Hollow. Luck would have it that his grandfather Elijah Murtaugh was just in the process of closing up his antique store.

Robert had taken over.

"You still haven't told me what's so significant about this particular store," Sarah groused and paused for a minute. The walk up to the store had led them through a beautiful, tony neighborhood, and up a steep hill for the past ten minutes. "How is this Robbie supposed to know about enchanted objects?"

"I'd suggest you don't call him Robbie right off the bat," Lily said, taking a huge breath herself. "At least not until he offers. Rumor has it—"

"Again, with the rumors."

"Honey, you're in New England, not Baltimore. Rumor is considered one of our prime sources of information around here. Might I remind you that in the case of the Luminus crystal—"

"I remember," Sarah snapped, pushing away the instant flash image of a human turning to ash in front of her—even if that human had threatened her with a gun. Pixie crowded a little closer as if she could sense her thoughts, and Sarah bent down to caress the soft, fluffy ears.

I sense something very powerful here.

Here? At this store?

Sarah crouched down a little more and put her hand on Pixie, which tended to strengthen their connection.

Is it because the owner was – is – a magician?

Pixie took a long time, staring at the little building with the red shutters and flower boxes at every window.

No. That's illusion. There is real magic here.

Real...

Be careful, Sarah. You will feel it.

At that moment, the heavy oaken front door to the store opened, and a wizened old man stepped onto the worn doorstep, gesturing to them. His white, almost silver hair cascaded down to his shoulders in a tangled mane. Deep lines etched a road map of stories on his face, indicating a life filled with wonder and secrets. His sharp, intelligent eyes, however, gleamed with a youthful sparkle that hinted at the magic he once wielded.

"If you are here to visit my store," he said with a surprisingly strong voice for such an old, frail body. "Come on in. I have many treasures waiting to be discovered."

"Whoa," Cory said and stopped, unable to tear his eyes away from the sight of the old man. Mr. Murtaugh wore a long, flowing robe made of deep midnight-blue fabric adorned with intricate patterns of silver moons and stars. Perhaps it was meant to add a touch of mystique to his antique store, or it represented a memory of his days as a magician. The celestial motifs caught the light in such a way that they seemed to shimmer with a faint, ethereal glow.

Beneath the robe, a simple yet well-tailored shirt and trousers in muted, earthy tones peeked out. The shirt, perhaps once crisp and white, had aged to a soft, off-white hue, and the trousers bore the signs of countless hours spent in pursuit of ancient artifacts.

Around his neck hung an antique pendant, perhaps an amulet, with a deep red gem at its center. To Sarah, the gem appeared to pulse with a subtle radiance, adding to the mystique that surrounded the old man. His fingers, adorned with rings bearing ancient symbols and runes, deftly waved them toward the door and into the store.

Sarah was the first to walk toward him as if drawn magically in. Her feet moved step by step, following the old man's invitation until she stood inside. Lily and the kids followed on her heels, all standing still just a step or two inside the door.

"Wow," Cory said, brushing back the hood of his sweatshirt, which, in typical teenage fashion, perennially obscured his face. But this – this was something he wanted to see.

Stepping into the store felt like entering a time capsule, a place where things had stood still for years. The creaky wooden floor supported a huge collection of treasures, so varied that the eye couldn't find a place to rest, all illuminated by the warm glow of aged brass lamps. Dusty windows filtered sunlight onto well-worn Persian rugs, and the air carried the scent of polished wood and old leather, mingling with the musty charm of vintage books.

Antique furniture, from ornate Victorian dressers to simple Shaker chairs, told the story of Rosewood Hollow through their design.

From somewhere, many old, ticking clocks reminded Sarah of time's passing and the soft tune of an old music box repeated again and again. Sarah fought to take a breath.

"I am sorry," the shopkeeper said, stopping the music box whose tune played over and over and smiling at them. I was repairing this little beauty. What could I find for you today?"

"Well – actually..." Sarah's eyes traveled around the room. It was hard, if not impossible, to find a single item to focus on.

"You are Sarah Anderson," the man suddenly said, offering his hand. "The new owner of Thompson Hall and its, uhh, history. Welcome to Rosewood Hollow. I am Robert Murtaugh. Most people call me Robbie."

"The way you pause when you say its history makes me think you know a heck of a lot more than you are letting on, Robbie," Lily said casually, turning a spinner with antique necklaces and bangles around to inspect the merchandise.

Robbie merely shrugged. The smile never left his face. "One does hear about things in this town. Lumarians are leaving in droves."

"Lumarians," Sarah said, finding her voice again. "You know the history then?"

"Ancient history now," Murtaugh corrected. "That crystal is gone."

"You know..."

Robbie Murtaugh wiped her sentence away and made a few complicated moves with his hands and fingers.

"All ancient history," he sang. "Today is all we have. Now, please tell me why you are here."

Pixie emerged from behind Sarah's legs and cautiously approached the old shopkeeper. Finally, she put a paw on his foot, and he crouched down to face her.

"I see," he said with a smile. "Interesting." Then he put his hand in the same spot Sarah used when she wanted to deepen her connection to Pixie and finally smiled.

"Such a precious little companion you have there."

He dug in his pocket for a little treat, which Pixie took and devoured before Sarah could intervene.

"Pixie, for God's sake!"

Relax, it's just a milk bone.

"Shhh," Robbie said gently and shook his head. "I would never harm the little one. It is just a treat."

Sarah felt a shiver creep down her back for reasons she couldn't grasp just then. The sheer variety of colors, shapes, textures, and items in the antique store put her brain on overload.

"Are you looking for something specific?" Robbie now asked as Pixie wandered around the store, sniffing and peeking in behind furniture and paintings, casually resting on the floor.

"Well, you see…" Sarah began and bit down on her lips.

"You are well acquainted with the young lady who was arrested for the jewelry theft just yesterday," Robbie supplied, and Sarah felt that dread in her stomach again.

"The neighborhood gossip is quite rich in this little town, and your young friend's arrival was spectacular. I well remember it."

"Katelyn didn't do it," Cory said with the absolute conviction only a sixteen-year-old could manage when he thought he was right.

"Hmmmm…" Robbie wagged his head back and forth and played with an exquisite silk tassel in his hand that Sarah had not noticed before.

"I know Katelyn—"

"Cory," Sarah said softly and raised a hand, and with a swish of her swing coat Lily took a step forward.

"Robbie, coming here was actually my idea. There are a few questions and rumors around that sapphire. Perhaps you know what I'm talking about."

"I might," Robbie nodded, his fingers wrapping the cord of the dark red tassel around and around, so fast their eyes could hardly follow it.

"It's said to be enchanted," Lily said, and Robert Murtaugh ceased all movement. From his hand dropped a tightly wound cord, deep red with golden strands blinking here and there. The fat tassel was nowhere to be seen. Sarah took in a quick breath, and the kids were mesmerized by the cord.

Lily never took her eyes off Robbie. "I don't know anyone who knows as much as you do about enchanted treasures and their magic," she said, her voice no more than a whisper.

"I wouldn't know," Robbie said, winding the cord into his pocket.

"Yes, you do."

"Look, I'm just a shop owner in a building the town keeps threatening to tear down. How would I even—"

"You were one of the greatest magicians of your time."

Robert laughed then, a papery, whispering sound that was no more than a gentle puff of air.

"A time long gone, Lily Morrison. So long, hardly anyone is left alive to remember it."

Lily pushed her hands into her sides.

"I know what I know, Robert."

Robert shook his head. The smile never left his wizened, crinkly face. Just at that moment, Pixie ceased her round-and-round exploration of the store and came to stand in front of the old shopkeeper. She put one paw on his foot again and looked up into his old, smiling face. Something passed there, Sarah thought and automatically reached for her little dog. However, with a speed and agility that belied his age, the old man bent down and swept Pixie into his arms.

Pixie didn't struggle or yelp, as she was wont to do when someone picked her up against her will, but she planted a quick little kiss on his cheek.

"Hello there, little one. You are quite – special, are you not?"

Their eyes held for a long silent moment. Sarah took two quick steps toward him to take Pixie back into her own arms, but she did not sense fear or terror from the little dog. Instead, there was curiosity, companionship, and a sense of a shared journey.

"Mom," Cory said urgently and elbowed her in the side. "Pixie. He has…"

Sarah held out her arms for the little papillon, and gently, almost reverently, Robert placed her into Sarah's embrace.

"She is yours?"

Sarah only managed to nod.

"I am sure you know she is—"

"Special," Sarah said softly, her heart hammering in her chest, blood rushing in her ears. "Very special."

Robert thought for a moment, his eyes unfocused, his mind on a silent struggle only he could fathom, and then he finally nodded.

"Very well, follow me." He fished in one of his robe's deep pockets for an ancient key and hesitated for just a moment, looking at Emma and Cory.

"Should the young ones…"

"We're fine," Cory said firmly and stepped toward him. "We have — experience — with ghosts, you know."

"I see." Robert laughed that papery sigh laugh of his again and nodded. "Very well, then."

Sarah clutched Pixie close until she felt the little dog squirming uncomfortably.

What did you do?

I let him know who you are.

How?

Pixie's dark eyes rested on her for a long, silent moment, and it might have been the lighting from an old oil lamp or the shadows in the deeper part of the store, but Sarah was sure there was a broad grin on her dog's face.

Robert deftly navigated through rows of ancient furniture until he reached a solid wooden door at the far end of the store. For a moment, he looked down at the old key in his hand, and his fingers rubbed it as if for good luck.

The ancient key, bathed in the warm patina of time, was a masterpiece of brass craftsmanship, its intricate patterns telling silent tales of forgotten eras. As his fingers traced the textured shaft, the key's golden hue glowed, revealing the countless hands that had turned it through centuries of secrets. The old man nodded as if to affirm himself then deftly pushed the key into a huge old lock. The door swung open on silent hinges, and for a moment, Sarah thought they had merely stepped into another storeroom of the antique store. Furniture, dishes, lamps, old books, and music boxes – so many ancient music boxes – were piled on shelves and boxes one atop the other. A mannequin wore what appeared to be three or four theatrical costumes at once, all with the hats to go with them. As they stepped inside, the dim light from a lantern by the door became brighter and brighter, without anyone touching the switch.

"I heard this room existed," Lily breathed, and her voice caught in her throat. "But no one will... talk about it."

"Besides you and your friends," Robert said, his voice now firm and strong, "no one has seen this room in many, many years."

"What is this place," Sarah asked, her voice automatically dropping low. "Another storeroom?"

"Of a kind. This is a store of thousands of enchanted items, and I am their keeper."

"Enchanted?" Cory asked skeptically and shoved his hands into his pockets.

"Indeed, young man. That light you just passed has lit up for hundreds of years, every time a person in need of illumination passes it."

"Motion sensors do that in the dark when you pass by."

"Perhaps, young man, perhaps. But this lamp requires neither cord nor batteries, neither oil nor any other fuel. Have a look if you are still doubtful."

Cory picked up the lamp to examine it, and Sarah forced her eyes away from the overwhelming multitude of everyday curiosities and artworks that threatened to overwhelm her senses again.

"And the sapphire? You must know of the sapphire and its supposed powers if you are the keeper of all these enchanted items."

"I know of the sapphire," Robert said, wagging his head side to side again. "Those fools at the historical society thought they could display it publicly, and an alarm and laser beams would keep it safe."

"Then you know Katelyn is innocent," Cory said, putting down the lamp with a thud and stepping up into Robert's space. "She did not do anything wrong."

Robert leaned back a little and fixed Cory in a stare that should, by all rights, have turned him to ashes. Robert raised a finger pointing directly at Cory's heart.

"Young man..."

"He didn't mean it," Lily hastened to say, but the storekeeper hardly heard her. Cory and Robert locked eyes and refused to let go, but the standoff abruptly melted into laughter when the old man smiled broadly.

"You have spunk and convictions. Cory – is it?"

Cory only nodded.

"And I do agree with you – to a point. For a young girl like her to steal the Royal Veritas Sapphire just as a plaything would be – foolish."

Cory spread his arms but didn't look away. But this time, he wisely did not speak.

"However, young man, you neglect to consider other possibilities. Your friend might have been coerced to assist in the crime, perhaps even paid. She may not even know what she has done."

Cory looked down at his feet. "I didn't think of that," he mumbled, just loud enough for Sarah to hear.

Robert nodded and went deeper into the room, touching an artifact here and there, speaking in a hushed tone only he could hear.

"Now, where have you gone," he muttered, and both Emma and Cory joined him in a narrow aisle between shelves of common household items and elegant bronze sculptures.

"Can we help you find something?" Cory asked, and Robert merely shook his head.

"Around – here…" Emma put her hand onto a thick leather-bound folio that made Sarah suddenly shiver with anticipation and – dread? Robert stopped, fixed Emma in a long stare, and cocked his head.

"This is it. How did you – I see… Come along now."

He took the book without another word and ushered them all back out into the main store. Sarah couldn't help but glance back over her shoulder at all the objects in the room, both precious and ordinary, intimidating and common. Could all of these…? Really? Pixie, she realized, waited by the threshold for the group to return.

Everything okay, girl?

Pixie, usually cheerful and cheeky, took a long time to answer just then, and she 'sounded' exhausted in Sarah's head.

There is – something – in there. What, I cannot tell you, but I am having to guard myself against it.

Robert plunked the thick folio onto his sales counter, an ancient oak structure polished by years of handling. It released a puff of dust that sparkled in the light from the window, and he wiped the cover with the sleeve of his ornate robe.

"Enchanted jewels and gemstones," Sarah read on the cover in gold letters, embossed deeply into the cracked brown leather covers. This book was nothing like the old ledgers and notebooks they had found in the attic months ago; this book looked and felt as if it had passed through thousands of hands and been consulted on questions for just as many years.

Sarah sneezed once and brought a tissue to her nose.

"The dust of all these years can weigh on a person," Robert said with a wink and began leafing through cracked handwritten pages. "Here we go then. The Royal Veritas Sapphire."

"I researched it," Cory said lightly, ignoring Sarah's hand on his shoulder. "It supposedly came from the mythical kingdom of Verdantia to ensure the truth was spoken in the courts."

"Impressive," Robert nodded. "And?"

"I guess they didn't think that something like that could be used by somebody who wanted to lie – but get away with it."

"Very good, young man. Come to me if you are ever looking for employment as a researcher."

"Robbie, we knew all of that," Lily said, a little impatiently. "As much as I like your shop and your – show – it doesn't get us anywhere."

Did Robbie twitch when Lily said, your show? Sarah was prepared for thunderclaps and lightning bolts; instead, Robbie merely laughed.

"Ah, Lily Morrison, impatient as always. You forget that this..." Gently he touched the book with a wrinkled old hand, making the gemstones on his fingers twinkle and gleam. "This came from the enchanted room. It has its own magic. It should be able to tell us the approximate whereabouts of the Sapphire right now.

"Now?" Cory asked and pushed forward before Sarah could hold him back.

Pixie jumped up on Sarah's leg just then, begging to be picked up and comforted. She automatically reached down and cradled the Papillon against her chest.

Watch out.

Sarah stood mesmerized. Robert turned another page to a blank one, and for a second, she thought she saw ants crawling on the page. But they were not ants, busy carrying a few crumbs to their lair; they were tiny precise letters in dark blue ink that were tumbling and sparkling and forming all on their own. Sarah felt her mouth go dry and reached with her free hand for Lily's, squeezing it hard. Cory exhaled hard, incapable of saying, whoa, this time, and then the words rested. Three words had appeared on the page.

Forum

Fresco

Filcher

Robbie looked up at them, smiled, and closed the book with a flourish.

"There you have it then."

"Forum, Fresco, Filcher – an alliteration? What does that even mean?" Sarah wanted to know, but Robbie shook his head.

"That would be for you to figure out. You have a lot of capable help in your own family."

He clapped his hands, releasing another bit of dust, and took the tiniest of bows.

"That's it for today, then. I have other things to do. Go on now, before you chase away all of the other customers."

"All of..." Lily looked around to see if a lineup had formed behind her, but they were still alone in the store.

"Robbie..."

"Go on now – it is for you to figure out."

A moment later, they found themselves on the sidewalk in front of the old antique store and heard the lock engage. The sign above the door turned to Closed as if by magic, and the four of them stared at one another. Pixie still rested in Sarah's arms and squirmed until she let her down.

"What was that," Sarah asked of Lily.

Lily stared at the store and shook her head. "I thought he was just eccentric."

"Eccentric!"

"He's a magician, that's the way they are," Emma said, primly adjusting the strap of her purse on her shoulder.

"Like you know any real magicians." Cory rolled his eyes, but even he couldn't quite hit the note of sarcasm he had been looking for. The store and its owner had impressed him deeply, Sarah realized, and put her hand on her son's shoulder, squeezing gently.

∞

Matthew, on the other hand, was not impressed when he came to the house later that evening, exhausted and in a foul mood from having to deal with museum board meetings all day long.

"You did what," he asked, the hand with his teacup frozen in midair, halfway to his mouth.

"We – went to see an antique dealer." Sarah opened the oven, checked on dinner, and closed it again. "That little old store down by the Shores condo building. Charming little place. The owner..."

"The owner is certifiably crazy, Sarah. A retired Vegas showman who was on trial for murder a few years ago. And the only reason he was not convicted..." Matthew saw the look in her eyes and put the teacup back down again. "Come here," he reached for Sarah and put his arms around her. "I am so damn proud of you for trying to help Katelyn, for believing in her, and for wanting to do the right thing."

"Just not with people who believe in the paranormal. Hmm." Sarah picked up Pixie, who squirmed and managed to escape to go see Cory.

"Touche, I get it."

"Do you, really? Because what happened at that store would have made a believer out of you. And Pixie..."

"Pixie?"

Sarah hesitated for just one second. "Pixie thought there was real magic there."

Matthew looked at her over the rim of his reading glasses. "OK, suppose you are right—"

"Hey Mom, did you know that the word 'Forum' can also refer to court proceedings, specifically 'the location or legal jurisdiction where a case is adjudicated and legal proceedings take place'?" Cory read off a page on his tablet while gesturing with an energy bar in the other hand. "So then — Oh hey Matt. What do you think?"

He completely missed the hand motions his mother made, urging him to shut up and not discuss it any longer.

"Forum?" Matthew asked, pushing up his glasses and looking from Cory to Sarah and back. "What?"

"Mom! You didn't tell him yet?"

Sarah slowly shook her head, and Cory pulled up one of the kitchen chairs and straddled it, facing Matthew. "It was the coolest thing ever. I mean, it was real Matt. It was one hundred percent real."

Out came the entire story. The strangely dressed Robert Murtaugh, the secret room full of enchanted objects, and the old book with the letters that formed three cryptic words.

When Cory was done, Matthew folded his hands and looked down at them for a long, silent moment. Then he raised his eyes and looked Sarah straight in the face as he asked Cory.

"That is an impressive trick, don't you think."

Cory put the rest of his energy bar down and rose from his chair again.

"If the sapphire was originally used to ensure fair and honest trials, a forum is a courtroom, and to Filch is another word for stealing, then we have a connection from two out of three of those words the book gave us. I think it sounds important, but hey..."

He shrugged, gathered up his tablet again, and headed for the kitchen door.

"Cory," Matthew called after him, and Cory would have ignored him and kept on walking if it had not been for Emma coming down the stairs at the same time.

"The news," she said flatly and nodded at the little TV in the kitchen. "Katelyn is being transferred to jail. They denied bail too, so she won't be coming home any time soon."

Sarah turned around and hid her face. It wouldn't do to grin broadly at Matthew with the pride she felt for her children and their sense of right and wrong. Matthew played with his teacup for a long moment, pushing it back and forth between his hands until he finally shook his head.

"Guess I'm outvoted around here, huh?"

"Matthew, you are not. If you are uncomfortable with this because of your job with the museum…"

"Nothing to do with my job, Sarah. I just remember two angry men breaking into your house last year and… what happened after. I keep trying to forget about it."

Pixie chose that moment to jump up and landed squarely in his lap. He put his arms around her just as she planted a little kiss on his cheek.

"And you," he said, affectionately ruffling the velvety fur between the Papillon's ears. "I only heard you speak once, but they say—"

They're right.

Everybody had heard that one. Nobody was sure if they'd heard actual sound or just knew in their heart, but they had all felt her voice. *They're right.*

Matthew took his hands off Pixie, looked at her, and continued patting her when she demanded he do so with insistent pats of her paw.

"Whoa," Cory said softly, and Emma went to take a cookie out of Pixie's cookie jar.

"Good girl."

"Now I am officially outvoted," Matthew said, stirring his tea with a lot more force than was strictly necessary, especially since he hadn't put any sugar into it.

Cory grinned broadly and pulled out his tablet again. For the next half hour, they went over various scenarios that could fit the three words the book had given them until Sarah had to call them to set the table and eat their dinner.

Still, they spoke of ancient definitions and possible meanings for the word 'fresco', and Matthew held a long discourse on old Roman frescoes. Sarah smiled quietly. Strange or not, paranormal or not, this was her family now, and she wouldn't have them any other way.

Chapter Nine

Matthew, feeling the pressure from the museum's board of directors, decided to take the next few days off. He told Sarah that the constant strain of the investigation and the accusations surrounding Katelyn had taken its toll on him. He needed a break, a chance to clear his mind and evaluate the situation with a fresh perspective.

Besides that, he planned to visit Robbie Murtaugh's old antique shop, a place filled with mystique and possibly the key to understanding the true nature of the stolen sapphire. Matthew wanted to stand within the shop's confines, surrounded by the artifacts and ancient energies, to determine for himself whether the rumors he'd heard held any truth.

"I feel like we're missing something," he said to Cory during one of their research sessions. "How could the sapphire, which was initially intended to safeguard truthful and fair court proceedings in Verdantia, suddenly turn up to allow the wearer to lie at will?"

Cory looked up from his online search and only shook his head.

"Furthermore," Matthew continued, " How would someone have found out about this and then decided to use it to their advantage? It isn't like this enchantment was all over the internet, at least before now. You would have to be specifically looking for it. And unless you were a professional in art or history..."

"You wouldn't suddenly go searching for an enchanted stone," Cory added, and his eyes acquired that glow again they always had when he became excited about something.

Sarah watched the two of them head off from the kitchen window and finally let the curtain drop. Seeing that room of enchanted things again was not top priority for her. She could still feel the myriad voices whispering in her head.

Matthew and Cory found her mindlessly staring at a nature show when they returned from town not an hour later.

"Back already?"

"The store was still closed," Matthew said with a little kiss on her cheek.

He gave her shoulder a little squeeze and went to make tea for himself and Cory. Their easy banter and comfortable jokes made them look more like father and son every day.

Sarah watched, a warmth blooming in her chest like the sun peeking through clouds. Matthew, with his kind eyes and gentle smile, brought a sense of peace and joy she hadn't known before, and even more so to Cory. His infectious laughter echoing through the house, felt like an extension of her own heart, a constant reminder of the love that filled their lives, and she whispered a silent prayer of thanks to the universe for bringing him into her world.

"Tea?" Matthew waved her mug at her, but Sarah never got to answer as Emma bolted down the stairs and into the kitchen, waving one of the literary magazines she often brought home from Lily's bookstore.

"Mom, Mom. I think I found something interesting – and creepy – but mostly interesting. It was in one of these magazines. They had that thing going on – a series about AI and whatnot. I skimmed most of it, but there was this one article."

"Slow down, Emma," Sarah laughed. "You're tripping over your own words. What magazine, what AI?"

"I'm looking for the exact one." Emma stood at the table furiously flipping through the pages of a book catalog, not even taking the time to sit. Cory glanced over his sister's shoulder.

"Basically," Emma said, "it was about one of the national libraries that deal with ancient manuscripts. They were planning to digitize a big part of their collection so people could study the texts without handling the books."

"Makes sense." Sarah raised her eyebrows and signaled Matthew to make the tea.

"So, they hired these students to do all of the photographing and putting these documents together – I don't know what it all entailed, but it sounded tedious. And there was this one guy who used an AI module to make the job easier."

"I would have," Cory grumbled.

"It wasn't allowed. I don't remember why. But then he wrote in an online forum that the AI tool he'd been using had discovered hidden text in one of the manuscripts he was scanning, and it transcribed it. It was the downfall of the Kingdom of Verdantia."

"It could be just a simple machine error." Sarah blew on her tea.

"Not at all. The guy wrote in an online forum that it was all about an artifact and how it could be turned from good to bad."

"Can we talk to the guy?" Sarah asked and groped on her coffee table for a pen and a piece of paper. "He might have more information."

Emma looked up and let go of her magazine, and Sarah knew this couldn't be good.

"Too late," she said softly. "He was widely discredited. Basically, they called him a kook who only wanted attention. He disappeared shortly thereafter, and he was found – um - murdered."

"Emma – no."

"Well, that's not everything. Every trace of his essay in that online forum has been removed – everything. The only way I knew about it was this scrawny footnote in a magazine story about AI."

Matthew put down the tea and Cory had lost all interest in what he had been doing previously.

"This is your link," Sarah finally said. "It has to be. Didn't you say you could never figure out how anyone would know that the sapphire could be used for nefarious intentions and now..."

"All artifacts usually have—"

"A shadow side, I know Matthew. But how many coincidences is that? Knowing about the sapphire's enchantment, knowing it could be turned. It has to be the reason."

"And you think..."

"I think someone read this fellow's article, decided then, and there he had use for the sapphire and would steal it."

"That still doesn't tell us who. I agree it could have gone down like that – could. But who and why? If we want to get Katelyn out of jail, well..."

"We need the whole story."

Pixie jumped into her lap and cuddled close.

You are on the right trail.

I think so too, but we still don't have enough.

Sarah shook her head and patted the silky soft fur between Pixie's ears absentmindedly.

"It's not enough," she thought again then she realized the words had actually been spoken aloud. By Emma, who still stood by her side, magazine in one hand. Cory grabbed his tablet again and typed furiously

"It's a start," she said slowly.

Emma put away the magazine and looked up at her mother from clear blue unwavering eyes.

"But it's not enough to save Katelyn?"

"Don't worry about that right now. You found this information so far. Let that be enough for now. And – I worry about you."

"There's nothing to worry about, Mom. I can't do what you do, but — I hear things."

"What kind of — things?"

"Mostly Amelia. She is getting weaker, though. I think she's going home. At the museum, there are lots of spirits if you make an effort to tune in. They're not scary at all. That store though, there is something very dark there."

"Emma..."

"Most ghosts aren't scary – they're fun." She giggled and gave Pixie a quick pat on the head. "But Katelyn is not safe. You need to go back to that store and see if you can find anything else to help. I'll keep looking for more from that article."

And with that, she darted back up the stairs, Pixie in hot pursuit.

"What – was that?" Matthew asked, and Sarah brought a hand to her mouth.

"I knew she could communicate with Amelia, but – other ghosts?"

"And by the store, I assume she means that antique store, not Lily's bookstore?"

"I think so." Sarah gripped her teacup a little tighter. "And what does she mean by 'Katelyn is not safe'? Did she hear that, read it? Where?"

Matthew didn't know. He had barely accepted that his girlfriend had certain abilities, and he wasn't quite ready to admit that her young daughter might have similar talents. He paced up and down in the living room, made a quick call to the lawyer he had arranged for Katelyn, and asked him to check on things. Ten minutes later, he answered a quick call and came back into the kitchen.

"They say Katelyn is fine, although quiet and withdrawn."

"Jail will do that to you, I guess," Sarah said, rolling her eyes.

"In any case, everything is good, for now."

"Thanks for checking," Sarah rose from the couch and held a hand out to Matthew. "Guess I'm going back to Robbie and his creepy store tomorrow."

"Are you sure you're up for that?"

"Honestly, I can think of more fun things, but the way Emma said 'Katelyn is not safe' unnerved me. So, I'm going to do everything to get her out of that place."

And I will have to come to terms with the fact that my daughter talks to spirits, she thought and stared into the dancing flames of the fireplace. That might be the hardest one of them all.

Chapter Ten

T he next day, Sarah waited patiently until Matthew was out on an errand, Cory had gone to play basketball for a bit of a mental break, and Emma was helping Lily at the bookstore. Grabbing her keys, she clipped on Pixie's harness and leash and took her for a drive into Rosewood Hollow.

After maneuvering the car into a parking spot, she clutched her purse in one hand and Pixie's leash in the other and climbed the windrow of snow to land on an icy sidewalk.

Not fun.

Pixie pulled up her paws one at a time to show her what she thought of walking on an icy sidewalk in the middle of February.

I'm sorry, girl, I didn't want to go without you.

I'm not a winter sports kind of dog.

We'll hurry – promise.

Sarah had no idea what she was going to tell Robert Murtaugh. He'd all but told her this was her own problem.

She pulled Pixie up into her arms and strode quickly toward the antique store.

You know you are a diva, Sarah thought.

No comment.

Sarah walked up to the store and automatically hugged the little papillon dog a bit tighter. The clouds around her appeared to want to pull in a little closer, to press down on her a bit harder. She was having a hard time drawing a breath.

Do you feel that?

The magic is closing in, Sarah. I don't like it. We need to go. Now.

Sarah walked up to the old antique store, not listening. No light showed through the old, stained windows. Pixie squirmed in her arms and pressed her paws into her chest, hard.

Sarah, leave.

Sarah didn't leave. She walked up to the store, holding on to a wriggling, squirming little dog, and finally stopped.

"Closed for vacation," she read off a large piece of paper tacked to the entrance.

Sarah, look at the paper.

She did. Her fingers found the old piece of printer paper, yellowed and stained. It looked old, Sarah thought, older than it had any right to be, considering.

Pixie, that can't be.

Automatically Sarah tightened her grip on the little dog until Pixie pushed her paws into her body.

We were just here yesterday. Sarah leaned against the side of the building taking deep cleansing breaths, trying to get her racing thoughts in order when an older woman stopped on the sidewalk beside them.

"Are you all right, dear? Do you need me to call anyone?"

Sarah shook her head and took a few more deep breaths. The woman had to be in her eighties, with a shock of curly grey hair and a heavy swan-necked cane. An antique carved cane.

"I was hoping to see Robert Murtaugh," she blurted as the woman was already walking away. "The man who owns this store. Is he away?"

"Robbie?" The old woman laughed, a sound that reminded Sarah of old clocks chiming and the tinny sound of antique music boxes. Automatically she shivered and clutched Pixie hard.

"Robbie? Oh no, my dear, he spends all of his winters in Florida. Or is it Arizona?"

The woman put a finger to her chin, and Sarah felt herself getting faint.

"Thank you," she said, her voice tinny and distant to her own ears. I'll try some other time."

The old woman walked away, shaking her head and chuckling to herself and Sarah stood on the sidewalk, leaning against the wall of the old antique store. She pushed her back in hard until she could feel every board of the old clapboard siding, and her heart finally stopped racing.

Pixie?

I'm here, Sarah.

What happened here?

I'm not sure. But it scares me. Let's get back home – hurry.

"Deep breaths," she mumbled. She looked around and found that the old woman with her cane had disappeared down the road. How could she have covered that distance so quickly? Again, Sarah shivered.

Pixie?

But instead of an answer, her little dog drew closer into the safety of Sarah's arms and thick down jacket until only a little black nose showed under the fringe of her scarf.

Sarah pushed off the wall and walked back toward where she had left her car in huge, ground-eating strides. Now and then, she paused and checked down the side roads, hoping to see the old woman lumbering along with her cane, but she didn't spot anyone.

Reaching the car, she opened the door and let Pixie hop in, reversed out of her parking spot, and drove out of the downtown core almost in one long movement.

Pixie, what was that?

Again, nothing. Pixie lay down and dropped her head onto her front paws, watching Sarah with dark, steady eyes.

I am always here.

Chapter Eleven

By the time they reached the house, Sarah could almost convince herself it had all been perfectly normal. Robert Murtaugh had decided to leave on the spur of the moment, and the old woman had gone into some nearby building. It was nothing unusual at all, just her overactive imagination.

Cory sat at the kitchen table, flipping through pages on his tablet while the kitchen TV was turned to a news station for background noise.

"Hey bud, how was basketball?" she forced herself to sound cheerful and unconcerned. Years of watching her former husband cheat and hiding that fact from the kids had given her that talent at least.

Cory looked up from the screen and searched her face for the longest time. No dummy, her oldest.

"Not bad – like always

Sarah reached down to hand a cookie to Pixie. "Homework?"

Cory gave her one of his famous eye rolls. His quick brain made him one of the top students in his class.

"Research. I'm working on those three words the books gave us."

"Forum, filcher..."

"Fresco, right. Trying to figure out if there is a way into this thing somehow. I'm getting nowhere."

His teenage frown told her all she needed to know about his mood.

"Leave it be for now, honey."

"I don't want to leave it be. I want to help Katelyn."

"Yes, but not all by yourself and not all on the same day. Maybe you should—"

"If you're going to tell me I need to let it go for now, well, just don't." Cory then nodded into the corner where Pixie had pulled her pink plush blanket into a huge pile in the dog bed and burrowed into it so only her nose showed. "But I don't think she's going anywhere for a bit."

"Pixie and cold temperatures are not two things that seem to go well together." Sarah laughed and sat beside her son. It felt so normal here in her warm kitchen, so beautifully normal and cozy.

She turned off the TV and pointed at the tablet, "What have you got so far?"

"Not much more. A fresco is a painting technique where pigments are applied to wet plaster on a wall or ceiling. As the plaster dries, the colors become an integral part of the surface, creating a durable and long-lasting artwork," Cory read and followed the paragraph with another eye roll. "One famous example would be Michelangelo's, *The Creation of Adam*. This iconic fresco is part of the Sistine Chapel ceiling in Vatican City, depicting the biblical story of God giving life to Adam."

He tilted the screen so Sarah could look at the famous image.

"It's beautiful."

"But I don't know what it means, Mom. There are more examples here, most of them...somewhere in Italy, I guess, but none of them has a sapphire in it."

"Well, these are by no means all of them."

"I know, and I looked up pictures of famous frescoes until my eyes bugged out, and still nothing."

"You don't give up easily."

Again, she squeezed his shoulder gently, and Cory shrugged, pushing the tablet away roughly, and got up to get himself a soda. For once, Sarah didn't give him a hard time about it.

"Maybe it's not about something that old," she mused. "Maybe..."

"What?"

Cory took most of his soda in one big gulp.

"Maybe it's not an old fresco but a recent painting?"

"Or the old guy was just full of it, and all of it was just a magic trick and a total waste of time." Cory came back to the table and gave the tablet another push. "I don't know. And I hate not knowing."

He left the kitchen then, most likely to go stew over one of the many computer games his father kept sending him. Her ex usually conveniently ignored his son's sharp mind and bought every variation of an ego shooter game he could find. Cory played with them once—if at all—and gave many of them away to his friends. Sarah found herself smiling. One of these days, he'd make a great scientist, this boy of hers.

☙

A little while later, Emma came home from the bookstore and didn't have anything to add to the fresco mystery either.

"Is Matthew coming over tonight?" Cory asked on his next snack trip into the kitchen, and Sarah checked her phone.

"I thought he was, but he's usually here by now if he comes straight from the museum."

Both her messaging system and texting app were suspiciously silent. It wasn't like him not to check-in.

Probably busy, she thought and tried to ignore the nagging feeling in her gut. *Probably endless meetings because of the sapphire. It's no wonder.*

The theft had been a colossal failure and embarrassment to the museum and the town of Rosewood Hollow. That sounded like meetings—lots of them.

Mindlessly, Sarah pulled some pasta out of the pantry and stared at it for a few long minutes before settling on a simple spaghetti dish.

"Hey, is Matthew coming over tonight?"

"I don't know, Emma. Why don't you ask him?" she snapped at her daughter, who had just stopped in the kitchen for some water. "Sorry, Em, I didn't mean to..."

"Did something happen? You guys have a fight?"

"No, no, of course not," Sarah blew out a big breath and ran suddenly shaking fingers through her long blonde hair. "It's just – I thought he was coming here after work, but I didn't hear, and now I can't get a hold of him. It's... I just had a long day, that's all."

Emma didn't believe it for a second. She stood before Sarah, quiet blue eyes resting on hers, and did not speak. Sarah thought she saw something in those eyes.

"You went to that store again," Sarah said.

"You know?" Emma shrugged and finally turned away, picked an orange out of the fruit basket on the counter, and peeled it slowly.

"Is it this house, or have you always – known things, seen things?"

"I'm not really sure. Amelia thinks—"

"Amelia! I think that ghost needs to mind her own business."

"She was shot by her own father, Mom, cut her some slack. Besides, I think she'll be moving on anyway."

"Where have I landed?" Sarah said at the table beside her daughter and buried her hands in her hair. "First Pixie, then Amelia, then it's me knowing how to do certain... things. And now you, and this...?"

Emma shrugged and segmented her orange, offering a piece to her mother, and savoring the others.

"Don't be afraid of it. That's the key. When I found Amelia's diary..."

"You knew back then?" Sarah made a fist, remembering Emma's fall and the accidental discovery of the diary – and everything that came after.

"I was drawn to it. Didn't know why, didn't know how. But it all worked out." Emma smiled brightly. "I do wish I could talk to Pixie the way you do, though."

"We don't really... talk, you know."

As if to disprove that statement, Pixie strolled into the room, took a leap, and landed on Sarah's lap.

Something is happening.

What is it?

I don't know – but the energy is off – everywhere.

Sarah shivered, hard, and clutched the little Papillon. "Something is going on," she said to Emma, who put down the remainder of her orange and closed her eyes.

"It feels off," she confirmed and looked toward the doorway that led into their games room. It was a comfortable room full of bookshelves, overstuffed sofas, and games. In the old days, it had been a fine parlor, and Amelia was often fond of appearing there. A cold draft blew into the kitchen from the direction of the games room, and Sarah thought she could see something wispy and white right there on the threshold, then it disappeared again.

"She can't come through," Emma said, and her face fell.

"It's okay, maybe she's happier on the other side," Sarah said and took her daughter's hand. "That was why you helped her figure out who killed her, right?"

Emma only nodded.

Sarah reached for the remote control and flicked on the TV, wanting only something mindless to stop her endlessly spiraling brain. Instead, pictures of huge crowds of angry people fighting and pushing one another assaulted her.

At the bottom of the screen, a red banner declared, Inmates riot at local prison, and, while the volume was quite muted, Sarah knew on location the noise had to be deafening. The feed from a security camera captured a roiling sea of people filling a narrow hallway, waving homemade banners, chair legs, and dinner trays, and shouting slogans that echoed through the room. Pushing and shoving, several men were busy jumping a counter, raiding a cafeteria, and guards in riot gear clashed with inmates, creating a chaotic tableau of flying debris and scattered trash.

Then the view switched to a helicopter circling overhead the prison, and a news anchor trying to regain his composure.

"Is that where Katelyn...?" Emma asked tonelessly, and Sarah only shook her head.

"I don't know, honey."

Although, if she had to be honest – most likely. How many prisons could there be in the area?

Just then, a door upstairs slammed, and Cory came thundering down the stairs.

"Mom, mom, turn on the — Oh, you're watching it."

"Yes, we just saw."

"That's the place where Katelyn is. She's in there – in – that…"

He pointed at the screen with an outstretched hand, his eyes wide and panicked.

"You can't leave her in there. Please, you have to get her out of there."

His eyes blazed with terrified emotions, and his arms waved through the air as if he could conjure up the solution he sought.

"Cory, there's nothing I can do about it right now. Katelyn's lawyers have been trying to get her out on bail forever and it keeps being denied."

"But now that is happening." He kept pointing at the TV. "Can't you – I don't know, write to a congressman or another politician? Doesn't Dad know anybody? He knows all of these powerful people, and the one time we need him – the one time…"

"Okay, okay, Cory – easy – sit beside me and calm down for a second. That's a good idea. We'll call your dad later. Perhaps he does know somebody. Katelyn did use to be his girlfriend, after all."

Cory dropped into the chair beside him, and she put her arm around his shoulders. For once, her usually tough teenage boy trembled with concern.

"It's all right, Cory; we'll do everything we can to fix this, promise."

Then she heard a familiar bike bell outside and a loud knock at the back door. Emma jumped up and let in Matthew.

"You know?" he asked, nodding at the TV.

"Cory thinks that's where Katelyn is," Sarah said. "Is that true, is she really – in there?"

The TV screen had switched back to images of the inmates rioting, clashing heavily with guards, and she shuddered.

"I only see men – surely the women are…"

"Different building," Matthew said and shook his head, but before she could take a relieved breath, he put down his bag and peered at her over the rim of his glasses. "They say it's...uh, just as bad on the women's side, if not worse."

Cory made a frustrated sound somewhere between a growl and a groan, and Sarah squeezed his shoulder again.

"Do they know what started this?"

Matthew stroked his chin and sighed. He looked at Cory and Emma and slowly shook his head.

Liar! Sarah thought, surprising herself with the intense emotion of that thought.

"I'm sorry. We decided to lock down the entire museum, so I'm a bit late. I hope you didn't worry."

When she looked up at him, he shook his head again, ever so slightly. Don't talk about this now.

Sarah pressed her lips together, hard. Why would they put the museum on lockdown because of a prison riot anyway?

Her heart sank for Cory, still staring at the TV and threading his fingers through one another. For some reason, he looked up to that girl like an older sister. Quickly she reached over and turned off the news.

"That's enough of that violence for now, I think."

Cory stared straight ahead and finally collected his tablet with a quick swipe of his hand.

"I'm going up to my room," he said without looking at anyone and headed upstairs, Pixie close on his heels. Emma stood there helpless for a moment and finally followed her brother.

Matthew sighed and went to the painted wood box where he kept most of the specialty teas he was so fond of. Nobody else would dare touch them, knowing that he went through great lengths to source and obtain the latest specialty blends and flavors. He dug through the box for a moment and finally closed it again.

"What the heck," he muttered, and when Sarah looked up again, he held a bottle of wine and two glasses. "This is a mess."

"I understand, but why…"

"What I didn't want to say in front of the kids was that some people think Katelyn is behind the entire riot."

"Katelyn? Surely not. Look, just because somebody…"

"Chooses an unconventional lifestyle and way to dress does not mean they are automatically involved in nefarious circumstances," Matthew recited. "I know – I heard you tell the kids a dozen times."

"Glad you are paying attention."

"The thing is," Matthew continued and slipped into a chair across from her, that somebody, he put the word in air quotes, "somebody had an entire box full of comfort items delivered to her and a bunch of money deposited in her commissary account."

"We didn't," Sarah protested. "I know we talked about it but decided to go with whatever her lawyer thought was best, remember?"

"I was the one who suggested that," Matthew took a big sip of wine, frowned, and looked at the label. He was not a drinker at the best of times, but the lines around his eyes and the disheveled appearance of his short brown hair spoke volumes. "I said, let's wait," Matthew continued and rubbed the spot between his eyes with the heel of his hand. "At least until the trial, and hopefully acquittal, her lawyers should call the shots. Fact is though, somebody did."

"Maybe Michael," Sarah mused, thinking of the children's father. His relationship with Katelyn had never made sense to her, but as she had told Cory, at least at one point he cared.

"That was my first thought. Now, I just heard about this in the meeting, so please don't shoot the messenger."

He paused to take more of the wine, and Sarah leaned back in her chair. "Why do I know that I'm not going to like what I'm about to hear," she said, running her hand through her hair. "Let me have it then."

"Apparently," Matthew said after checking that neither Cory nor Emma had snuck back down the stairs again. "Apparently, whoever had this box of stuff delivered used some rather unconventional methods to do so."

"Unconventional?"

"Going around normal channels," Matthew said, peering into his glass. "There are rules to be followed, and whoever wanted to give Katelyn a gift made sure they were not and did not have to be followed."

"All right, all right, that does sound like something Michael would do," she said, "but still, that's no reason to blame Katelyn for a prison riot."

"Maybe not, but..." Matthew pressed his lips together hard and got up from his chair. Folding his hands behind his back, he began to pace up and down in the kitchen, peeking out into the entrance hall now and then. Not a peep came from upstairs and the children's room, and Sarah only hoped they were not listening somewhere.

"Katelyn's cell mate had some issue with that since she's been waiting for her birthday presents to be cleared and delivered to her for weeks now," Matthew sighed.

"Yes but..."

"And she complained about it and got right up in Katelyn's face, and Katelyn started to argue that she had no idea who sent the care package or who paid to get around the rules, and before you know it..."

"A fight started," Sarah closed her eyes and brought her hands to her face, palms together. "I'm guessing special treatment, even if you don't know from whom, is not a good way to endear yourself to others in a place like that. But to make her responsible for a riot?"

Matthew said nothing, standing by the kitchen window and staring out into the dark yard and the road beyond. There was something else, Sarah thought, right there in the tense lines of his shoulders, the clenched hands, and the way he refused to look at her now.

"Matthew?"

"You saw it on TV," Matthew mumbled. It was... everybody against everybody—police, riot unit..."

"Matthew? What is it you're not telling me?"

This time he did turn around and brushed an invisible speck off his dark jeans. Upon joining the museum's board of directors not long ago, he had ditched the quirky slogan tees in favor of sophisticated, muted-tone sweaters, instantly elevating his style. Sporting an air of unshakeable confidence most days, he appeared impervious to any challenge. Yet, at this moment, a sudden shift revealed a vulnerability etched across his face, transforming it into a canvas of palpable hurt.

"Katelyn was hurt pretty badly," he said softly. "Just before I came here, I got word that she'd been taken to the university hospital. No idea of a prognosis just yet."

"And you waited till now to tell me," Sarah jumped up, looking around for her purse as if she wanted to leave for the hospital right then. Automatically her thoughts spooled off a list of tasks – who would sit with the kids, she didn't want either of them along, who would tell them, they'd be devastated, was there gas in her car, how much of this wine...

"Did you want me to tell you in front of the kids?"

"No, of course not – I have to go see her."

"Not now, Sarah."

"Yes now, Matthew. We've all failed this girl for… ever since that damned sapphire was stolen. I am not going to let it happen again. If indeed it was Michael who sent that package to her, who started all of this…"

"It wasn't."

There was more. Sarah had just found her car keys and carefully, almost reverently, put them back into the little ceramic bowl by the back door, where all of the odds and ends that needed to go out were being kept.

"Yes?" she asked, not daring to look at Matthew.

"I called him when I found out? Michael swore up and down he had not sent that package."

"But who then…"

"My question exactly. We did not, Michael did not, and there's nobody she knows here in Rosewood Hollow who would have done that. So I just don't know. What in the dickens is going on here?"

For a fleeting moment, Sarah thought of Cory and Emma and dismissed that theory almost instantly. They were young, but not dumb. Cory specifically knew better than to do something like this without checking with her.

"And I'm sure it wasn't the kids either," Matthew added needlessly. "Somebody knew just how to cause enough trouble to harm Katelyn, but not enough to trigger an investigation," Matthew said and struck the table with his flat hand. Matthew never lost his temper – never. Sarah shivered when she thought of her strange afternoon and saw the hard set of his jaw. Without a moment's hesitation, she told him the story of the old woman on the street who had disappeared, and Robbie's store that looked like it had been closed for weeks.

Matthew's eyes narrowed and glittered with a fire she hadn't seen previously. "Let's call Lily," he said, phone already in hand. "She knew this guy, she took you there."

He'd barely dialed a few numbers when they heard a series of impatient knocks at the back door, and he admitted Lily.

"Speak of the devil," he said, ushering her in. I need to ask you a couple of really important questions—"

"Any news about Katelyn?" Lily interrupted, and Sarah only shook her head.

"How do you already know about Katelyn and the riot?" Matthew put himself between Sarah and Lily, straightening up to his full height and shoving the phone back into his jeans pocket. Sarah raised a hand, but Lily wheeled on Matthew.

"That riot has been all over the news, and Katelyn—well, I have my sources in this town. I've lived here as long as I can remember." *Unlike either of you*, the sentence stood in the room, even if she didn't say it aloud.

"Answer me honestly now, Lily Morrison," Matthew ground out from between clenched teeth. "Did you send a package with all sorts of high-value goodies to Katelyn?"

"A what? To jail?" Lily sat hard on the nearest kitchen chair. "No, of course not. I didn't even know you could do that."

Matthew said nothing for a moment, then blew out a hard breath and poured some water from a carafe on the table.

"What about this guy you took my family to, Robert Murtaugh?"

My family? Sarah felt her heart open when she heard him say that. A smile tugged at her lips, but it died there. Her phone felt heavy in her hand, where she would have phoned Lily to share this perfect moment.

Lily looked from Matthew to Sarah and back. A tiny wink told Sarah she had not missed that moment entirely, but immediately she shook her head.

"Robbie is an oddball, Matthew. He's strange, he's weird. He does things nobody else does, and that store of his – can be downright creepy."

"To say the least," Sarah said, hugging her arms to her body, remembering the message of dancing letters the strange book had given her.

"I didn't know he would scare the bejesus out of everybody with his magic show," Lily insisted. "He was a professional magician, he seems knowledgeable about enchantments. We were talking about that damned sapphire having an enchantment, so I thought why not visit Robbie. He'll be entertaining and spin a good yarn. That's all, that's everything."

Matthew took that in and looked away. Finally, he drank most of his water in one big gulp and took a kitchen chair.

"Sorry," he muttered in Sarah's direction. "I don't usually react like this, but when the people I care about get hurt – physically or emotionally..."

"It's fine." Sarah put her hand on his, and this time, she smiled when he said the people I care about. "We're all feeling helpless."

Lily stared at the two of them and got to her feet again. "I can see I'm in the way here," she said, and was gathering her bag when Sarah grabbed her arm.

"No, stay. Nobody in this house has had dinner yet, and the kids are upset and confused. A little bit of normalcy would be good for everybody. Please." Lily looked at Matthew, who only shrugged.

They called the kids back down again, telling them as gently as they could that Katelyn had been hurt and was at the hospital. Sarah made some pasta dish no one really noticed, and by the time the evening was running out, they had decided they would go see Katelyn at the hospital the next day. Even if there were rules and regulations about it, even if another officer had to be there and the kids most likely wouldn't be allowed in, they all felt they had to try.

Chapter Twelve

Matthew, with some difficulty, was able to secure a brief visit with Katelyn at University Hospital – one person, thirty minutes, no exceptions. Sarah, the chosen visitor, steeled herself for the strict procedures.

The car ride mirrored the somber mood – Matthew, laser-focused, gripped the wheel. In the back, Lily chattered to a distracted Emma while Cory stared out, lost in thought. Pixie, perched on Sarah's lap, scanned their surroundings with worried eyes. Sarah longed for a word, any word, but Pixie remained stubbornly quiet.

At the hospital, bureaucracy tightened its grip. Sarah endured ID checks, pat-downs, and a confiscated purse before finally approaching Katelyn's door. The weight of the situation pressed heavily.

She had known Katelyn as the vibrant, energetic young woman with cascading raven-black hair who had unfortunately found herself entangled with Sarah's former husband. Sarah often speculated whether Michael had brought her to Rosewood Hollow merely to provoke a reaction from Sarah, showcasing his penchant for younger women more akin to Cory's age.

However, confronting a ghost and thieving neighbors together tends to change one's priorities, and Katelyn had stayed behind in Rosewood.

Katelyn seamlessly integrated into their circle, joining in video game sessions with Cory, engaging in literary discussions with Emma, and exchanging unconventional fashion tips with Lily. She became a friend.

Closing the door to the heavily guarded hospital room with a hushed click, Sarah scanned the space, momentarily perplexed. Had they directed her to the wrong place? The pristine white bed appeared vacant until she spotted Katelyn.

Hidden beneath swathes of white bandages enveloping her head, her once lustrous raven hair was obscured. One eye nearly swollen shut, and a leg encased in a cast protruding from beneath the covers. Crimson scratches etched across her cheeks and neck, vanishing beneath the hospital gown. Three fingers taped together hinted at further injury. Sarah could only envision the ordeal Katelyn had endured.

"Katy," she said softly, trying to sound confident and jovial but failing miserably. "What have they done to you?"

Katelyn tried to smile even though it visibly pained her.

"Didn't make any friends in that place," she said with an effort and pulled herself up in the bed a little. "Go figure."

"I am so sorry."

"What on earth for, Sarah?" Katelyn's hand snaked out from under the bed covers, mindful of the sensors attached to the back of her hand. Gently she squeezed Sarah's fingers and winked with her unhurt eye. "Not like you did this."

"I thought Michael might have sent the gifts that started all of this."

"No, no, he didn't..." Katelyn reclined, briefly closing her eyes. "Those cops listening at the door?"

"They're outside. There's only one—and I don't assume he's listening." Sarah looked over her shoulder and then back at Katelyn.

Sarah impulsively approached the door, peeked through the central window, and returned, edging her stool closer to the bed. "What's this all about, then?"

"I'm not safe."

"It's that damned prison. Matthew, and all of us, are working so hard to get you out of there—"

"No, Sarah – I'm not safe outside either."

For a moment, Sarah felt something hard and tight clamp around her heart, and she hugged her arms close. Katelyn still had her eyes closed, and the only sound in the room was the far-off hospital noise and the overly loud ticking of a wall clock.

"Nobody gave me that gift box," Katelyn finally said, in a voice so low Sarah had to lean in. "It was just a way to get a message to me."

"A message? But what...?"

"To stop investigating the sapphire theft, or I'd be dead. And just to prove that they could get to me anywhere, they had someone start that riot over that thing."

The ticking of the wall clock seemed to become louder so that every second hammered into Sarah's brain with the force of a sledgehammer. *Stop investigating the sapphire.*

"Katelyn, if we stop looking into this, you may go to prison for the rest of your life. That is not an option, at all" she said. She wanted to take Katelyn's hand, but the bandaged, broken fingers made her hesitate, and she touched the pillow beside the girl's head instead. "We can't stop now. We have found—"

"They will kill me, Sarah," Katelyn's voice became urgent now, and a lone tear crept out of her uninjured eye.

"Who is they?"

"I don't know."

"Then how do you know?"

Katelyn struggled up into a more upright position as best as she could.

"I told you, that damned gift basket. And a note warning me to stop looking into the sapphire. It wasn't exactly signed, okay? But it was explicit enough to make me want to stay in jail for a very, very long time."

"I can't accept that." Sarah got to her feet again and peeked out the window into the hall. "Maybe we can find that note in your cell, then we would have all we need—"

"Sarah." It took her a moment to realize that the choked, strangled sound from the bed was Katelyn's vain attempt to laugh. "Do you really think that a person, or persons, with enough clout to start a riot in prison just to get a message to me, would be dumb enough to leave any incriminating evidence behind? Anyway, my lawyer already had it checked out."

"Still..."

"You guys have got to back off before something happens to you or the kids. Do you think they would care that Cory is only sixteen and that he just happens to love researching things with his hero Matthew?"

The effort was taking its toll, she could see the strain on Katelyn's face. A red light in the bank of monitors behind her began to blink, and a soft, rhythmic beep started. Katelyn sighed, forcing herself to relax a bit, and slid back down in her bed.

"Promise me—"

Just then, the door to the tiny room opened, and a nurse appeared, together with the police officer.

"All right now," the nurse said and busied herself at the bank of monitors. "Enough for today, young lady, you are getting far too excited."

"Sarah, promise me."

"Not right now, ladies. Tomorrow is another day. Time for another checkup and some meds now. Lie back down"

The nurse nodded at the police officer, who took another step closer and took Sarah's elbow.

"Ma'am,"

"I don't need an escort." Sarah snapped, tearing her elbow away and turned toward the door, turning around one last time. "I will be back, Katelyn, promise, I will."

"Sarah."

She heard Katelyn's voice even as she collected her things in the hall, slung her bag over her shoulder without looking back, and stalked down the hallway.

∞

I am not safe.

You have to promise me.

Stop looking into the sapphire.

The hell I will, she thought, coming off the elevator into the ground floor lobby, looking around for her family. I never promised anything. The hell we are leaving her in that place.

"Mom." Cory waved at her from across the lobby, where he was sharing a hot chocolate with Emma.

Mentally gathering herself, she forced a smile and joined them. Matthew could read her like a book. He said nothing while pushing another decadent cup of hot chocolate toward her.

"How's Katy?" both kids wanted to know before she could get out a single word.

"Healing." Again she forced that godawful smile, thinking of Katy looking so tiny and frail in that bed. *I am not safe.* "Unfortunately, it will be a while before we'll be able to see her again."

She looked up to find Matthew's dark eyes resting on hers. His face did not give the slightest hint of what he may be thinking, but Sarah knew. He understood that their fun amateur sleuthing experiment had just taken a serious turn.

"Hey, you told me you broke your arm riding your dirt bike a few years ago," he said and playfully cuffed Cory on the side. "If you remember what that felt like, you probably know that Katy needs nothing but rest right now."

"Yeah, it was my BMX bike, and we were in the skate park," Cory muttered, looking down at his hot chocolate. "I thought we could..."

"I'm sure you can film a few videos for her, and I'll take them in," Sarah said quickly and looked around the cafeteria. Was someone watching Katelyn's room and visitors? Were they even at this moment keeping an eye on her and her children?

"Why don't we let Pixie out for a minute? Let your mom catch up on these hot chocolates," Lily suggested, lifting the handle of the purse carrier that held Pixie—guaranteed to fool most no-pet rules.

"Yeah, sure."

Neither Cory nor Emma were enthusiastic about stepping outside. Cory specifically was smart enough to understand there was something she wanted to discuss with Matthew. Something he wasn't meant to hear, and he dragged his feet an awful lot on the way out of the cafeteria.

∾

"You look white as a – ghost," Matthew finally said and put his hand on hers. "Is Katelyn in really bad shape?"

"No. Injury-wise – she's not even all that bad."

Sarah lowered her head, checked that Lily and the kids were out of earshot, and finally told Matthew the entire story. By the time she reached the end, Matthew had tightened his grip on her hand, and his face was set in hard, angry lines.

"Any idea who *they* are?"

Sarah only shook her head.

"If they come anywhere near you or those kids," Matthew clarified, his tone ominously stern.

Sarah hid a weak smile behind her napkin, wiping her mouth.

"Now I'm worried I may have endangered everyone by coming here and seeing Katelyn."

Matthew stared off into the distance, eyes unfocused, hands folded at his chin. Finally, he ran his hands through his hair then folded them behind his neck.

"We have got to figure out who this is. Who has taken the sapphire and is threatening Katelyn, or we'll end up looking over our shoulders for years?"

"We?"

Matthew looked at her as if she'd grown a set of horns suddenly. "Of course, we. Did you think I wanted to let you figure this one out on your own?"

"No, but it could be..."

"Dangerous?" Matthew laughed out loud and drew a few curious stares from neighboring tables. "Sarah, since I met you, Cory, Emma, and Pixie, almost everything we've done together has turned out dangerous in one way or another. I'm used to it by now, and to be honest, I kind of like it."

"Really." Sarah took his hand again. "Thank you."

"Hey, other people go skydiving," he said with that mischievous grin that could make her agree to anything he said—anytime. "I just hang with the people I love. It works."

Sarah squeezed his hand, hard, and tried to hold on to that moment for all it was worth. All too soon, Matthew moved again, and reality came flooding back.

"That doesn't mean we need to be reckless, Sarah. If anything out of the ordinary happens – anything – I want to know about it. Are you using that alarm system I installed for the house every day?"

"We did, but..." Sarah looked down at her hands.

"But what?"

"Amelia kept setting it off."

"Am..." Matthew closed his eyes and blew out a breath. "Of course she would. Your ghost—"

"She's not really my... It's complicated. And anyway, Emma thinks she's leaving soon."

"You let Emma talk to that, uh..."

"Apparition?"

"I was going to say thing." Matthew rolled his eyes.

"Emma has a strong connection to Amelia. And there's always Pix-ie."

"Pixie, I see. All five pounds of her." Matthew folded his hands in his lap. "You want to know what I think? Maybe best if I were to move in with you all at Thompson Hall. Only until this is all over, of course."

"Really?" Sarah grinned broadly, and once again, her spirits lifted, and she caught a ray of sunshine through the great front windows.

"If it's okay with you, of course."

"It would be more than okay, thank you, Matthew." She got up then, threw her arms around him, and held him in a tight embrace. Long enough for the people at the neighboring table to glance over yet again with barely hidden smiles.

"Not that I'm not enjoying this tremendously," Matthew whispered in her ear. "But Lily and the kids are just coming back in."

By the time the kids reached their table, Matthew and Sarah were back sitting across from one another, albeit both sporting broad, silly grins.

Lily put down her purse and stared from one to the other.

"All right," she said. "I'll bite. What has you two grinning like – like, I don't know," she shrugged.

"We thought that it would make things easier if Matthew would stay with us for a little while," Sarah said, looking down at the tablecloth.

"Yeah." Cory pumped his fist, and Lily looked a little suspicious, searching Matthew's face.

"Easier, huh?"

"You know how it is," Matthew spun a finger in the air. "We just want to help Katy, and with all of the research and looking up things... It would just be easier."

"I see." Lily sat again and finally burst out laughing. "Congratulations, you guys."

"Lily, it isn't really..." Sarah started until Emma put her hand on hers.

"Mom, if you think nobody in the family has noticed, I have very bad news for you. Besides, Cory and I love Matthew, and Pixie does, too."

A subdued little ruff out of the purse carrier confirmed Emma's words. Matthew suddenly blushed a deep crimson and looked around to see where he could pay their bill. Lily only grinned, delighting in Sarah's discomfort.

Cory chimed in, "There's a spare room beside mine, Matt. You can totally grab that."

"Y – yes. We'll talk about it." He glared at Lily, whose grin had only become broader in the last few minutes, and finally got to his feet. "I'll go pay, then let's get back on the road. We have things to do."

Chapter Thirteen

Matthew, despite his Ph.D. and prestigious position at the University, the museum, and historical society, lived in a relatively small condo close to the center of Rosewood Hollow. Sarah had been there a few times. Mostly they hung out at Thompson Hall, since there was more room for everyone.

He owned a few high-quality antiques, a few pieces of art, and an exceptionally high-end computer system Cory admired. That was it. Consequently, it took Matthew a very short time to pack a few things to stay at the house until they had solved the mysteries around the sapphire.

"That's all?" Sarah asked skeptically as he emerged from the bedroom with a silver rolling suitcase and a laptop bag.

Matthew looked down at his suitcase, up again, and shrugged.

"Do I need more? I seem to remember you own a washing machine, and if I need something – I'm ten minutes down the road. Cory even offered to ride my bike back to the house."

"Sure, but..." The implications of sharing her home with another man once were making Sarah question her impulsive decision to say yes when Matthew had offered to move in – for a while. There would be mornings without the airbrushed glow of getting ready first, moments of losing her temper, screwing up a meal, or totally misplacing her house keys, something she was known and famous for. After he moved in, Matthew would realize that *perfect* did not exist in a world with two children, a dog, and a resident ghost in the house.

"Cold feet?" Matthew asked, seeming to read her mind, and Sarah busied herself with a bag containing groceries from the fridge, trying to hide a sudden fierce blush.

"What, no of course not. It's just…"

"Having somebody move into your sanctuary is scary?"

"Not that either, exactly," Sarah squirmed, trying in vain for words that would neither be hurtful nor silly. "Our every day is a lot – less glamorous than you might think."

"Well, hallelujah," Matthew laughed out loud, put down the laptop bag, and wrapped his arms around Sarah. "If I have, in fact, convinced you that mine is, I must have some sort of special gift." With one arm around her shoulders, he led her toward the door of the condo. "I want you to feel safe. We'll just have to come up with a code word for when we get on each other's nerves, and we'll deal with it."

"If you're sure."

"Absolutely sure," he confirmed. "Besides, I'm still worrying about how your ghost will feel about me suddenly being there 24-7."

∞

Amelia, it turned out, did not appear at all. Cory tidied up the room next to his, busily ignoring the pointed looks between Matthew and Sarah. Emma kept peering into dark corners and closets, hoping Amelia would appear. Pixie bounced around barking happily, and Lily filmed their escapades on her phone, providing a running commentary.

"If I find any of this on social media," Sarah warned after they had finally put the last of his things into his room and were sitting relaxing in the big former parlor, which everybody called either the front room or the games room. Emma still looked around, waiting for Amelia to make one of her grand entrances.

When Lily asked Cory and Matthew to explain the latest camera features on her new phone, using a sleeping Pixie as a willing model, Sarah put her hand on Emma's shoulder and nodded toward the kitchen.

"Do you want to help me get a few snacks on a tray? We've had a busy and exciting day, might as well have some fun."

"Sure," Emma shrugged and rose, still peeking into the dark corners.

"You know this might be the time that Amelia has – gone home for good," Sarah said when they were in the kitchen. "That was the reason for helping her, after all."

"I know." Emma merely nodded and pulled a few trays out of the cupboard. "These ones?"

"Emma?"

"What? Blue ones or green ones?" Emma held up the two trays until Sarah took both of them out of her hands.

"I think you have some new, um, abilities we've never talked about. Do you want to tell me about them?"

"No big deal," Emma shrugged. "Amelia can communicate with me, that's all. No big deal."

"Are you sure that's all," Sarah asked. "You know you can talk to me."

"Mom, can you let it go? It was nothing." Emma closed the door to the cupboard a lot harder than she needed to and rolled her shoulders. "I guess it's intuition or whatever you call it. It's nothing weird. Just because you can hear things, feel things, and talk to Pixie doesn't mean I am going to turn into—into..."

"What?"

"A weirdo," Emma said, making a face and turning her back on her mother.

"Is that what you're worried about?"

"Mom, I don't know how you do all of that stuff ever since we moved here, how you can talk to ghosts and dogs - and whatever – but I'm normal."

"Of course, you are – Emma." Sarah put down the trays and took two giant steps toward her daughter putting her arms around her.

Emma only rolled her eyes and extricated herself from her mother's embrace. "It's been a while since you've gone to school, hasn't it? Harry Potter is over, ghosts are not cool right now."

"I'm not sure they ever were," Sarah tried for a laugh. "I just don't want you to be afraid. Come to me if anything—"

"Mom—Mom, look," Emma whispered and pointed toward the back door leading out into the garden.

The door suddenly became wispy and unfocused, as if a fine layer of mist were developing between them and the frame. The mist grew and became a small cloud, and as quickly as it had formed, it was gone again. Emma's face fell.

"I thought..."

"Wait."

Sarah pointed. There by the door, the mist formed again, grew, and changed shape, and the faint image of a woman appeared. She wore a beautiful flowing white dress, her dark hair pinned up with lethal-looking hairpins, and her face contorted by effort.

"It's Amelia," Emma said reverently and stepped toward the apparition. She held out her hands as if she wanted to embrace the ghost, and the image wavered and solidified again.

"Hello, Amelia," Sarah said, finding her voice trembled a little. She felt something brush her leg and looked down to find Pixie had come into the room and moved to stand between her and Amelia.

"It's fine, Pixie," Emma said, her voice a strange, soft whisper just then. "Amelia is not here to hurt us."

Sarah slowly took another step toward the apparition. While she absolutely didn't doubt Emma, she still remembered the first time she had met Amelia — the shortness of breath, the dizziness. How well she remembered the power that had suddenly surged through her mind and her hands, to repel the spirit and protect her family.

Amelia raised her hands in a surrendering gesture. She showed her hands being empty and her image flickered for a moment.

Her mouth formed frantic words, but Sarah could not hear anything except static in her head. The tiny tinkling sound of collar tags told her that Pixie crowded even closer to her side.

Amelia? Pixie's voice.

Pixie was silent for a long moment and took a step closer.

I can't hear her. Odd. This has never happened before.

"Emma, are you speaking to Amelia?"

"I'm trying, but I can't hear her. Why?"

"Come here," Sarah said, stretching her arm toward her daughter without taking her eyes off Amelia. "Give me your hand for a minute."

Why the hand-holding suggestion? Sarah, shivering with a sudden chill, longed for answers. Why her, and these unwanted powers? She felt Pixie by her leg and knew the little Papillon had the same idea.

Amelia still gestured wildly with her hands, and her mouth kept moving as if she were trying to get a story out as fast as she could, her hands drawing trails of white luminescence.

"I can't hear you," Sarah said, shaking her head. The image of Amelia dissolved and wavered again like a distant radio station.

For a moment, Sarah feared she would disappear into nothingness again, leaving them no wiser than before. She felt dizzy and squeezed Emma's hand a little harder. "What is it you are trying to tell us?"

The three of them moved even closer together, standing as one, focusing on the ghost. Amelia, the name stood in the room, thought or spoken by all three of them.

Amelia's image coalesced a bit more. Her dress suddenly appeared like a white cloud, as if she couldn't waste time manifesting it properly. Again, her mouth was moving quickly, and again, they couldn't hear the words she was speaking.

"Art."

The word suddenly hung in the room, and Amelia disappeared as if someone had suddenly turned off the lights.

"What's going on in here?"

Matthew's words shattered the dreamlike moment, and Sarah let go of Emma's hand and wheeled around to find him and Cory standing in the doorway to the game room.

"Who were you talking to?" Matthew asked.

Sarah exhaled a huge breath and scooped Pixie up in her arms. "Amelia just appeared out of nowhere, and I think she wanted to tell us something, but we couldn't hear her."

"Take it easy, you're trembling." Matthew took Pixie from her and led them all back to the games room, settling her into the big couch. "Let's start over - what just happened?"

"We were in the kitchen, getting snacks," Emma supplied, handing a glass of water to her mother. "She just appeared out of nowhere."

"Appeared?" A smirk played on Cory's lips, and he rolled his eyes.

"You know how Amelia shows up. And she was talking, trying to. She wanted to tell us something."

"She's a ghost, Em. What do you think she said, boo?"

"Yeah? Well, if you'd seen her…"

"Easy, both of you." Matthew sat on the couch beside Sarah and put his arm around her shoulder. "Are you all right? Do you need anything?"

"I'm fine," Sarah gently pushed his arm away. "Art? That was it. Just that one word. Didn't you hear that too, Emma?"

Emma scrunched up her face and cocked her head, but she didn't say anything.

"That's the only word I actually heard. She said it, didn't you hear?"

Emma only shook her head.

"Pixie?"

I don't know.

"Art? What's that supposed to mean?" Cory wondered, turned away, and sat in his game chair again.

"I know I heard it, I know it," Sarah said, striking her thigh with her hand. "I heard it."

"Easy." Matthew took her hand. "Maybe it was a message, but it's not much to go on. Maybe Amelia will come back."

"Not if she's finally gone home," Emma said softly and snuggled closer to Sarah's other side.

Emma wrapped her arms around her and rocked back and forth with the sadness over losing her spectral friend.

Just as Lily stood to throw her five cents into the conversation, Matthew raised both index fingers as if he were in front of the class.

"Okay, everybody, let's relax. It's been a long day, and we're all on edge because of Katy."

Cory looked away as if his collection of games held all the vital clues in the world. Lily sat quietly, her eyes firmly on Sarah.

Finally, Sarah gathered herself, stood, and rolled her shoulders.

"You're right, Matthew. I thought Amelia was trying to give us a message, and I thought it was important. But who knows? Maybe she was just trying to say goodbye because she's finally moving on. I am sorry, Emma, I know you were fond of her."

Emma's eyes glittered with unshed tears, and Matthew shot Cory a warning glance.

"Then let me finally get those snacks."

"No, sit," Lily got to her feet and nodded at Cory. "You there, why don't you come help me in the kitchen for a minute and make some tea for your mom and Matthew."

Cory did, not without his usual bored teenager eye-roll, and Matthew flipped through the takeout menu from a restaurant everybody liked. "Any particular preference?"

Maybe she really did say art.

Thanks, Pixie, but I'm just not sure.

Pixie jumped off the couch, stretching her tiny body leisurely, and gave Sarah a long stare. Then she followed Lily and Cory into the kitchen.

"It had something to do with Katelyn," Emma said suddenly.

"What did?"

Sarah, who'd been about to go help Cory and Lily, stopped dead in her tracks and stood before her daughter.

"What had something to do with Katelyn?"

"Amelia's message."

"But it couldn't have. We couldn't hear what she was saying…right?"

"I felt her, Mom," Emma's eyes became unfocused, and a sweet smile spread on her face. "I didn't need to hear because I felt her in here." She put both of her hands over her heart and fully closed her eyes for a moment. "She was showing me pictures because she couldn't speak, and I didn't understand them, but I saw Katelyn."

Sarah sat down and stared at her daughter. No matter how much she had tried to ignore it, it was becoming obvious—Emma was developing powerful abilities similar to her own.

By then, Emma had picked up the remote control and idly flicked through the TV program guide, leaving Sarah utterly speechless with that realization.

"Hey – Katelyn just called," Lily came into the games room waving her cell phone. "She'll be transferred to physical rehab tomorrow. Is everything okay?"

"I have to tell you something."

Lily hardly blinked when Sarah hurriedly whispered about Emma's newfound abilities.

"Makes sense," she shrugged.

"Makes sense? She's barely a teenager. Barely. And now…"

"She is your daughter, Sarah. Did it not occur to you that she might have inherited your, whatever they are?"

"Nothing I can teach or pass on, or even describe or anything. Every now and then, I seem to…do something. That's all."

"Really?"

"Really. And only when Pixie tells me what I have to do."

"Uh-huh." Lily nodded towards the stained-glass transom window, where the luminous crystal had been replaced by a piece of deep blue glass. "And what happened when Mortimer Jenkins killed Pixie?"

"He didn't, he just..." Sarah looked away.

"Don't tell me she was just stunned because I was there. You brought her back, you! So don't tell me there is... are no abilities there."

Sarah didn't speak. She'd tried her best to forget that moment in the kitchen last year: the attack, the Jenkins', and the glass maker. And Amelia telling her to use her powers.

"I'm terrified," she finally whispered. "Not only for me, but for Emma."

"Don't be, Mom," Emma suddenly stepped out of the shadow into the pool of light around the hall lamp. "It's perfectly fine."

She raised her hand, and Sarah felt a deeply comforting wave of love and joy wash over her. Tears choked her voice as she reached out to her daughter. Emma stepped into her embrace, and together they stood, enveloped in that wave of joy.

"I'm not scared because I know I have you," Emma said softly. "But Katelyn has nobody, and that means it's up to us to help her."

Chapter Fourteen

"**H**ey, what's going on out here in the hall? You going some-where, or is this a secret girls-only meeting?"

Matthew came out from the kitchen, a dish towel casually slung over his shoulder, Cory not far behind him.

"Girl talk," Sarah waved a hand through the air. "Nothing you boys would be interested in."

Cory made a face, but Emma couldn't resist the sibling rivalry.

"I can talk to ghosts just the way Mom can," she said proudly, sticking her tongue out at her brother.

"You…" Cory's face fell, and he took a step back.

"We think Emma can," Sarah corrected quickly. "We'll have to work on that first. And besides, everybody has their own abilities. Emma, there's not one more valuable than the other, okay."

Emma was about to say something snippy, Sarah could feel it, but Emma surprised her by staying silent. Emma smiled instead and gently elbowed Cory in the side. "We need to help Katy," she said, pulling the ribbon in her ponytail tighter. "And that's going to take all of us."

Lily looked from one to the other as if she were in a school play. She picked up Pixie and she and Matthew watched the Anderson family huddle for a moment and grinned at one another.

"Guess it's us for the dishes," Lily pointed at the dish towel Matthew had brought and gave Pixie's nose a quick swipe.

"No, we'll all help," Sarah said. "And I distinctly remember buying a brand-new dishwasher."

Matthew took the dish towel off his shoulder and wanted to say something when suddenly the lights in the house flickered, went out, came back on, and went out again.

"Oh great," Matthew toggled the flashlight on his cell phone. "The joys of living in an ancient house. Let me check the fuse box. It's probably just...Whoa."

Matthew stopped in his tracks just as the power, and with it, the lights came back on. They would have had a laugh at this, as it happened quite often at Thompson Hall, except for one thing. There in the door to the games room, backlit with the blue glow from the television Emma had left on, stood a young man of about twenty.

Pixie emitted a deep growl that sounded like it came from the center of the little dog, and only Sarah could hush her. Pixie jumped down and cautiously approached the apparition in the doorway. Finally, she sat quietly and regally between the family and the young man.

The man looked at them with a cautious smile and raised his hands, indicating he meant no harm. His dark tailored trousers, well-fitted shirt, and black vest looked homespun and a little threadbare, Sarah thought. He wore no tie, but his hair was well-groomed, parted to the side, and his mustache appeared neatly trimmed. Curiously, he looked from one to the other and brought a leather-bound sketchbook close to his chest.

"Simon," Emma said brightly. "Where is Amelia?"

Simon had been Amelia's fiancé at the time she died, although her wealthy father had planned to do everything he could to break up that relationship.

"Emma," Simon asked, and his image flickered for a moment like an unstable movie. "Amelia is here. She only crossed over a little while ago. It's taking her a lot of energy to visit, but she wants to thank you for reuniting us."

He seemed to flicker and disappear for just a second.

"Thankful," he said with an effort. "Happy. And she wants you to remember..."

"Remember what Simon?" Emma ran toward him, but her hands reached into nothing. Simon was already gone.

"Art."

This time they all heard the word. Art. Just as Sarah had heard before.

Cory sat open-mouthed, Emma reached with both hands to where Simon had been as if she wanted to grab onto him, and Lily hung on to her glass with a monumental effort.

"That was – Simon?" Sarah asked and went to the spot where Amelia's fiancé had appeared as if she could leach an echo of his presence out of the very air. "How do you know?"

"I just knew," Emma shrugged. "It was Simon. And Amelia is with him now."

"And he was carrying a sketchbook," Cory said. "And even I heard him say the word *art*. Simon was an art student if you remember."

"Right," Sarah came back and put her arm around her son. "I wonder why he suddenly appeared?"

"To let us know Amelia made it safely to the other side? That they are together again?"

"Yes, and that's nice. But why here, and why now?"

"Why don't you just ask Emma? She knows everything about ghosts."

Cory pushed away from her again and picked up one of his game controllers, pointing it at the TV. Pixie, who always appeared to know what the kids needed, jumped on the couch beside him and pushed her little nose into his hand again and again.

"Stop it, Pixie; I don't want to play."

Pixie didn't stop. Instead, she put her paws on the boy's shoulder and snuffled his ears until he curled up with a serious case of the giggles. "Stop – stop, Pixie – you're tickling. Mom."

"She loves you, Cory. As do we all. And if you're upset..."

"What, because I can't talk to ghosts the way Emma says she can."

"Perhaps that's a good thing."

Cory finally sat up straight again, threw a little ball across the room for Pixie, and gave Sarah a sideways look from under his long bangs.

"Nobody I know does research the way you do."

"Yeah, but..."

"Face it, you're good at it. And if we want to help Katelyn – really help her – then it's going to take all of our talents."

"Matthew could do it," Cory muttered and looked down at the controller in his hands again.

"No, Matthew has a job he needs to be going to every day," Matthew corrected. "And he's taken a lot of heat over this sapphire theft. And I have no idea half the time what your mother and Emma and Pixie are doing. Sometimes they scare the dickens out of me, so welcome to the club."

Cory looked up again, slowly put away his game controller, and ran a hand through his messy brown hair.

"You're not going to give up anyway until I say okay and go apologize to Emma, are you?"

"Nope."

"Fine." Cory rolled his eyes and looked at Emma. "Sorry I snapped at you," he said with as little conviction as would get him out of trouble and at least sound halfway sincere.

∽

Around the dinner table, they were laughing and joking around, alternately making fun of Matthew and Lily and the way Pixie hung around their chairs, hoping for a little tidbit. A normal family dinner – except now and then one of them would look up and peek into the games room where their ghostly friends apparently could most easily manifest, or stare off into the distance, trying to figure out something connected to Katelyn, sapphires, thefts, or ghosts.

No more apparitions showed up, though, and when Lily had gone home and the kids to bed, Sarah turned off most of the lights and took Matthew's hands.

"Thanks for putting up with all of us."

"Wouldn't have it any other way," he said softly and kissed her behind the ear.

"That's quite the family you inherited here."

"Yup, and I'm thankful every day."

Together they walked up the wide double staircase, followed by Pixie's ticking little nails on the wood, and peace settled over Thompson Hall.

Chapter Fifteen

"I didn't know you were a drill sergeant," Matthew said the next morning, watching Sarah orchestrate children getting up on time, washing up, getting breakfast, tidying their rooms, and, in fact, getting out the door on time for their school bus.

"It takes practice, that's all."

She handed him a small lunch bag and nodded at the front window. "Looks grim out there. Your bike is outside, but I can drive you if you want."

Matthew opted to be driven, and Sarah decided to drop by the hospital's rehab center to pay another visit to Katelyn.

∞

"She wouldn't see me," she said to Lily in the bookshop a few hours later. "Just left word with the nurses that she didn't want to be disturbed."

Rather than driving back home, she'd stopped by the store and was helping Lily organize a shipment of new books. Pixie had abandoned her purse carrier and was snuggled in one of the many comfortable reading chairs scattered around the bookshop, snoozing, likely dreaming of juicy treats and tidbits falling from the sky.

"Katelyn has a lot to think about," Lily said diplomatically, taking books out of Sarah's hands that needed to be shelved.

"She's trying to protect me and the kids."

"That too."

More books followed. Lily served a customer, went to the back to make a fresh pot of tea, and came back with two mugs.

"But we're trying to help her, for god's sake," Sarah said, scalding herself with the hot tea. "We are the good guys."

"How was the first night with Matthew in the house?"

"Matthew has…" Sarah blushed and put away her tea. "Not like he hasn't spent the night before, but it was – nice – to have him there."

"Nice? That's all you're going to give me? Nice?"

Sarah grinned and held up a few new books. "Where do these go?"

"Back there, business section." Lily only pointed. "You know the least you could do is let me live vicariously."

"Nobody told you to live like a nun," Sarah countered.

"If you hadn't noticed, Sarah, I am not exactly the prim and proper standard that's expected around here."

"Now you sound like Cory when he's feeling sorry for himself," Sarah said and threw up her arms. "Do you see prim and proper here? I talk to dogs and ghosts and knew absolutely no one in this town a little over a year ago. There are nice people coming and going from this store every single day, no?"

She nodded toward a tall, good-looking guy who had stopped by the chair Pixie had chosen, squatted down beside it, and gently scratched between the little dog's ears. Pixie opened one eye and continued snoozing. "Want me to ask him?"

"Don't you dare, Sarah. Here." She handed her another stack of books. "Art section. On the wall to your left."

"365 Days of Creativity: Inspire Your Imagination with Art Every Day," Sarah read off the top book on the stack and put them back down again.

"Why would both Amelia and Simon say the word *art*?"

"I've wondered that." Lily broke apart the box the books had come in and nodded toward the shelf on their left again.

"I'm not the ghost whisperer here." A woman browsing the cookbooks section looked up and cocked her head. She'd likely heard the words *ghost whisperer*.

"Nothing to do with Katelyn, you don't think?"

Lily shook her head and walked away to serve the cookbook lady. Finally, she came back to where Sarah was still unpacking books.

"Listen, I love you helping me and all, but in here, maybe we shouldn't talk about..."

"Amelia?"

"Her. Exactly. People already think I'm a little crazy." Lily winked and elbowed her in the side. "Besides, I want to hear all about Matthew now living at the house. Did you really drive him to work this morning?"

"Sure did."

The morning passed with gossiping and helping customers, and Sarah felt herself relaxing just as much as Pixie in the chair snoozing in the mystery section. Just past lunchtime, she headed home again to be there when Emma and Cory came back from school.

The empty house gave no clue to a ghostly presence. But perhaps if she asked? Sarah burned to know what Amelia and Simon had meant by that one word.

She stood in the games room by the old fireplace, took a few deep breaths, and closed her eyes, listening.

Nothing.

Neither one of the ghosts felt compelled to come forward.

After a few minutes, Sarah opened her eyes again, only to find Pixie sitting in front of her, with a curious look on her little fox face.

"Ghosts," Sarah said and made a face. "Can't trust them to be around when you need them."

I don't think they mean to shut you out.

"All I wanted was a clarification, Pixie. This whole cryptic thing is a little frustrating."

Pixie shook and came to stand by Sarah's side, putting her paws on her knee to be scratched between the ears.

I don't mean to alarm you, but I have had a feeling something is going on ever since this morning.

Something? Anything I need to worry about?

Pixie slid back down into a sitting position and finally stretched through her entire body. Her little face looked like she was indeed thinking about what to say.

I can't tell. But I can feel something. I can feel it – I just don't know what it is.

Sarah, who'd learned to pay close attention to Pixie's feelings, looked into the entrance hall at the piece of glass that replaced the Luminus crystal. Everything seemed fine, nothing amiss, nothing out of order. Still.

"Keep an eye out, little girl," she said softly and scratched between Pixie's soft fringed ears again.

The slam of the front door announced Cory and Emma's arrival, and at the same time, she heard her cell phone ringing in the kitchen. Torn for a second, she went to the front door only to find that her children had disappeared up the stairs and into their rooms already. By the time she came back to the kitchen, the caller had hung up, and Sarah grabbed a dog treat and tossed it to Pixie.

"Can't win today, girl."

I think he left a message.

"He?"

Sarah reached for her phone, just as the message notification arrived. She gave Pixie the side eye and pushed the mailbox button.

"Sarah, I don't know what's going on, but my store has been burgled. The entire store, even the back room, which they shouldn't even have been able to open... I mean – nobody should be able to open. I mean — I think you should come here as quick as you can. This could be dangerous. To you too... I mean. This is awful. Just awful."

A long pause. Then the voice continued. "Oh – it's Robbie, Robbie Murtaugh from the antique store. Just hurry."

Sarah's hand with the phone dropped to her side, and she looked down to where Pixie sat at full attention, her shiny white and sable coat standing on end, making her seem even fluffier than normal.

"Mom, why does Robbie want you to come to the store?"

Sarah wheeled around to find that Emma had come into the kitchen for a snack and heard the last bit of the message.

"Something happened at his store?" she asked, trying to keep the alarm out of her voice.

"And he thinks you can help?"

Including the back room, no one should be able to open the back room.

She looked down at Pixie and stretched out her arms, and the little Papillon jumped up to be snuggled close.

Pixie, is this what you were sensing all day?

It might be, and I think you should go see about it as soon as you can.

That back room...

It's where all of the enchanted items were being kept.

Pixie's eyes rested on her unblinking.

That means it could have something to do with the sapphire.

"Right, I think I have to go out for a bit," she said and let Pixie hop to the ground again. "I won't be—"

"We're coming with you." Cory had now joined his sister.

"No, you're not." Sarah raised both of her hands like a cop trying to stop rush hour traffic. "I'm just going to see him, find out if I can help him in some way. You wait here for Matthew."

"I am going." Cory took a step forward and stood square to his mother. "There's no way I'm going to hang out here, waiting."

"And I'm going in case you need help with...stuff." Emma now took another step to stand beside her brother. For another moment, the three of them stood staring at one another, until the slam of the front door announced another visitor.

"Guys," Matthew came almost running into the kitchen. "Good thing you're all here. Something happened—"

"Robbie's store got broken into," Sarah said, still looking at her children. "We know."

"How? He called me when he couldn't get a hold of you. He thought you all might be in danger."

"Why?" Sarah pressed her lips together ard automatically took a step closer to the children. "His message said something like that, but what kind of danger would we be in?"

"I don't know, but he sounded panicked out of his mind, and he told me to get there quickly. With you. So, what are you guys waiting for?"

Cory and Emma had already put their coats and boots back on, Pixie had climbed into her traveling bag, and they were waiting by the front door. At this point, neither Matthew nor Sarah took the time to argue with them.

They piled into the car and drove at top speed out to the old section of town where the antique store was.

∾

"Doesn't he usually go down south for the winter," Sarah asked. "I mean – somebody told me that, I think."

Matthew only shook his head.

"He probably should have. Honestly, I've rarely heard anybody in such a panic."

"Why call us?"

"We're about to find out."

Two police cars left the antique store just as they pulled up. Right in front of the building, a local handyman's van stood in the no-parking zone, and two men were busy mounting large sheets of plywood over what had been the front store window. A large pile of glass shards, hurriedly swept together, told the story of what had happened there.

"Mom," Emma grabbed her mother's hand to stop her. "There is a lot of – anger – there." She nodded at the old antique store. "Do you feel it?"

Sarah stopped for a moment and tuned into the feeling. What Emma called anger actually felt like the sharp, cutting edges of fierce, untamed violence, and she automatically recoiled from it.

"Yes," she said softly. "Tune it out." And she kept Emma's hand in hers as they walked up to the store.

The anger and violence wasn't coming from Robbie. The old man sat on a stool in front of the scarred old counter, his head buried in his hands. Fear and frustration rolled off him in giant waves.

As they cautiously stepped deeper into the store, a familiar sense of nostalgia and history hung in the air, mingling with the musty odor of aged wood, forgotten treasures, and raw fear. The dim light filtering through the dusty windows now revealed a scene of utter chaos. Shattered glass crunched beneath their feet, a testament to the force with which the intruders breached the entrance.

The once neatly arranged shelves, adorned with delicate porcelain figurines and weathered books, now stood in disarray, some toppled and thrown over. Antique clocks lay shattered on the worn wooden floor, their once melodious ticking silenced forever. Tattered lace curtains, remnants of a bygone era, hung forlornly, partially torn from their moorings.

The burglarized store bore the scars of a relentless search. Cabinets had been flung open, their contents spilled onto the floor like a jigsaw puzzle missing crucial pieces.

In the midst of the wreckage, Robbie slumped on his stool, radiating none of the mystery and magic he had a few days ago. He sat amidst the ruins, his shoulders slumped, and eyes reflecting a mix of sadness and fear. His trembling hands clasped an antique pocket watch, a family heirloom that miraculously had survived the onslaught.

Robbie looked up as they entered, his eyes widening with a mixture of relief and apprehension. The creaking floorboards beneath their feet seemed to echo the heaviness in the room as if mourning the violation of the carefully curated memories that once adorned the shelves. The silence was broken only by the distant sounds of the city outside, a stark contrast to the quiet haven of history that now lay in ruins.

Robbie raised a visibly trembling hand and only pointed. The heavy, ornate door at the back, the portal to the secret room filled with enchanted treasures, hung precariously on its last hinge. Its violated state mirrored the disarray within.

Hesitant steps carried her and Emma toward the breached entrance of the clandestine chamber. The air inside was thick with the sense of violation, as if the room itself mourned the intrusion into its hidden sanctum. Antique manuscripts, once carefully preserved, now lay scattered like autumn leaves in a storm.

In that room, shelves that once held mysterious artifacts and ancient relics were now barren, their contents pilfered by unseen hands. The dust of ages disturbed the air, swirling in it.

Sarah looked at Robbie, and she saw a flicker of desperation in his eyes. The violated sanctuary of the secret room was a wound that cut deeper, a loss that transcended mere material possessions. The old man's vulnerability deepened, his frailty echoing the shattered state of the once-sacred space. The silent plea in his eyes spoke of a desperate hope that some remnants of the store's soul might yet be salvaged from the ruins.

Sarah stood stunned, fighting the onslaught of anxiety that hung in the air. She took Emma's hand and felt her daughter's fingers trembling. Matthew and Cory took charge almost automatically.

"Mr. M," Cory said, placing a hand on the man's shoulder. "Are you okay?"

"Look," Robbie said, his shaking hand pointing all around him. "Just look..."

Sarah noticed that the old amulet he'd worn was gone now. All that remained was a broken chain around his neck, and she shuddered to imagine how it had been taken from him.

"We saw the police leave," Matthew said, holding Pixie in his arms to protect her paws from the shards on the ground. "Have the EMT's been here and checked you out?"

Robbie only shook his head, and as his long hair fell back, it exposed a nasty cut and bruise on his right temple. Seeing the cut, Sarah finally broke the spell and moved into action. From her bag, she retrieved the little emergency kit she always carried and cleaned and bandaged the cut.

"Sorry—a superhero bandage is all I have for the moment."

Robbie managed the faint ghost of a smile.

"Anything else? Did they hurt you? Head trauma? Should we go to the hospital?"

"Sarah, you sound much like the policemen," he said, straightening up slowly and with a fair bit of effort. It was not me they came here to hurt."

Sarah put the emergency kit back into her bag. "What did they want, and most of all, why did you call us—me?"

"Can you not guess, Sarah?"

"We could," Matthew cut in. "But if we play twenty questions, we'll still be here in a couple of hours, and I'd just as soon you straight up tell me why you called my—Sarah—and then me when you realized your store had been broken into."

"And don't you usually go away over the winter?" Sarah added, taking Pixie from Matthew.

"Not this year," Robbie reached out and stroked Pixie's chin with a trembling forefinger. "Turns out that was a mistake. But I did put a note on the door anyway because I figured you would be back, and I didn't care for more of your questions about that sapphire."

"The sapphire?" Sarah cast around for another stool, found one half lying under the counter, and sat beside the old man. "From the top now, why did you think I would ask more about the sapphire, and why did you call me when your store was broken into?"

"It does make sense," Emma's said. Sarah looked up to see her daughter taking Robbie's hand. "You know all about enchanted items, don't you?"

"Well—I wouldn't say all."

"And you've written a book on the power of gemstones."

"You know about that?"

"The Enchanted Gleam: Unveiling the Mystical Powers of Gemstones," Emma said, smiling. "I've seen it at the store, although it is tucked away in an obscure section."

"No doubt it was, but the original manuscript for that particular book was about ten times longer than the final product, and it was taken, Emma. That is what they came looking for."

"Your—manuscript." Matthew had finally found a chair and set it down, straddling it to face the old magician.

"A story about gemstones?"

"Enchanted stones."

"Enchanted then. But why steal it? And what about the sapphire?"

Understanding dawned slowly, and Matthew looked at Emma. "I guess that means this break-in and the theft of the enchanted sapphire are connected? How?"

"Sapphires are deep blue, and the color blue is connected to the throat chakra," Robbie said, touching his throat ever so gently. "Associated with communication and self-expression. It symbolizes calm, clarity, and open communication, fostering the balanced flow of energy for authentic expression."

"And the enchantment?"

"Allowed that connection to be subverted," Robbie said, nodding. "So, the sapphire could be used to hide the liar's words and make them appear to be truthful."

"We know all of that," Matthew said, throwing up his hands. "I presume that's why the thieves took the sapphire. Why break in here?"

"Because they didn't know how," Cory said, taking a step forward. "They had no clue how it worked, did they? Maybe messed around with it for a bit. Then they figured—why not go to the authority? The guy who's written the book on it, literally."

Robbie only nodded. "They took—everything," he said, wiping his eyes.

"Didn't you have a backup?"

The old magician looked forlornly at Cory.

"Okay, okay," Matthew said raising his index fingers and putting them together, as he was wont to do. "So, we know that as of yet unknown persons stole the sapphire for its ability to mask a lie, then stole the—ahem—manual to figure out how to use it. What we don't know, as of yet, is who they are and why they need it so desperately because," he pointed at the carnage around them. "To me, this looks like the work of desperate people. If you just wanted to steal a manuscript, there are easier ways."

In Sarah's arms, Pixie began looking around the room. Sarah could feel the restless quiver of the little Papillon, and the tip of her tail acquired that little bit of golden glitter that seemed to indicate Pixie was using some of her more extraordinary talents.

Are you sensing something? she thought, stroking her hands down the sides of the little dog.

The anger, the violence I felt earlier, Pixie sniffed at the air repeatedly, shook her head, and tried again. *There's an unusual... something, but I can't catch it.*

Sarah let her eyes drift shut just a little and concentrated on her own senses: the smell of old furniture, books, and rugs, the far-off rumble of the ancient furnace, murmured words between Matthew and Robbie, a gentle touch on her searching thoughts. Sarah smiled; that was Emma, doing the very same thing.

She opened her eyes again and looked at her daughter.

"Pixie thought she sensed a presence," she whispered. "I can feel — something. But I don't know what it is."

"What are you two whispering about?" Matthew asked jovially, and Sarah did her best to ignore Cory's crestfallen look.

"We felt a presence in the room," Sarah said, "but we can't tell what it is."

"Of course, there's a presence," Robbie spat. "The room of enchanted objects has been broken into, and the peace disturbed. Every object in there—"

"Was anything taken beyond your own manuscript?" Matthew wanted to know while looking at the broken door into the back room over the rim of his glasses. Sarah could feel his reluctance in dealing with what was in there. If he did, he would have to acknowledge the existence of things that his professor's mind insisted couldn't exist.

"No, no, that was the first thing I checked." Robbie took the cold pack Sarah had taken out of her first aid kit and held it against the side of his head. "Just the manuscript, although I did hear them say something about — about..." He scrunched up his face and pushed the cold pack against his head even harder. "About art, I think."

"Art," Sarah said, jumping to her feet. The word hit her like a slap to the face. Art.

"That was the word both Amelia and Simon used," she continued. "So it does have something to do with the stolen sapphire."

Matthew got up and put his hand on Sarah's shoulder.

"What are you thinking?"

Just then, Robbie let out a raspy, terrified sound that raised the hair on their arms. He jumped to his feet with a speed and agility she wouldn't have thought him capable of, and pointed into the corner of the store with a trembling hand.

"No – please." Automatically, he reached for the amulet on his chest, his hand coming away empty from where it had been torn from its chain. "God help us all." He began to mutter an invocation or spell or something, and Sarah narrowed her eyes to see what had frightened him so.

It's just Amelia, she heard from Pixie and sat back down.

In the corner of the store, the familiar white, wispy form began to take shape, separate into two, and reform again. Two spirits? She and Emma looked at one another, and Emma grinned broadly.

"It's both of them, Simon and Amelia."

"By the light within..." Robbie was mumbling and gesturing. Then a bit louder, "By the light within, I invoke divine protection."

"Take it easy," Sarah put a hand on his arm. "This entity means you no harm."

"It's a dark spirit that has escaped. Dear God." He crossed himself and began muttering again until Emma rose and walked toward the wispy white cloud, reaching her hands for it.

"Don't touch it, child."

"It's just Amelia, hi there," Emma touched the edges of the white vapor, and suddenly, a couple in old-fashioned clothing stood in the corner of the antique store. One was the young man they had seen earlier—Simon—and the other was Amelia, who had fought them for dominion over their house last year and who had finally found the peace she required to cross over to the other side and be with Simon again.

"Emma," Amelia's face trembled a bit, her version of a smile perhaps, Sarah thought and approached another step, shushing Robbie with a hand behind her back.

"Amelia," she said, raising her hands open in front of her to show she meant no harm to the specters. "We need some information about—"

"Listen to me," Amelia whispered, reaching over and holding Simon's hand tightly. Simon, at the same time, became unfocused and appeared to weaken. Perhaps they shared the available energy.

"We don't have much time. I need to gather strength, and if you want to help the girl..."

The lights in the store all turned off at the same time, and Robbie wailed again, repeating his incantations even louder now.

The lights came back on, and a very translucent Amelia came closer to Sarah.

"It's the stolen art," she whispered, even as her image dissolved and then dissipated in a puff of air. "Follow the stolen art to help..."

Then she was gone, as if someone had flicked a switch. Robbie kept repeating his spell, and Sarah sat down on the chair, stretching a hand out for Emma to stand beside her.

"Are you okay?"

"Yes. Amelia was drawing on Simon for energy, but he only had so much to give. Do you think they're okay?"

"Why shouldn't they be," Cory scoffed. "What do you think, they'll die or something?"

"Easy, Cory, we—but mostly Katelyn—need your help." Sarah stretched her other hand toward Cory and held both of her children. "You're disappointed because Emma and I share this... energy."

"S'alright." Cory mumbled and shrugged. "It's weird as all get out, though."

Matthew stood behind Cory, and for a moment, the little family stood as one, holding on to one another.

"Please leave my store now," Robbie grumbled. "You brought this here—this thing, this..."

"If I remember correctly, this break-in happened because of a manuscript you wrote," Matthew said sharply, turning around to face the old magician, narrowing his eyes and dominating with his height. "And who knows where they got the idea to steal the sapphire and subvert its energy in the first place. Perhaps another manuscript? Perhaps one of—"

"Out." A trembling old hand pointed at the entrance door, its broken window covered with a large piece of plywood. "Out now."

"It's nothing to be afraid of," Emma said, breaking free from the group and taking Robbie's pointing hand. Amelia and Simon died long ago, and all they wanted was to be together. I helped them do that, so they would never hurt any of us—or you."

"Leave, please." Robbie pulled his hand back and eyed the devastation around him. "I have to set this right. You're no help here, so you better go."

"Let's go, Emma," Cory said, wrapping his arm around his sister's shoulder. We have to figure out what Amelia meant by 'follow the stolen art'. He can't help with that."

Robbie said softly, "The only art thefts I know of are the string of robberies happening the last few years in a few museums, but how can that tie in with this.? Again, he pointed at the door and nodded.

Pixie scurried out from under a table and put her paws on Sarah's legs to be picked up. She hugged the little dog tightly and hurried after Matthew, Cory, and Emma, who stood outside on the sidewalk, waiting.

∞

"What could it mean, follow the stolen art? Any ideas?"

"I don't know," Cory said, wrapping Pixie's leash around his wrist and walking deep in thought. "It's like I remember something; I just don't know what it is." His free hand knocked against his temple. "It's right in there; I just can't..."

"It'll come to you when you least think about it," Matthew said. "Want to go back to the house to play hockey for a bit? Take a mental break?"

"You play hockey?" Cory asked, giving Matthew a long curious look that didn't exactly suggest confidence.

"Not as well as you, I'm sure," Matthew shrugged, falling into step beside Cory.

Sarah fell back a bit so Matthew wouldn't see the broad smile she leveled at both of them. He'd never had children or been around them, other than the students in his university classes, but he'd painstakingly built a little ice rink in their yard where Emma would practice figure-skating moves, and Cory shot endless pucks at a red net

"Yeah, we think Matthew is pretty cool, too," Emma said beside her and winked at her mother.

"You didn't read my mind just now, did you?" Sarah asked, a horrified suspicion spreading inside her. "Because that would be…"

"Relax, I can't do that – yet. But it was written on your face clear as a book."

"What was?" Matthew asked, turning around, and they both giggled.

"Nothing. Nothing at all. Perhaps you guys should go off, and the girls will go to the library and then Lily's bookstore and see what shakes loose. Sound good?"

Cory smiled, and they headed off toward the car.

Chapter Sixteen

Only a few customers were browsing at Lily's bookshop, which was normally a haven for local gossip, good books, and a generous cup of coffee.

"It's just too cold for people to be out," Lily complained, blowing into her hands, and smiling at Pixie. The little Papillon, by now, had tested all of the chairs in the store and found the one she felt was most comfortable for a princess of her tiny stature.

"You know, any time you want to leave her here at the store for a while. People think she is the most adorable little mascot—ever."

And well they should, Sarah heard, just as Pixie's head sank down on her paws and her eyes softly closed.

"Oh, she's special, alright – as you well know." Pixie had belonged to a friend of Lily's who'd passed away in a tragic accident.

"Now, let me fire up this," Lily fussed with the massive copper espresso machine she'd acquired. "And you tell me what drives you out of the house on such a miserably cold day."

"You heard anything about stolen art lately?" Sarah asked, looking after Emma who had already disappeared between the rows of bookshelves.

"Stolen art? You're gonna have to be a bit more specific than that," Lily said and pushed a few more buttons until the machine emitted a satisfying hiss and a cloud of steam. "What are we talking about here? Paintings, anything specific—can you narrow it down a bit?"

"Not really." Sarah frowned and tried to recall details of what had come up at the scene of the break-in, and Amelia's appearance and statements.

Lily took a sip of her cappuccino. "Maybe something to do with what you heard at the house, *art,* wasn't it? Matthew can't help? He has all of these university professors he could ask."

Sarah only shook her head. "He's playing hockey with Cory," she said with a smile. "Cory thought something sounded familiar. I think Matt's hoping a distraction might help him get it out."

"I see," Lily lifted her cup again and grinned broadly at Sarah. "I'm still waiting to hear a thank you, you know."

"Thank you for what?"

"Thank you for setting you and Matthew up in the first place. I did know the two of you would hit it off."

"Well," Sarah blushed and lowered her eyes to her coffee for a moment. "Thank you," she finally said, a broad grin still splitting her face like it had not in a long time.

"Now, about that follow the stolen art comment."

"No idea, sorry," Lily said, cupping her mug with both hands. "Stolen art...

"You talking about the trial at Claremont Superior Court?"

A young man had approached the cash register with an arm full of books, and his eyes raked Lily from head to toe.

"Um – maybe?" Lily blushed, looked down at the cash register, and fussed with a button.

"It's been all over the news, man," the young man continued. He had the brush cut of a soldier about to ship out and wore olive green fatigues, but no identifying badge revealed his name. "They're supposedly this—gang—that apparently steals famous art on order for wealthy collectors."

"No kidding," Lily said, ringing up the purchase.

"One of them was caught, and he's going up on trial. Everybody is waiting to see if he'll give up the rest of the group in exchange for getting off or just plead guilty, do his time, and keep his mouth shut."

"Or testify on his own behalf," Sarah said, as a horrible realization began to dawn on her. She heard a jingle of collar tags, looked down, and found Pixie standing at the ready beside her.

"Yeah, right," the young man chuckled and took his change and book bag from Lily. "And who'd believe him if he pleaded not guilty? He got caught red-handed, as they say. Anyway – you ladies have a great day now."

He waved a greeting and disappeared, making the bell above the door twinkle brightly.

"Forum, fresco, filcher," Sarah said, her words tumbling over one another in her hurry. "It's been in front of us all along, albeit in archaic language."

"What are you talking about?"

"The words that book at Robbie's formed," Sarah pressed on. "Forum, fresco, filcher. Cory researched it — we've got to go."

"Wait, why…?"

Emma had appeared by her side as if summoned by Sarah's urgent thoughts.

"I think I see the connection now," Sarah said, pushing her half-finished cappuccino back at Lily. "Forum is an old word for court, and fresco is an art form. Court, art, thief. A trial for a man accused of art theft. It's been staring us in the face, and we didn't see it."

"But then who stole the sapphire if that man is in jail?" Lily wanted to know. "And why?"

"We have to tell Cory and Matthew," Emma said, already shrugging into her coat. Sarah did not even question how her daughter already knew what she was only suspecting: They had finally solved the mystery of those three words they'd been given and maybe even the theft of the sapphire. Tenuous as their lead was, they finally had something in their hands that would, maybe, help Katelyn.

Sarah scooped up Pixie with one hand and hit her phone for an Uber with the other.

"Wait, give me a minute to find someone to sub. I'll drive you," Lily called out even as they were turning for the door.

Sarah shook her head. "Follow us when you can," she called over her shoulder. "But I wouldn't wait too long."

Chapter Seventeen

At the house, laughter and cheers rang out over the front yard. The skating rink Matthew had built had become somewhat of an attraction to the neighborhood kids, and when the cab pulled up at the curb, at least five other kids were playing hockey with Matthew and Cory, gliding effortlessly over the smooth ice and taking turns shooting at the goal.

When the cab pulled up and Sarah and Emma all but ran toward the house, Matthew stopped mid-shot and dropped his hockey stick. "Everything okay?" he asked, even though he could see something was up.

"We've got something," Sarah called out without breaking stride. "Hurry up."

Matthew left Cory to explain why their game was so suddenly interrupted and followed up the stairs and into the house behind Sarah and Emma.

"What?" he wanted to know. "What did you find? Is it about Robbie's store? Is it…"

"Wait." Sarah stripped off her gloves and coat and carelessly flung her bag onto a kitchen chair. Pixie came storming in through the doggie door and uncharacteristically sat in front of them instead of begging for a treat. Her tail, Sarah noticed, the tip of her tail had that golden glimmer about it.

Cory came in and slammed the door shut behind him. "You solved it," he called out, surprising Matthew.

"Wait, how do you..."

Cory only pointed at Emma, Sarah, and Pixie. "What does it mean?" he urged. "Come on, Mom, I know you figured it out. What have you found?"

Sarah nodded at the kitchen table to sit and went to put on hot water for tea and hot chocolate. "Sorry to interrupt your game."

"Forget the game. Spill."

Sarah told the story of seeing a book about art, wondering about art thefts, and a customer coming to the cash register and talking about a trial.

"Yeah, I remember that," Cory said and slapped his hand on the table. "I heard about it somewhere."

"You did?"

"Yes." Cory wanted to strike the table again, but Matthew gently took his wrist. "It was some gang," he said. "Now I remember, they all had weird names like Opal and Onyx and sh- stuff like that."

"And?" Sarah asked.

"And—one of them got caught, the one who hacked together their electronics. Garnet, I think," Cory rolled his eyes dramatically. "That was what's been bugging me all day." He looked sideways at his sister and down at his hands again. "Guess you figured it out first."

"I didn't. It was Mom," Emma said, putting a hand on her brother's shoulder.

"Guys, it doesn't matter who came up with it first," Matthew said, picking up the TV remote and scrolling through the list of old shows they had watched. "Let me see if I can find that show."

Another slam of the door announced Lily's arrival, who had only caught the end of Matthew's sentence. "You have something to help Katelyn? What is it? You stormed out of the store like there was a band of zombies after you."

"Sorry," Sarah said as she touched her friend's arm. Everything fell into place suddenly, and we had to tell Matthew and Cory. This—this is the solution to this puzzle."

"Why, how," Lily only asked, stripped off her coat, and took one of the chairs. "That seems like old news. Why now?"

"Hang on." Matthew had finally found the short documentary he'd been looking for. "Not sure if that's the one Cory watched, but it doesn't matter. Listen."

On the screen, a preppy, handsome young announcer smiled into the camera and looked back at his notes, eerily reminding Sarah of the moment when the break-in at the museum had been all over the news and Katelyn had been arrested.

"There is encouraging news in the art scene," he said, smiling. "In a major breakthrough, law enforcement has apprehended a key member of an infamous art theft ring responsible for a string of high-profile heists across the United States. The suspect, identified only by the alias, Garnet, was nabbed during a recent operation, sending shock-waves through the criminal organization that had eluded authorities for months."

"Garnet, I knew it," Cory said softly.

"This group," the announcer continued, "operated under a mysterious network of aliases such as Opal, Onyx, and others, specialized in stealing priceless works of art. Garnet was the tech whiz responsible for orchestrating the group's sophisticated electronic systems used during their meticulously planned heists. His arrest has prompted intense speculation about whether he will cooperate with authorities and reveal information about his accomplices. Investigators are hopeful that the captured member may provide crucial details that could lead to the dismantling of the entire criminal syndicate."

The screen now showed a dark-haired man in his twenties, wearing prison-issue orange, his hands shackled, his eyes down at the table in front of him. He had no intentions of talking, Sarah thought, but there in the tense set of his shoulders and back, she thought she could see fear. And if he was afraid, he could be persuaded. Maybe.

"So far, the art theft ring is suspected to have carried out approximately ten high-profile thefts, targeting museums and galleries holding priceless masterpieces. The stolen art includes pieces of significant cultural and historical value, raising concerns about the fate of these irreplaceable works. To date, none of the stolen art has been recovered, leaving museums and art institutions anxiously awaiting news of potential leads that could lead to the return of the missing masterpieces. The investigation is ongoing, with law enforcement agencies collaborating with international counterparts to trace the artworks and apprehend the remaining members of the art theft ring."

Matthew finally lowered the remote and sat back in a chair, his face taut, his lips a hard, drawn line. He probably knew every one of the stolen pieces, and he knew their value.

"Authorities are urging anyone with information related to the stolen art or the whereabouts of the other suspects to come forward, emphasizing the importance of community cooperation in solving this intricate case."

As the show went to a commercial break, Matthew muted the TV and set the remote down on the table gently, almost reverently. For a long moment, no one talked.

"I'm still missing something," Lily finally asked. "This guy's already in jail and has been for a while. He couldn't have taken the sapphire."

"No, but his gang probably did," Cory said softly. "If they can get the sapphire to him, they can question him forever and a day – he'll give them any cockamamie story he wants – and nobody will know he's lying."

"So, they are..."

"Protecting somebody. Their leader, the other members, maybe even their headquarters, depending on how much this guy knows." Matthew worried his bottom lip with his fingers. "I don't like it. That, together with the staged attack on Katelyn and the meticulously planned theft..."

His eyes met Sarah's across the table, and she could see concern written there, for all of them.

"Should we be afraid?"

Automatically, she put her arms around her children's shoulders, waiting for him to say, no, of course not. Those words didn't come out.

"Oh, come on," Lily slapped her hands onto the tabletop. "Criminals like that, here in Rosewood Hollow? Surely not. I mean... that's big city stuff, right" She stopped when she met Sarah and Matthew's serious eyes.

"They've already broken into our museum," Matthew said. Bypassed one of the most sophisticated security systems I know of. Then, they staged an attack on a correctional facility. It's got to be the same group, and I think they've proven they are here, in Rosewood Hollow."

"But..."

"We still need to help Katelyn," Cory protested, and Sarah shook her head.

"Cory, this is starting to get dangerous, perhaps even deadly." She paused for a moment to let that last word sink in. "Don't for a moment think I'm letting any of us get near the people that hurt Katelyn."

"So, we just sit here and leave her be?"

"The authorities—"

"The cops don't care, Mom. As far as they're concerned, she's guilty. You think they'll just listen to your side of the story? Come on, get real."

Cory talked so fast that his words tumbled one over the other. His cheeks had turned bright red, and his eyes had a wild gleam in them she'd not seen before.

"Cory."

"Easy, folks, easy." Lily rose and raised her hands. "Cory, your mom is right. This is one size too large for folks like us."

"But nobody will help Katelyn, Aunt Lily. She's going to jail for the rest of her life, and how long do you think that's going to be? If they are that dangerous, then maybe..."

Cory trailed off and hunched his shoulders. He was disappearing into his shell again, and the thought of it broke Sarah's heart. She got up and stood behind him, putting her arms around her son.

"I'm sorry, but I have to think about you first. Do you understand that?"

He nodded ever so slightly. They'd all grown fond of Katelyn. Sarah swallowed hard, remembering the day they had fought with Amelia.

"You forget I'm still here."

She blinked once, twice, looked at Matthew, and found his mouth agape. Then she looked again. She wasn't remembering Amelia, but seeing her, standing there in the doorway to the games room. She wore one of the long, flowing white dresses she seemed so fond of, her hair piled in an intricate pattern on top of her head and secured with large, sharp pins. But beyond Amelia, there was the door frame, and the faint blue glow of the blank TV screen shimmering through her. She was translucent, yes, but a lot stronger than she had been at the store.

"Amelia," Emma jumped up as if she wanted to run up to the ghost and throw her arms around her until she thought better and simply grinned broadly. "I knew you would come."

"It has been – harder than I expected getting used to the other side," Amelia said, her voice rough and gravelly with disuse.

Her eyes, her eyes were the one thing that gave Sarah cold shivers. She'd seen portraits of Amelia, and she'd been a lovely woman with long blonde hair and serene blue eyes, but this apparition had coal-dark circles where her eyes would have been, deep and featureless, and every time she looked, Sarah felt something cold gripping her heart.

"Don't be afraid," Amelia said and attempted something that probably should have sounded like a laugh.

"We're... not," brave Matthew said hesitantly.

"We thought – you were on the other side, with Simon." Sarah opened her hands. "But you are always welcome. This used to be your home too."

For a moment, she felt those dark circles focused on her and hid her trembling hands behind her back, and then Amelia's specter made that odd laugh sound again.

"Yes, of course. Simon and I are forever grateful that you solved the mystery that reunited us. Without you, I would have been stuck in the attic forever, and Simon would have remained alone."

"What do you mean by, you forget I am still here?" Matthew asked. "It sounds a bit – ominous."

Amelia looked at him from head to toe, like one might check out a specimen under glass, and finally moved all the way into the kitchen. Her flowing dress, Sarah noticed, ended in a little cloud where her knees might have been. Handy if you wanted to glide around the house.

"You were here last year."

"Yes, but—"

"Then you know that I can protect you – from many things."

Matthew closed his eyes for a moment and sucked in a mouthful of air, probably remembering the black smoke entity.

"Cory and Emma," he began, only to have all of the lights in the kitchen go out, and Amelia light up like a column of pure fire.

"You doubt me?"

"No, I guess not."

"Then you should know that Cory and Emma are far safer with me than anyone on your so-called police force." She spat those last words, and her head wavered and became unfocused for a moment. "Anger is a strong force. It drains me."

"And you are angry?"

"That girl they have accused chose to stand with you against Mort Jenkins—to help me. If you had seen the tactics they used to get her to stop saying she was innocent."

"They coerced her? You saw that?"

"Yes."

Pixie shook and moved to stand before Amelia, and the ghost actually managed a smile.

"You're still here," Amelia said, and for the first time in a long time, everyone in the room could hear Pixie.

Thanks to you.

"It was not me." Amelia gave Sarah a long look, and finally, the lights turned back on. "Enough of this. We do not have much time. We need to help the soul you call Katelyn."

"And how do you suggest we do that," Lily asked, finally finding her voice. "It's not like any of us here are real detectives."

Amelia became a little brighter as she turned on Lily and settled down to her white glowing mist again.

"You must prevent the sapphire getting into this man Garnet's hands," she said, her voice trembling a little and becoming very low key, like an old-fashioned radio losing its station. "He cannot get the sapphire, then he will have to tell the truth, and Katelyn..."

Amelia disappeared mid-sentence, and Lily stepped into the empty space she had vacated, looking around.

"We have to help," Cory said with the kind of determination even his mother couldn't override, and opened his laptop.

"Cory, maybe we should..." Sarah met her son's eyes, and all of the arguments she'd been thinking of died in her throat. He was determined. No – he wasn't merely determined; he was a force of unyielding will and relentless dedication.

"Look. Claremont Superior Court," Cory announced, lowering his eyes to the laptop again, where his fingers danced so fast she could barely follow them. "The first trial day is a week from today. We don't have much time."

"And how are we going to get our hands on that sapphire," Matthew asked. "I don't think we can just walk up and ask if we can have it, even if we knew who."

Cory chewed on his thumbnail, thinking, and, at that moment, he looked so much like his father that it made Sarah's heart ache.

She wanted to take him and keep him safe, somewhere inside a locked box where no one could steal his innocence and enthusiasm, ever.

At the thought of the word, *steal*, Sarah blurted out, "Robbie."

"Robbie? What about him?" Cory asked.

Sarah poured more hot chocolate and walked to the window, staring out at the snowy expanse of the garden, the now-empty backyard rink, and the bits and pieces of left-behind hockey equipment scattered about.

"Whoever broke into Robbie's store was looking for a compendium on enchanted stones," she said, and Cory nodded.

"Assuming there was a process to it," she continued.

Then the realization struck him, and his eyes lit up. "He needed to know how it works. We figured that."

"Yes," Sarah nodded.

"But the book was stolen. They probably have it, no way for us to look it up."

"Yup," Sarah turned around and smiled at them. "But they don't have Robbie. He's the one who wrote the book. He can tell us what they have to do to make the spell work – and how we can, uh, interrupt it. I assume you need to hold or touch the stone in some way, perhaps even an incantation or spell. But he would surely know."

"He isn't the most helpful person around," Lily said, getting to her feet and coming over to Sarah.

"There's no other way," Sarah said and picked up her bag again. "We're asking him, and if he has an issue…" She looked over to the spot where Amelia had disappeared a few moments ago. "Our friendly ghostly helper can have a little talk with him."

"That's not how Amelia works," Emma protested, and Sarah grinned.

"And that's not what I was going to do, but Robbie doesn't know that."

"Whoa, whoa, whoa, everybody…" Matthew now raised his hands and physically stopped Sarah. "What I am hearing is that you want to force some information out of this guy, then drive to Claremont and try to interfere with official court proceedings?"

"That's about it," Sarah confirmed.

"No." Matthew stood between her, Lily, and the kids, looking from one to the other. "I'm – worried, I guess."

"You saw Amelia."

"Yep, still hard to wrap my head around that."

"Seems she was impressed when Katelyn chose to stand with us," Sarah said, putting her purse back down. "So, do you want to tell her we don't want to do anything, or should we wait for her to find out?"

"Damn." Matthew let his arms drop. "There are days when I hate…"

"Yes?"

He looked toward the door from the kitchen to the hall and further on into the games room again. "When it's not that easy having a ghost around," he said, his voice raised. "Geez, I can't even believe I'm even saying that."

Emma giggled at that, and Sarah gave her a long mom look. "This is going to require all of us, Emma. Matthew and Cory don't communicate with Amelia the same way we do, but we need Cory's research and Matthew's help, all right."

"So, how are we going to do this?" Matthew asked and touched his fingers to his forehead. "After your experience with Robbie, do you think Lily and I should go see him, and get the details on how the sapphire works, and you do more research on Claremont and the court case?"

"That would work," Sarah nodded and stood with Cory. "Anything you can find out about this group…"

"I'm on it, Mom."

In the time he'd spent with Matthew, Cory had become a first-rate researcher. Give him a topic, give him a question, Sarah thought, and he would sit there until he had the answer. His interests by now included history, technology, and sciences, and he could still beat Katelyn in one of the many, many video games they owned.

She put her hand on his shoulder and squeezed gently, remembering the moody sixteen-year-old he had been when his father left. And a large part of it was due to the time he spent with Matthew.

Matthew now came around in his beat-up old leather jacket and kissed her on the cheek.

"We'll hurry, okay? Meanwhile, would it be too much to ask you to figure out a way we can solve this without having to deal with actual criminals?"

"We'll try." Sarah winked and watched Lily and Matthew head out to Lily's old orange VW bug. She dropped the kitchen curtain again and busied herself and Emma with cleaning.

Pixie hopped up on a chair beside Cory and curled her beautiful fluffy tail around her paws, looking for all the world as if she were helping him with his research.

"It says here," Cory told her now, "that this art theft ring is suspected to have stolen around ten million dollars' worth of famous paintings and sculptures over a number of years."

"What I don't understand," he continued. "If these pieces are so valuable and so famous, wouldn't they have shown up by now? How do you even fence something like that?"

"Maybe you don't." Sarah stepped behind him to read the article he was looking at over his shoulder. "Here, you see." Her finger followed a line. "Detectives from the art crimes unit discovered that several of the paintings were found to have been moving through the criminal underworld for an extended period, serving as a form of security or guarantee in various illicit transactions, such as drug deals and arms deals, over the course of several years." she read. Again, she had to swallow hard.

Are we sure this isn't too big for us, she thought and felt Pixie's reassuring paw on her arm.

Amelia...

I know Amelia is here, and she kind of likes Katelyn – but this is our family we're talking about.

"You see," she said slowly. "It's entirely possible these pieces are tucked away in secure storage somewhere and never see the light of day."

Cory cocked his head, his eyes full of questions.

"Selling stuff like that would be incredibly difficult; they would be far too recognizable. But imagine one of these paintings as a kind of secret currency in the criminal world. Instead of money, people use the art as a promise or guarantee when they're involved in illegal deals, like buying drugs or weapons. So, if someone wants to make sure they won't get cheated in a shady transaction, they might use a painting as a sort of IOU or security deposit. It moves around between different criminal activities, being like a valuable token that helps keep things in check among those involved. And if it's a very famous piece, everyone knows how valuable it is. Millions and millions of dollars in some cases."

Cory looked at her and back down at his laptop screen.

"I can't even imagine paying that much money for a simple picture," he said, wrinkling his brow, and Sarah chuckled.

"You see…"

"But Matthew is right," Cory continued, "these are some pretty bad dudes."

"They are," Sarah said, taking her son's shoulders and looking him in the eyes directly and for a long moment. "Look, we do not have to go there; we can quit this right here and now."

"But Amelia…"

"Amelia is not your mother, I am. We can ask Matthew to give your research to the police and let things fall as they may."

"And Katelyn?"

"Honey, Katelyn is a lovely girl, and I have to believe that if she's innocent, it will eventually come out."

"Right." Cory snorted and pulled his laptop close again. "Think again, Mom. Besides, you're a lousy liar. I can tell you don't believe that for a minute."

He's right, you know.

Do you mind? Sarah glared at Pixie, even though the little pap was right. She had no doubt what would happen to such a police report.

❦

About an hour later, Lily and Matthew breezed back into Thompson Hall, and Lily headed straight for the refrigerator and an open bottle of wine.

"That man." She said and her facial expression left no doubt who she meant.

"Didn't go that well?"

"No, Sarah, it did not. Robbie was being really obstinate and was not going to tell me anything, until…"

"Until I got there," Matthew said, taking the wine bottle away from Lily and putting it back into the fridge. "Then he finally came out with the goods. Turns out you were right; you have to hold the sapphire in your hand and maintain contact with it at all times, in addition to speaking a brief request beforehand."

"Hmmmm," Sarah drummed her fingers on the countertop. "Are you sure he told you everything? How come he spoke to you anyway but not to Lily?"

Matthew looked at Lily and snorted.

"She's not the one who has a ghost at home."

"You didn't…"

"Oh yes, he did," Lily said, heading for the fridge once again. "You should have heard the details he gave him, about the things Amelia could and would do – none of which I believe are true."

Matthew only shrugged, thumbing through his metal box of specialty teas, finally selecting a very specific bag. "Worked, didn't it," he said, putting on the kettle.

"So you were lying then?" Cory asked.

"The way you say that…" Matthew raised his eyebrows and finally chuckled.

"Okay, you have to say a spell and hold the jewel in your hand," Sarah repeated. "That doesn't sound easy to do in the middle of a courtroom."

"Could wear it as an amulet or good luck charm," Lily said and shrugged. "Nobody would think twice about it. There are lots of ways."

"None of which are going to be easy to figure out." Sarah accepted a hug and a mug of tea from Matthew and stood, holding the heavy earthen mug in both hands.

"There's a B&B in Claremont, close to the courthouse," Cory said, still bending over his computer. "I think we should go there when the court case is going down, don't you?"

"Cory..." Sarah looked up and swallowed whatever she was going to say. The bright light in her son's eyes made up for all of the arguments crowding in her mind. It was going to be dangerous and complicated... and Michael would hate the idea.

"Unless somebody has a better idea," she finally said.

Lily had already opened her bag and handed her credit card to Cory for the reservations. "Lily, you don't have to..."

"But I do. I haven't had this much fun since we nailed those Lumarians. This will be a riot."

Chapter Eighteen

Sarah, Emma, Cory, Matthew, Lily, and Pixie settled into an old bed and breakfast that resembled a charming, smallish motel.

The quaint inn exuded a nostalgic charm, with its white wooden exterior and cozy ambiance promising a comforting refuge during their stay in Claremont for the court case. Sarah kept wavering between the excitement of solving the case of the stolen sapphire and sheer anxiety about the Canvas Collective, as the press was fond of calling the art thieves. Sarah thought that was a little silly, and it made them sound like something out of a Saturday morning cartoon instead of violent criminals.

She noticed Matthew looking carefully around the parking lot when he parked their rented van and behind and around the sides of their B&B. She could feel his concern.

Their rooms were spacious yet adorned with vintage furnishings, each carrying a distinct personality. As they unpacked, Sarah marveled at the floral wallpaper, instantly transporting her back in time. The antique bed frames and quaint bedside tables added a touch of rustic charm, creating an atmosphere that felt like a haven away from the hustle and bustle of everyday life, such a counterpoint to the violence she knew their adversaries to be capable of.

Nothing will happen. She repeated the mantra in her head and surreptitiously checked the corners and shadowy alcoves for a sign of Amelia.

Excitement filled the air as the group chattered away, discussing their plans for the upcoming days. Emma and Cory, eager to explore their temporary abode, scampered from room to room, claiming their sleeping quarters with playful giggles. Pixie wagged her tail in approval, seemingly delighted by the new surroundings.

Matthew and Lily joined in on the lively conversation, filling the air with anecdotes and laughter. Their camaraderie softened the edges of the impending court case, creating a supportive atmosphere that helped alleviate the stress looming over them. But the laughter, Sarah thought, was a little too loud, and the jokes a bit too forced.

∞

The group gathered in the common area, a cozy sitting room with a crackling fireplace, to unwind. The worn-in couches and vintage décor added to the welcoming atmosphere. Lily shared travel stories while Pixie curled up on the rug in front of the fire, content to be surrounded by her pack.

As the day transitioned into evening, Matthew rose from his cozy position in a stuffed wingback chair and stretched.

"How about we all go outside for a little evening winter stroll?" he said to the group. "I'm sure Pixie could use a bit of relief. We can get the lay of the land and maybe find a cool place for dinner. Anybody?"

"That sounds like an idea," Sarah agreed and rose as well. "Kids – you want to get your jackets and boots and Pixie's leash?"

"It's cold out," Cory said, barely looking up from his tablet. "Do we have to? Isn't it enough if you and Matthew go? I was about to look up something."

"Maybe a bit of exercise wouldn't be too bad for you."

"Mom..."

"I'm in," Lily said. "I've been cooped up inside for too long, but if you kids want to stay here, it's okay."

No, actually, Sarah thought, she wanted the kids with her. She didn't want to take her eyes off them, but the old B&B had become their haven, a place of shared laughter, support, and moments of respite amid the challenges they faced in Claremont, and finally, she relented.

"Fine, but stay here," she said. "In the common room or in your rooms – do not go anywhere, understood."

"Yes, Mom," Cory rolled his eyes dramatically, hardly looking up from his tablet. She'd likely find him in that very position on the couch when they returned, she thought, shrugging into the coat Matthew was holding for her. It was fine. Nothing was going to happen.

❦

The air in Claremont carried a distinct chill, the kind that seeped into bones and whispered of winter's lingering grasp. Matthew hooked his arm into hers, and they walked close, Lily a few paces ahead of them. Bundled in coats and scarves, they navigated the labyrinth of cobblestone streets. The dim glow of streetlights painted a delicate tapestry of shadows on the ground, enhancing the historic charm of the town. The echoes of their footsteps bounced off the brick facades, creating an ambiance that felt both intimate and slightly haunting.

Sarah relaxed a little, her breath forming small clouds in the frigid air. She tightened the scarf around her neck and pulled her coat closer, a futile attempt to ward off the relentless cold. Matthew followed suit, their breath visible in the night air, mingling with the mist that hung above the streets.

"Look," Lily suddenly said. "It's even closer than we thought."

Her mittened hand pointed at a rectangular metal sign, so institutional and out of place in this old town. "Claremont Superior Courthouse."

Approaching the courthouse, the heart of the upcoming legal happenings, the atmosphere shifted. The imposing structure rose before them, a monolith of justice that seemed to scrutinize their every step.

Sarah's gaze lingered on the courthouse doors, each step towards them feeling like a march towards an uncertain fate. The seriousness of their mission enveloped them, and the camaraderie that had buoyed their spirits waned in the shadow of the imposing structure.

Sarah shivered again and felt Matthew pull her a little closer.

"Everything will be fine," he whispered and released Pixie from her leash, so she could sniff around the bare, snowed-in bushes and scraggly trees that bordered the walkways and parking lot around the courthouse.

"I keep wondering if Amelia is near," Sarah whispered and peered into the deep shadows around them. The institutional-type lighting around the courthouse cast long angular shadows around her, but she couldn't spot the familiar, comforting mist that meant Amelia was close by.

"I don't think that's how it works," Matthew whispered, and Lily, who'd been checking the public notice board at the entrance, came back, hugging her arms and with it her distinctive, orange wool coat with its plush collar closer to her body.

"First hearing is the day after tomorrow, guys, but honestly, I think Cory is right. It's freezing out here. Can we not walk back and order takeout? Isn't that what the internet was invented for?"

Matthew went to take a picture of the announcement of upcoming court hearings, and Sarah stomped her feet. "You're not wrong. I underestimated how cold it would be tonight."

"It is February."

"I wanted a bit of fresh air. Oh well. Where'd Pixie go."

Sarah looked around, but the little white and sable Papillon was nowhere to be seen.

"Matthew," she called out, trying to hide the panic in her voice. "Matthew – is Pixie with you?"

"Hmm – what – no, I let her off to..." Matthew checked the photos he had taken and pointed to the spot in the parking lot where he'd let off Pixie.

"No – wait, I let her off right here. Pixie?" As he called out, his voice took on a tinge of panic. "Pixie – come out here, girl; time to go home."

"She's gone. God, she's gone," Sarah cried, turning on the flashlight on her phone, calling out again and again.

The once-carefree atmosphere now hung heavy with anxiety and fear, casting a chilling shadow over the previously cheerful group. Sarah's heart raced in her chest, the rhythm echoing the urgency of her calls for Pixie.

"Pixie! Where are you, girl?" Sarah's voice trembled. Her pleas were accompanied by the worried calls of the others. The cold night air seemed to steal the sound of their voices, leaving an unsettling silence in its wake. The town, once charming and welcoming, now felt like a maze of uncertainty, every corner holding the potential of hiding their beloved Pixie.

The group scattered, eyes darting around, each face etched with urgency. Their movements were sharp and hard, body language screaming a silent search. Their breaths, visible in the crisp air, added to the sense of urgency as they checked every hidden corner, hoping to catch even the slightest glimpse of the adventurous Pixie. The courthouse steps, usually a symbol of justice and order, now served as a stark reminder of the chaos that had unfolded in their midst.

"She couldn't have gone far," Matthew said, squeezing Sarah's hand. "I just let her off so she could… Just for a minute. God, Sarah. She couldn't have gone far." The night seemed to conspire against them, the darkness swallowing their desperate calls. Each passing second intensified their anxiety, and the cold air, once refreshing, now carried the weight of their collective worry.

In the midst of their rising panic, a distant but familiar bark pierced through the oppressive silence.

"Pixie, I'm here," Sarah screamed and ran in the direction she heard the faint little bark. Behind her, she could feel Matthew and Lily trying to keep up with her. "Sarah, wait," Matthew called, trying to reach for her. Sarah had no intention of waiting for anything. She only stopped when she stood at the mouth of a dingy, barely lit alley behind the courthouse. She couldn't see past crates, garbage containers, and a few old cars parked there. The alley was entirely quiet – too quiet. "Pixie," Sarah cried and heard all the fear and anxiety in her voice. "Come out, please."

Matthew finally caught up with her and put his arm around her. "Hush, Sarah, we'll find her, okay?"

"I don't want to wait," Sarah tried to tear away, but he held fast. Lily had a flashlight in her hand and began to light up and down the alley. Step by step, she walked in, Matthew and Sarah close behind. She shined the beam of her light under and behind the garbage containers and bins, a pile of old pallets, and under the old cars. Nothing. "But she wouldn't just run away," Sarah said. "Not Pixie, not after everything…"

"Be still for a moment," Matthew said, physically holding her and putting his hands on her shoulders. Close your eyes. See if you can feel her. You two still have this bond."

Sarah nodded. She closed her eyes and tried to block out the alley, the smells, the silence of the night, and the cold creeping into her coat. *Pixie…?* She felt nothing. *Pixie??* Again, more frantic this time. And again, she didn't feel anything. For the first time since she'd welcomed the sweet little Papillon into her house and heart, she couldn't feel their connection. "She's gone, Matthew." Her hands clawed into Matthew's woolen coat, and she cried out her anguish. "Pixie's gone."

"No, she's not gone," Matthew held her tight. "Don't say that. She just wandered away a bit. She's curious. She probably got lost and is trying to find you just as desperately as you're trying to find her."

"I can't feel her."

"You're both frantic. Look at you, you're trembling head to toe. I'm going to take you home…"

"I'm not going, not until I find Pixie, don't even try."

"Sarah, look, I…"

Sarah tore away from him and ran after Lily, who had disappeared into the shadows of the alley. Together, they went all the way to the end, shining into every shadow. "I don't get it, Lily. I heard her. I know it was her; I heard her little bark."

"You think somebody might have taken her to the pound?"

"Without checking around for her owner first? We were right there in the park in front of the courthouse."

"We'll find her, Sarah. You're all but panicked."

"What if something happened to her?"

"Nothing happened. She's micro-chipped; she has your information on her collar. Somebody's going to find her and bring her back."

"What if they don't, what if…"

Just at that moment, her cell phone rang, and Sarah whipped it out of her pocket without hesitating for a second. "Anderson – do you have my—"

"Mom?"

Cory. She would have to tell them both about Pixie. Matthew had caught up with them by then and wanted to speak, but she raised a hand to silence him.

"Cory, I am sorry. I – we have…"

"Where are you, Mom? I looked out the window, and there was Pixie all by herself."

"Oh, thank God." Sarah felt her knees buckle and her body go limp. If Matthew hadn't been standing close and holding her, she would have sat on the hard, icy ground. "Cory, I don't know what happened."

"Mom – she's covered in blood." Just like that, her relief turned into panic once again. She shoved the phone into her pocket and began running toward their inn, only a few blocks away.

"Hurry," she called over her shoulder. "Pixie made it to the inn, but she's bleeding."

"Bleeding? What in the…"

"Look up 24-hour veterinary hospitals," Sarah called over her shoulder, knowing Lily wouldn't be able to keep up.

"I'll get her ready for transport. Call us in if you can."

She ran. Cobblestones pounding under her feet, refusing to look left or right. The only thing she could keep her mind on was sweet little Pixie.

Her adorable white and sable Papillon, that broad smile, the fluffy ears moving this way and that when she was trying to tune into something, and the golden sparkling glow around the tip of her tail when she used her magic. *Hang on little Pixie, I'll be right there.*

At the inn, she tore through the front door and down the hall to their rooms without as much as nodding at the proprietress in the front room.

"Pixie?"

All the towels the inn had given them were spread around the floor in their room, and they all were stained with grisly dark red splotches.

So much red, so much red everywhere. Sarah thought her heart would explode out of her chest. There in the middle of that sea of red and white sat Pixie, upright, tail wagging as best as she could, tongue lolling out of her open mouth.

"What the..." Sarah stopped dead in her tracks, tossed her coat into a corner, and dropped onto the floor beside the little Papillon.

Pixie was covered in red alright, but she wagged happily and gave Sarah a little kiss on the cheek.

I'm not hurt. I'm so sorry, I can see you were worried.

What on earth happened out there?

Sarah ran her hands over the little dog's body. She could feel her heart beating strong and evenly, the sweet tongue gave little kisses, but her hands still came away covered in a red, sticky substance.

"Paint," Sarah asked and looked at Cory. "Paint? She's covered in red paint?"

"I thought it was blood, I swear, Mom. But then Emma said she looks so happy, and we saw it was just paint. Sorry. It made a bit of a mess."

A bit was an understatement. Everywhere Pixie had walked, a little trail of red footprints tracked. In the glass patio door, through the sitting area, up on the couch, the chairs, the blanket. Cory and Emma were both covered in red, and Sarah brought her hands to her face.

The release of adrenaline made her laugh out loud just as Matthew, Lily, and Cheryl, the owner of the inn, came through the door.

"Dear God," Cheryl said and stood thunderstruck. "It looks like someone got murdered in here."

"It's just paint." Sarah picked up Pixie and held her close to her chest. "We'll pay for the damages, of course. She got away, and some joker must have thought it was funny throwing paint at her."

"Who would do such a thing to the adorable little dog" Cheryl said and touched a tiny, unblemished spot on Pixie's head.

"I'm so sorry; I am so sorry," Sarah repeated, heart pounding in her chest. "Do you have any place where I could clean her up – in the garage maybe…"

"Nonsense, bring her into the kitchen. We'll bathe her in the sink in some warm water. I've had kids, my dear, I've cleaned up my share of messes in my life. Come now."

Not a bath, Pixie protested, but Sarah held fast.

"Can you try and clean up," she asked Matthew. "Best as we can, I don't know what kind of paint this is."

"On it." Lily called the veterinary hospital back to cancel the emergency and was already looking up how to get paint out of furniture as Sarah carried Pixie into the kitchen.

I was frantic.

I'm sorry. I didn't mean to...

What on earth happened to you?

That's the part I don't understand. One minute, I was sniffing on a tree—the next, somebody grabbed me and threw me into a car. I barked once to warn you.

I heard that.

Then he just drove me over here, put me in the parking lot, and dumped this—stuff—on me. Is it grisly?

Very.

Together with Cheryl, Sarah shampooed Pixie and rinsed her off in the big old ceramic sink in the kitchen. The water ran blood red off the little dog's coat and disappeared like a red river down the drain, and Sarah shivered.

When they were done with the first round, they soaped up the little dog again, massaged baby shampoo into her coat, and rinsed her clean. Pixie had murder in her eyes, and her coat still had a slight pink tinge here and there.

Sarah kept babbling about the damage to their rooms and how they would pay for everything until Cheryl finally took her wrist.

"Stop worrying about it, Sarah. Whatever doesn't come off with a good clean, we'll just have to replace it, that's all. I'm much more concerned that somebody would do this to one of my guests. Here in Claremont, of all places. It's not a little village, but still – up to now, we've described the town as a place where you can raise your kids in peace."

"Perhaps it was just... teenagers," Sarah muttered, wiping the soap off her hands and wrapping Pixie in an old utility towel. Now that her usually fluffy white coat was wet and plastered against her body, she looked no bigger than a little fennec fox. She shivered even wrapped in the towel, and Sarah held her close to her body.

"I don't think there were any teenagers involved here," Cheryl said darkly. "For one, it's about zero degrees out there, and I don't know any teen who'd be out voluntarily at that point."

"Perhaps…"

"For another, harming an animal is a terrible thing to do. I don't want to think any of the teenagers living in the area would be able to do something like this."

Also, those were no teenagers holding me, Sarah heard Pixie say. *Those were men with a bad attitude.* She squirmed a little in her towel, and Cheryl tapped the tiny nose peeking out of the terry folds.

"How about this, little one," she asked, holding a small cube of cheese in front of her nose, which Pixie took carefully and gracefully.

"You spoil her."

"I hope so. Now let's sit in front of the fire and dry the little sprite."

Half an hour later, Pixie had come out of her towel cocoon. She had been dried and brushed, pampered and fussed over. If one looked close, a faint trace of red remained here and there, but it would wear off in time, Sarah thought. In time.

She still couldn't wrap her mind around the random attack on her little dog when her phone chimed with an incoming text. She didn't recognize the number and unlocked the screen with one hand.

This time it was only paint, the text read.

Next time it will be her blood. Go home.

Sarah dropped the phone and began to shake violently. Cheryl had gone to fetch tea, and without calling out to her or saying another word, Sarah scooped up Pixie and took her to their rooms.

Chapter Nineteen

Matthew and Lily were busy scrubbing red paw prints off the caramel-colored fabric couch.

"You know, I wonder if it would be less work to just go and..." Matthew started, then stopped as Sarah walked back in, and he saw the look on her face.

"What is it?" he asked

"It was them," Sarah said and held out her phone to him. "It was them. They took Pixie, they dumped paint on her. It's a warning."

"No..." Matthew took the phone.

Lily read over Matthew's shoulder. "'Go home.' That's fairly direct."

"Where are the kids?" Sarah asked.

"In their room, I think." Matthew nodded at the connecting door.

"Are they okay?" The panic growing inside her. "Has anyone checked on them, are they okay?"

"No, I figured they were watching TV."

Panic in full bloom, Sarah tore open the connecting door, stopping just short of storming in there. Cory had dozed off watching

something, the remote control still in his hands. The other bed was –
empty. The door leading into the main hallway and straight to the back
staircase stood open just a bit, as if someone had left in a hurry.

"Emma," Sarah screamed and flicked the light switch, watching the
overhead chandelier and all wall sconces blaze to life. "Where is Emma?"

For the second time in the same evening, her heart exploded with
fear, panic, and utter agony. Not her child, not her youngest, sweet little
Emma.

"Emma."

Matthew came tearing in behind her and gently shook Cory.

"Cory, what's going on in here? Where is Emma?"

"Huh, what…" Cory sat up in a daze and blinked a couple of times.
"I dunno. I – what…?"

"Mom, you're back – how is Pixie?"

Sarah turned around in slow motion. There in the door to the hall
stood Emma, in her pink pajamas, holding a glass of water. "Why are
you looking like—"

Sarah flew into the room and threw her arms around Emma. "Thank
God, thank God – where on earth were you?"

"Let go of me, Mom. What's the matter? I just wanted to get a glass
of water." Emma raised the glass she'd barely managed to hold. "I took
the back stairs, okay?"

"It's all right, baby, all right. I just thought…" She sat on a chair,
forked her fingers through her hair again and again, and forced herself
to breathe evenly.

"After what happened today…"

"I'm sorry, Mom."

"Okay, guys, new rule," Matthew raised his hands to his shoulders,
silencing them all. "Nobody goes anywhere alone. Buddy system. If you

want to use the bathroom, use the one in our rooms. If you're going out, go with a buddy. Preferably an adult. Cory, I'm looking at you to keep your sister safe."

"Why? Did something happen?" Cory now sat up fully and wiped the sleep out of his eyes. He still looked so much like the little boy she took by the hand to walk into his first-grade classroom, Sarah thought.

"Let's just say – we have a strong suspicion that what happened to Pixie may have been the work of this Canvas Collective or their supporters."

"But why." Cory turned off the TV and checked his tablet for the news. "How would they even know we're here?"

"Your mother went to see Katelyn in the hospital. I was the one who got her the job at the museum. And most people think she came here with us. If they had been keeping an eye on the house, they could have followed us. I'm afraid we may have underestimated this group."

"What about Amelia?" Emma asked, scanning the corners of the room.

Pixie strolled into the room with a tinkle of collar tags and put her paws on Sarah's knees to be picked up.

I'm afraid Amelia might have overestimated her ability to manifest outside the Rosewood area.

"She can't appear?"

Sarah pulled in her shoulders and fought the impulse to pull her family in close, asking them to pack their bags right then.

I only get a weak sense of her. Usually, I know when she's coming in. Now – almost nothing.

"But why?"

Energy – distance – who knows? Ghosts are strange that way. And she can't rely on Simon to give her his energy forever.

"God." Sarah squeezed Pixie and sat hard on Cory's bed.

"What happened? What did Pixie say?" Matthew asked, and when she had told them, they all looked down and sat in stunned silence. One of the reasons they had felt secure coming on this escapade had been Amelia's promise to keep them safe.

A tiny paw touched the center of Sarah's palm, and She took it and closed her eyes.

You have the power. Listen.

Sarah listened. With her eyes closed, she listened, hard.

Her mind picked up the background noise of hundreds upon hundreds of people around her, almost like being in the center of a busy airport with your eyes closed. She knew the signature of Amelia's presence, how it felt when her entity was trying to come through, how the hair on her arms started to stand up, and her senses tuned to the ghost. This time – nothing.

She took Pixie's paw a little harder until she could feel the little dog joining in her effort to locate the spirit.

"Nothing," she finally said, opening her eyes again. "I think we're on our own."

"But Mom..." Matthew hushed Cory with a quick gesture.

"Are you sure, Sarah?" Michael asked, and she nodded.

Matthew sat on Cory's bed and motioned for him to sit beside him. "Bud, I'm sorry, but there is no way we can do this without Amelia."

"That's not fair. You said we would help; you said we would try to find the real thieves so Katelyn could get out of jail," Cory yelled.

"No, it isn't fair." Sarah took her son's wildly gesticulating hands and held tight. "It isn't; I totally agree with you, but after what just happened to Pixie, do you think I want to risk the same thing happening to you or worse?"

The hard words made Cory stop short. He sat by Matthew and pressed his lips together hard. "No, of course not," he finally mumbled. "I just thought..."

"You thought we could do something good, and you have no idea how immensely proud that makes me," Sarah said. "But this is a no-go. Tomorrow morning we will pack up and go home."

"And Katelyn?" Cory still looked down at his hands.

"Just promise me you won't do anything on your own, Cory. Please promise me. Matthew and I will try to figure out if we can maybe get an anonymous tip to the police, maybe direct their investigation a bit, maybe leak something to the press – I don't know yet. But this here," her finger spun around the little room at the inn. "This whole idea only seemed possible with the help of Amelia. And it looks like we're not going to have that."

"Okay." Cory still wasn't looking up.

"Cory? Please promise me – really promise – you won't do something like sneak out in the middle of the night to try something on your own."

Cory sighed and looked up at her. The corners of his mouth twitched, and somehow, Sarah thought, somehow she had known he would be planning just that.

"Okay, Mom," he said with a sigh. "I promise I will not do anything without checking in with you or Matthew first."

"Thank you." Sarah got up and squeezed her son's shoulder. "Thank you. Now, let's all get some sleep, and tomorrow morning, we will head back to Rosewood Hollow."

Cory nodded, and Pixie hopped up on the bed to cover his face with little kisses until the boy squealed with laughter. Emma joined in the game, and a moment later, Sarah couldn't help but giggle and laugh with her children.

"Okay, you little troublemaker," she finally said and caught Pixie, holding her close. "Let's leave these two to go to bed and sleep, and you come with me."

Shouldn't I keep an eye on them?

I think they are good now. Let's go.

Matthew and Sarah tried watching a movie in their room, but Sarah couldn't concentrate. She got up every fifteen minutes or so to peek into the other room to make sure they were in bed, sleeping.

Getting up to check again, Matthew held her hand and said, "It's okay, Sarah, they haven't gone anywhere."

"But..."

"They'd have to go through this room or down those old stairs to the back door. As wired as you are, you would have heard them."

"Maybe..."

I would hear them, Pixie said, and Sarah dropped heavily onto the sofa. "I know I'm overreacting. But losing Pixie, and then seeing her covered in – in paint." She shuddered, and Matthew pulled her close. "Hush. I'm here. We'll go back home, and nothing is going to happen. Promise."

Even after they had gone to bed and she could feel Matthew's arm around her and hear his steady, quiet breathing, she still worried. Worried about the children, worried about the Canvas Collective gang, worried that somebody would break in, or Cory would break his word and try to go out.

At some point in the grey morning hours, she finally fell asleep, dreaming of sapphires, and gangsters, and so much blood.

Chapter Twenty

When Sarah woke again, she was alone in the great four-poster bed with Pixie cuddled up close beside her, snoozing peacefully.

The heavy curtains were drawn, but through a tiny gap on the side, Sarah could see the grey February morning light, and she smelled the delicious aroma of freshly roasted coffee from downstairs.

"Hey, baby," she said to Pixie. "Looks like Matthew decided to let us sleep in, huh? Bet you any minute he is going to come up with fresh coffee and croissants."

Pixie rolled on her back to have her tummy scratched. Sarah happily obliged, and doing just that, she dozed off again.

A little while later, she woke violently and automatically reached for Pixie. The little Papillon sat upright on the bed now, the hair on her back raised, making her impossibly fluffy and large. A low growl coming from her tiny throat.

"Pixie?"

Sarah sat upright and pulled her close.

Something is happening downstairs. And it is not good.

Sarah's eyes fluttered open as she slowly emerged from the depths of slumber. A loud crash sounded from down below, shattering the tranquility of the morning for good, and she could feel the unusual commotion that reverberated through the creaking floorboards.

Something is happening downstairs.

Sarah swung her legs over the edge of the bed, her bare feet meeting the cool, worn, wooden floor. The distant echoes of raised voices and shouts reached her ears, sending a chill down her spine.

Hastily, she slipped into jogging pants and a big sweater she had discarded on a chair the night before. She wanted to pick up Pixie, but she was already at the door.

Walking on bare tiptoes, she crept down the narrow staircase, wincing every time a tread groaned beneath the weight of a step. The air thickened with tension as the commotion grew louder, blending with the acrid scent of fear.

The cozy, quaint ambiance of the bed and breakfast now felt like a distant memory, replaced by an unsettling atmosphere.

At the bottom of the stairs, she snuck to the door leading into the kitchen, from where all of the commotion seemed to stem. With trembling fingers, she opened the door ever so slightly and clapped her free hand over her mouth, so she wouldn't scream with horror at the scene unfolding before her.

There, in the middle of Cheryl's cheerful kitchen, where she had bathed Pixie the night before, a sinister figure with his face obscured by shadows held Emma and Cheryl at gunpoint. He screamed at them and gestured with the grey, terrifying gun in his hand.

"Where is the woman," he screamed.

The woman. He likely meant her. The room seemed to tilt, and Sarah's heart raced as her mind struggled to comprehend the nightmare unfolding.

Matthew, Cory, and Lily were not there. If they showed up now and walked into the middle of this… Sarah's eyes stayed glued to the gun.

Don't lose sight of it, she thought, as a stubborn, unrealistic idea grew inside her head that if she just kept her eyes on that gun, nothing could happen.

She could feel Pixie, uncharacteristically quiet, sidling up next to her, touching her leg.

We are the only ones in the house.

Emma cried out, and the sound sent a surge of panic through Sarah's veins. The acoustics of the room amplified every terrified whimper and plea, intensifying the desperate ambiance. Sarah's hands trembled as she clutched the railing for support, her breath catching in her throat. The once comforting surroundings now felt like a trap, the silence of the missing trio echoing louder than the commotion around her.

"Where are they," the gunman screamed again and jabbed the gun hard under Cheryl's chin. The rotund, sweet owner of the inn whimpered weakly.

"They've gone out," she said. "I don't know when they'll be back. Their car isn't there, can't you see?"

Help me out here, Pixie. How can we get out of this without either of them getting hurt?

Stay hidden for now.

At that moment, the gunman grabbed Emma roughly by the arm and yanked her around, spinning her hard into the stainless-steel prep top where cut fruit for breakfast lay scattered.

The knives, Sarah thought, where was Cheryl's set of kitchen knives? Were they anywhere accessible?

Pixie? Can you spot Cheryl's knives anywhere?

I can't. But wait… I can smell them. He threw them into the big trash bin.

Too far to get at them.

The masked assailant tightened his grip on Emma, pressing her even harder against the cold, solid prep top. The edge of stainless steel dug hard against her vulnerable form, the metallic edge unforgiving. Sarah felt the sharp chill of the steel against her own skin.

The gunman was no more than a figure draped in shadows and blackness. Every inch of his attire, from head to toe, was black; the absence of light and darkness came to life. A large medical mask concealed the lower half of his face, transforming him into a faceless terror, his eyes gleaming with inscrutable malevolence.

Under the shadow of a tattered black baseball cap, strands of dirty blonde hair hinted at a hidden identity, adding an unsettling touch to the assailant's mystery. The cap cast a shadow over his features, obscuring any glimpse of humanity and amplifying the sense of dread that hung thick in the air.

Sarah hardly dared to breathe and pushed back from the door frame ever so slowly, one inch at a time. There had to be something in the foyer she could use as a weapon, some solid, sharp object.

She barely heard Pixie's warning before she backed into the little table Cheryl used to hold the day's mail.

Her hand automatically flew out to steady the little hall table, which was more decorative than sturdy, but the damage was done. A stack of mail landed on the floor with an audible splash.

"Who's there," the gunman called out.

Too late. Too late for so many things.

Hide, Pixie, her mind screamed desperately.

If Pixie kept free, perhaps they still stood a chance.

"Come in here or this little girl..."

"Wait... wait. I'm here."

Sarah slipped out of the shadow of the foyer into the rectangle of the kitchen door.

The gunman held Emma close to his chest, the muzzle of the gun pressed to her temple.

"What is it you want – money?" Sarah asked, although she already knew the answer. Money was the last thing on this man's mind.

"You don't get to ask the questions here, lady. The famous Sarah Anderson, I presume."

Sarah lowered her head, biding for time. She couldn't feel Pixie beside her but sensed her strong presence in her heart.

I'm going to get help.

Hurry. Hopefully, they had that much time.

"You seem to already know that," she said, defiantly raising her chin and glaring at the gunman.

"Where's the rest of your family?"

"Out, I presume." Sarah shrugged. "Do you see them around here somewhere?"

"Don't get cute with me."

"Trust me, 'cute' goes out the window when someone shows up with a gun." *What are you doing*, she thought to herself. Why get him mad? While another portion of her mind said keep going, keep him distracted.

The gun wavered between Emma and Cheryl, and Sarah dug her hands into the edge of the countertop. Her teeth ground together, and she couldn't look at Emma. Keep him distracted.

"Mom, please..."

"It's okay, sweetheart, this – man – hasn't even told us what he wants yet."

"Shut up!"

What am I doing, she thought? Why am I babbling? Where is all of this coming from? Dear God, help us now. Her fingers cracked, holding onto the counter top hard. Then she felt it. The electric tension in the air, the way the hair stood up on the back of her arms – and she smiled.

"What is it you want from us, huh? First, you took our dog, dumped paint on her, and now you're here waving a gun around. What exactly do you want?"

"That mangy mutt." The gunman muttered as he came closer, dragging Emma all the way, until he stood face to face with Sarah. She could smell the odor of sweat, garlic, and stress, but she refused to blink or back up.

"You got our message, and you're still here. You had a chance."

"Okay. So again – what exactly do you want?"

She could feel it building now, as she had experienced it before, and she knew what it was now: that far-off feeling when energy gathers into a bigger and bigger cloud and rolls toward you, gathering more energy, more power, crackling and burning with all of that build-up.

The kitchen lights flickered and went out. Almost immediately, the backup generator kicked in, and the emergency lights around the kitchen came on, casting the entire scene in an eerie blood-red light. Emma whimpered again, and Sarah stared right at her.

"Just stay calm, Amelia," she said, praying Emma would get the message. "Stay calm. It will be over soon."

"If you think this will be over any time soon..."

The gunman sneered and raised his hand with the pistol in it, and at the same time, he screamed as if a lightning bolt had struck him.

The gun left his hand, flying through the air, struck the kitchen wall on the opposite side, and crumbled into a thousand pieces. Crumbled, as if it were nothing but cheap Play-Doh, Sarah thought irrationally and held a hand out to Emma.

Emma ducked under the gunman's arm, ran around the kitchen island, and tucked in close to Sarah.

"I thought she couldn't come," Emma said, her entire body trembling.

The gunman screamed again and pointed. Sarah looked toward where he was pointing. There, in the doorway, a giant grey cloud hovered. Deep grey and impenetrable, it moved, flexed, and wavered around its outer edges, flashes of lightning blazing through it.

It reminded her of the entity she had seen only a few months ago, and yet – not.

Emma screamed.

Cheryl began praying loudly.

The gunman looked at his hand, and then at the entity in the doorway. He let loose a string of curses and backed up, but it kept coming, advancing on him, bit by wavering bit.

"That's enough of this." And was at the back door in two giant steps. With one look over his shoulder, he ran outside, the door slamming behind him.

For a moment, all they could hear was the far-off rattle of the emergency generator. Then the lights flickered, flashed once, and came back on. The red emergency lighting snapped off, and the furnace in the basement started up with a comforting rumble.

"What in the name of…" Cheryl said and blinked at the kitchen doorway, looked again, and shook her head. There was nothing there.

With a little tinkle of collar tags, Pixie came strolling around the corner. She looked fresh and sweet and entirely harmless, if you didn't notice the strong golden glow just around the tip of her tail.

What did I miss?

Pixie – you...

"Mom, what just happened? Was that Ame—"

"I don't know, Emma," Sarah said quickly, not wanting to explain to Cheryl who, or what, Amelia was.

Smiling, she strolled over to the sideboard and poured a cup of coffee with all of her remaining concentration.

"There was a man with a gun in my kitchen," Cheryl intoned carefully, her hand clutching a rosary she had found in a drawer. "They were looking for you and your family, Sarah. First, the red paint on your dog – now this. I don't think I'm quite equipped for this."

"I know," Sarah said, her nerves ebbing only slowly as she clung to the solid white mug of strong coffee. "I don't know what to tell you..."

"But Mom..."

"I know, and I can't blame you, Cheryl. As soon as Matthew, Lily, and my son got back, we were going to tell you we are going back home today. Perhaps you want to put our bill together."

She put her arm around Emma's shoulder and directed her toward the kitchen door and upstairs again.

Sarah waved a hand over her shoulder and took the stairs two at a time, only to drop onto her bed and bury her hands in her face.

"You were awesome, Mom. And Amelia protecting us."

Sarah raised her head and forced a smile, welcoming Pixie into her arms as well.

"Thank you, Em, but that wasn't Amelia, was it?"

She took Pixie's little face and planted a kiss on the shiny black nose.

"How do you know?"

"I just... know."

Sarah looked deeply into Pixie's eyes. *I saw that entity – and it wasn't the same one as before.*

No, I think you are right.

Pixie... How did you do this?

Amelia is still sorting out her issues. She's never traveled. So, I borrowed her energy – and a bit of the house's power. I have to tell you, she lifted a little paw *Electricity bites.*

Sarah grinned and hugged both Pixie and Emma a little

"You're talking to Pixie, aren't you?" Emma said, and Sarah nodded.

"I'll teach you how to do it too if Pixie is okay with it," she said, and in her heart, she knew this to be true: she could teach Emma. She could feel abilities awakening inside her that had been dormant before.

"Just then, the door flew open with a resounding crash, and Matthew rushed in, trailed by Cory and Lily, laden with bags and packages. Matthew took her hands and pulled her close, then pushed her back a little again.

"A gunman, Sarah? Threatening you and Emma?"

"Yeah. One of those Canvas Collective guys," Sarah said and rolled her shoulders. "He all but admitted it. It was them who attacked Pixie to drive us out of town."

"And you – oh my God..." Matthew dropped into a chair and rubbed his face with both hands for a moment, trying to get his mind around what he was hearing. "Cheryl said something about a power surge and you calling Emma, Amelia? So, I'm guessing..."

"A little more complicated than that."

"Wait, Mom. How did you get rid of the guy anyway? Was it Amelia? I thought she couldn't come through here."

"She couldn't – or can't quite yet. I'm not so sure myself. I could feel her trying to come through, but...." Sarah rubbed her arms, remembering the electric atmosphere in the air when Amelia and Pixie had joined forces.

"But," Sarah pointed at Pixie, happily playing with a random sock she had found. "Pixie took over, gathered Amelia's energy, shorted out the power to the house, and created a pretty good entity for a five-pound dog."

Pixie threw the sock in the air and caught it again, shaking it furiously.

"This entity," Matthew blanched visibly. "She didn't – there wasn't..."

"Nope." Sarah quickly looked from the children to Lily. The children had seen the original entity, and the results, a fact for which she would be forever grateful.

"Not this time. The guy took one look and hightailed it out of there. He might need some emotional support for a while."

"Yes," Cory struck his palm with the fist of the other hand. "Score one for us."

"It's not quite that easy, Cory," Matthew warned. "These people definitely know we are here. Just because we got rid of them once doesn't mean we're safe."

"And also, I told Cheryl we'd move out as soon as you guys were back," Sarah admitted ruefully. "She really was not up for a repeat performance."

"Mmmm, can't blame her. I don't know how you are taking this so calmly." Matthew pulled her close again. "They threatened Emma, and you. If something had happened to either of you..."

"It didn't – it won't." Sarah couldn't even explain to herself how she could stay so calm, so centered when she had watched someone holding a gun on her youngest child. She closed her eyes for a second and listened inside. Nothing. Only the feeling that whatever was happening, she and her family would find their way through it.

"Sarah," Matthew said so low she had to close in to hear him. "I won't risk all of your lives."

"I know, Matthew," she said, pushing back from him. "But I think we know we can't just watch them win and hope they won't come after us after. The moment we showed an interest in Katelyn, in the sapphire, and in this case, we were inextricably in." Her words hung in the room, and Sarah hugged her arms to her body.

"I am sorry," she said, softening her words a little. "I don't feel as if we have a choice."

Matthew pressed his lips together.

"Okay, look." Lily got up and put her hands on the kids' shoulders. Why don't you two go into your room and pack up your things? Either way, it looks like we are going to have to leave here."

"Are we staying, though?" Cory asked, looking from his mother to Matthew, and Sarah shook her head.

"Not here at the inn. We'll find a hotel or something."

Cory tried to catch Matthew's eyes, but he had walked over to the window and was staring out into the cold February morning.

"Matthew...?" Sarah asked

"I'm just...worried, Sarah. And not sure we should be pursuing this."

"I know."

"But there you have it."

"I bet if we talked to Cheryl," Lily suggested, "maybe we could just—"

"You know what," Sarah forced herself to smile at her friend. "Matthew is unsure, and likely for good reason. Why don't you guys pack up? You and he and the kids can head back. I'll make arrangements with Michael to pick them up, and Pixie and I will stay on here and see this through, okay." She took her coat and looked around for her purse. "Tell Cheryl I'll be back as fast as I can, please. I'm going to look for a hotel and get a room."

Without waiting for a response, she walked out of the room, down the stairs, and through the back door.

Her open coat billowed in the cold wind, and she finally buttoned it and tightened her scarf. Of course, she hadn't brought the car keys or one of the tourist maps that littered the rooms and the foyer.

Looking down she realized that Pixie had followed her out, and she also hadn't thought of bringing a leash.

I'm sorry, girl. Can I trust you to stay with me and not run out chasing a squirrel or something?

I don't really chase squirrels. They're lame.

"Squirrels are lame," she said out loud, and that made her smile a little. At the same time, she could feel hot tears pricking at the back of her eyes.

I know it was dangerous, Pixie. But you were there, and you were drawing on Amelia and...

And you have more energy than either of us.

So you say. We can't just go back home and pretend nothing happened. For one, it's not right; for another, they will come after us.

Probably.

I'm not sure Matthew sees that.

Because he can't.

Sarah stopped and looked down at Pixie.

What do you mean he can't?

He doesn't feel the power, Sarah. The power you felt when you knew Amelia was trying to come in, or when you were goading that gunman so he wouldn't look and see us building the entity.

Mmmm, even I didn't know that's what I was doing, Sarah admitted ruefully.

You see? But you did know. For some reason even I don't understand, you share the power my original Mom, Serena, her grandmother Selena, and I share. Matthew doesn't... sense any of that.

Sarah bent down and let Pixie snuggle into her arms. She found a park bench close by and sat down with her tiny but powerful companion. As near as they could determine, Serena had transferred her 'powers' in the last moments of her life, during a fatal car crash, and the only being close enough was Pixie.

She wrapped her arms around the little dog and buried her face in the silky long white fur. Pixie gave her little kisses on the cheek.

He's worried about you, Pixie said. *Probably the first time in his life he has had to worry about a gun. And I can... sense... he is terrified of guns, all weapons as a matter of fact.'*

And here I am, and you think I have powers that rival any weapon.

Concentrate, trust yourself, and learn. You'll find out just what you can do.

A shadow fell over their park bench, and someone scooted in and sat next to them. Pixie's fluffy tail began wagging furiously.

Sarah looked up and saw Matthew. She shivered, pulling her coat tighter around her as she met Matthew's gaze. His expression showed only concern. She could see the worry etched into his furrowed brow, and it tugged at her heart.

"Thank you for coming to find me, but I just can't…"

"I know, we just can't go back home to Rosewood Hollow and hope those… men will just forget about us."

"Right. So you know I have to see this through." Her brow furrowed, and she met Matthew's eyes again. "Wait. Did you just say, 'We can't go back?'"

Matthew nodded.

"You're right; we know about the sapphire, and heading back without resolving this will probably only make things worse."

Sarah leaned in, with Pixie squirming between them, and allowed herself to be held in Matthew's arms. She'd been prepared to see it through alone – but this was so much better.

"Thank you," she said softly.

"Now we better get moving. It's freezing cold on this bench, I left Cory looking for hotel rooms, but we need to get ready. The first hearing is tomorrow morning."

Sarah only nodded and burrowed her face in Matthew's coat to hide the broad smile on her face.

Chapter Twenty-One

Cory had found some rooms in a large, nondescript hotel chain. It was a far cry from the charming and homey feel of Cheryl's inn, but it was generic anonymity – exactly what they needed. Sarah hugged her son despite his squirming.

They moved into adjoining rooms that very afternoon and had a light meal in the downstairs cafeteria. Also nothing like Cheryl's home cooking – but the mass of people ebbing around them made them at least feel safer.

Sarah, who'd been an avid artist in her youth, dug out her sketchbook and pencils and drew sketch after sketch of everything she remembered about the gunman. Looking at her sketches and the menacing look of the masked man in them, she could see and finally understand why Matthew was almost blinded with fear for them and reached under the table to hold his hand.

When the evening news came up on the big screen TVs in the cafeteria, the upcoming hearing for the captured member of the fabled Canvas Collective was the leading topic as the News Hour started.

Sarah held up her sketchbook and looked from it to the screen and back again.

"Not him."

"Duh, Mom, he's in jail," Cory said with an eye-roll and stabbed at his meatloaf listlessly. "This tastes like cardboard."

"I know. Another one, I guess."

"There's one supposed to be an expert at disguises," Lily said, reaching for the sketchbook. "I read somewhere that in another heist, he had a silicone mask made of the museum's director, then had a Zoom call with the head of security, saying a restoration expert would come by about a painting. Walked right out of the museum with it, even got an escort."

Sarah looked down at her sketch. "This guy was muscle," she finally said, "probably hired to clear the way for the rest."

Someone turned up the volume on the TV, and the general dinner buzz in the room hushed just a bit.

"In a daring series of heists that have rocked the art world, a notorious gang known as the Canvas Collective has once again made headlines for their brazen criminal activities," the news anchor said. "Comprising four key members, each with their own specialized skills, this elusive syndicate has been identified as the orchestrator of a string of high-profile museum robberies."

"The recently apprehended man is so far known mostly by his code name, Garnet. He will be on trial in Superior Court Claremont tomorrow for his involvement in at least one of these high-profile thefts. His expertise is said to lie in remotely interfering with security systems. His recent apprehension and subsequent questioning shed light on the gang's sophisticated methods of bypassing state-of-the-art security measures. Will he or won't he identify the remaining members of the gang, that is the question we are all asking tonight."

"Not if he has the sapphire; he won't," Sarah muttered, looking left and right to make sure no one was listening in.

"With the Canvas Collective's audacious exploits continuing to confound law enforcement agencies, authorities remain vigilant in their pursuit of justice," the news anchor continued. "The art world anxiously awaits the next move of these master criminals. Four members of this legendary gang remain free, 'Amethyst', also known as, 'The Infiltrator,' 'Onyx,' dubbed 'The Enforcer,' 'Topaz,' alias 'The Con Artist,' and their leader, who seems to have no further designation. Tomorrow's trial promises to be quite a spectacle."

Sarah squeezed Matthew's hand a little tighter.

"I don't even want to ask," she said, staring at the TV where an ad for a cruise line had taken over. "Do you have any thoughts on how we should tackle this tomorrow?"

"None," Matthew shook his head. "I thought once we were here, it would become kind of – obvious."

"We know this Sinclair dude has to hold the sapphire during his trial," Sarah mused.

"Could have it on a leather string around his neck, too." Cory pulled out a little silver dog on a black leather string that had been hidden under his sweatshirt. "Lots of guys do, though it would have to be very well disguised to not be recognized."

"I don't recognize that one you've got."

Sarah reached for the silver dog that looked suspiciously like Pixie before Cory snatched it away again.

"Where did you get it?"

"Nowhere... girl at school gave it to me." Cory blushed furiously and hid his face in his tablet once again.

"At least you're not just researching," Sarah grinned. "You can tell me..."

"Mom! Never mind. What are we going to do tomorrow?"

"Given the notoriety of the case," Matthew said. "I think perhaps only two of us should try to get into the court. Sarah because of her – abilities – and you, Cory. Nobody can resist a sixteen-year-old doing research."

"Okay."

"Pixie and I will stay outside and close by."

"I would rather have Pixie with me," Sarah argued, and Matthew shook his head.

"You don't know if they'll allow her in the courthouse. And by the time you're through arguing with the clerk, the room will be full. It's a public trial, so there will be a lot of spectators wanting to watch."

That's a whole lot of baloney, Sarah heard and automatically scratched Pixie's ears. *Mmmm baloney.*

"It's baloney," she said, "but I see your point."

Lily and Emma looked a little crestfallen, and she smiled brightly at them.

"You two will be my backup and getaway team. I need you close as well, with the van, ready to get out of there in a hurry. If something does hit the fan, we need to be able to get out of there with that sapphire as fast as we can."

"You're really going to steal that thing," Lily wanted to know. "You're not worried you'll be... arrested on the spot for, uh... stealing?"

Knowing the kids were looking at her, Sarah folded her hands and rested her chin on them.

"I don't know what I'm going to do yet, Lily. The sapphire is stolen property in the first place. Essentially, I'm just trying to stop a criminal from getting away with it."

"And help Katelyn," Cory tossed in. "Don't forget Katelyn."

For a minute, Sarah worried that Katelyn could be the girl who had given him the dog necklace. She was only five or six years older than Cory. With an effort, she pushed the thought away and nodded at her son.

"Right. Make sure the right person is in jail. So, I'm afraid I have no idea what I'm going to do yet. We are flying by the seat of our pants here."

She put a hand on Pixie who was sitting under her chair rather listless. The food in the cafeteria didn't interest her in the slightest – something new for her.

Any ideas girl?

Amelia indicates we should wait. I think... she's trying to figure out how to get through this time.

In the middle of the courtroom?

It would make a statement!

"Brother," Sarah said out loud and grinned when they all looked at her. "Never mind – Pixie."

⦵

Lily, looking for distractions, unearthed a board game that evening, which fell flat. Matthew paced the confines of their room like a caged lion. Meanwhile, Cory and Emma huddled together, exchanging hushed whispers.

Sarah sat staring out the window into the neon-lit hotel parking lot, watching cars come and go, people arrive and depart until she felt a heavy hand on her shoulder. Half-turning, she found Matthew smiling at her.

"Hey... You've been staring out that window for the past hour."

"I know, I just can't..."

"Let's go to bed, okay? I checked on the kids; they're zoned out. Lily is watching TV. We should try to get some sleep."

"I don't know if I can," Sarah said, shaking her head. "I have a thousand things on my mind."

"I'm pretty sure you will. We've had quite a day."

"And tomorrow will be even bigger."

Matthew pulled her to her feet and into his arms. "Everything will be okay," he said softly. "I am going to do everything I can to make sure of that."

"Yes, but there is one more thing we haven't thought about," Sarah said, leaning heavily into him.

"Which is?"

"What happens if we actually do get that darn sapphire, Matthew? That power – it's always going to attract people who want that. And what about us? Is it going to affect us? That's the problem with magic, nobody really knows—"

Don't.

Sarah felt something touch her foot and looked down to find Pixie in a luxurious, long stretch that raised her hindquarters and stretched her front paws.

Don't think about that – yet. You will figure it out.

"That's easy for you to say," Sarah said, laughing out loud.

Matthew was right, she had fallen asleep almost instantly, but the gray light of dawn through a gap in the curtains woke her and brought all of her worries tumbling back.

I can't let them use the sapphire to cover up his lies in court, and then come after us, she thought.

Dressed in jeans and a sweatshirt, she let Pixie out behind the hotel for a minute. By the time she came back upstairs with two cups of coffee from the breakfast room, Matthew had showered and organized the kids to do the same.

He and Lily had arranged transportation, planned out meeting points, and saved all vital information on both their phones. They were ready.

Showered and changed, Sarah only picked at the pastries room service had brought up.

"I paid for the rooms," Matthew said casually. "Assuming we are going to leave the courthouse and Claremont in a hurry."

"You ready, Mom?" Cory's eyes all but glowed, and she forced herself to sound as confident as she could.

"Yup, ready, willing, and able."

She felt as if she were jumping off a cliff without knowing where to land, but she'd done that before, right? Usually, just before she found out about another magical ability she'd supposedly always had without knowing.

"Let's go then," she said and wrapped her coat around her tightly.

Chapter Twenty-Two

At the courthouse, two police officers at the entrance checked all visitors trying to get a seat inside courtroom seven. Their eyes brushed over Sarah, barely acknowledging the woman walking with a teenager and carrying a large sketch pad under her arm.

Sarah squeezed into the third row of the public area, Cory close beside her. Her heart was racing, each thud echoing the tension that suffused the courtroom. The ancient wooden benches seemed to groan under the collective weight of the audience, their varnished surfaces polished by decades of use. The air was thick with anticipation, a tangible presence that seemed to press down on Sarah's shoulders. Murmurs swirled around her, blending into a low, indistinct hum that filled the space. Every whispered conversation, every shuffle of feet, added to the mounting suspense that hung in the air like a heavy fog.

Sarah glanced at Cory, his face etched with worry, mirroring her own apprehension.

Sinclair, or Garnet, as he was more often referred to, the accused art thief, had been led into the courtroom and sat at the defendant's table, seemingly unruffled by the gravity of the situation. His posture was straight, his expression composed, but Sarah could sense the tension simmering beneath his façade. She knew the truth. Beneath that calm exterior lurked a cunning mind. Off and on, he'd whisper with his attorney seated beside him, and his hands appeared clenched tightly under the table.

As the minutes ticked by, Sarah felt the weight of anticipation bearing down on her. Each second stretched into an eternity, the silence punctuated only by the occasional cough or rustle of papers. The atmosphere crackled with electricity, charged with the anticipation of what was to come.

Sarah's gaze remained fixed on Garnet, her eyes narrowing as she studied him intently. She could practically feel the sapphire's presence, hidden away somewhere on his person.

The prosecutor stalked the courtroom, a predator circling its prey. His voice, a honed blade, sliced through the tense silence, each word an accusation aimed at Garnet's impassive facade. The polished floor gleamed under his relentless pacing, a metronome marking the rhythm of Garnet's crumbling defense. Every gesture, a calculated strike, designed to shatter the illusion of innocence. This wasn't a courtroom - it was a battlefield, and the prosecutor was a general leading his troops to a decisive victory.

Garnet fidgeted with his fingers, yet his palms remained pressed together, never breaking contact. What an odd position, Sarah thought, tuning out the prosecutor's brilliant speech, never taking her eyes off Garnet's hands.

She leaned in close to Cory at the same time he turned to her.

"His hands," Sarah whispered, and Cory nodded.

"He's holding it loose," Cory whispered. "That's pretty dumb."

"Dumb?"

The heavy air in the room became even more charged, and this time, the hair on the back of her neck began to rise. Sarah hugged her arms to herself and grinned secretly. This was a good sign.

"Why dumb?" she asked, but Cory never had a chance to answer. A piercing scream echoed from the hall just outside the courtroom, followed by shouting and the sound of scuffling feet. Garnet, startled by the sudden noise, jumped up from his seat to stand, his eyes flicking around.

Someone opened the door to look out into the hall and thick white mist spilled into the room from the outside. Spectators screamed, the judge banged his gavel and shouted for court clerks, and over all of it, Sarah could hear a sweet sound – barking.

Pixie!

Be ready, Amelia can't materialize – that smoke is all you get.

As another scream sounded outside, people began to rise to their feet, craning their necks to see what was happening. The judge banged his gavel again and shouted for order, but the chaos only escalated.

Sarah took Cory's hand. "Get ready," she whispered, though he gave her a mildly annoyed look. What teenager wants to hold his mom's hand?

"Pixie?" he whispered back, and Sarah nodded.

For a moment, the overhead lights flickered and buzzed, but this time they didn't go out completely. Smoke began to creep into the room like a grey, winding snake, rolling around the defendant's table. A tendril reached out and touched Garnet's pant leg.

"Get me out of here!" he yelled, trying to back away from the advancing smoke. "Taylor, do something!"

Taylor, presumably his lawyer, looked around frantically, then gestured for Garnet to stand by him. Garnet did and accidentally opened his hands a bit too much. Something small, shiny, and blue dropped to the ground.

He cursed and dove to retrieve his lucky charm, banging his head in the process.

"Is there a fire? Should we all be evacuating this building?" Taylor shouted, looking annoyed at his client.

The court clerk was still trying to get an answer on his walkie-talkie, but at the door, something tiny, incredibly fast, white, and sable streaked into the courtroom. It raced under the cover of the billowing ground smoke to the defendant's table and dove underneath.

"Ouch, let go of that! What in the—"

Garnet emerged from under the table, his head bright red.

"Mr. Taylor, please control your client," the judge admonished. "This is not a circus. What are you doing under there?"

Sarah felt as if she were at a tennis match, trying to look from the door to Pixie and the defendant at the table. Taylor had his hand on Garnet's sleeve, but the man had already taken two steps toward the door.

Sarah could just barely spot something tiny and lightning-fast disappear through the open door of the courtroom, and she let out a massive breath.

"Cough a little," she whispered, elbowing Cory in the side. He did as she asked.

"Excuse me," Sarah tapped the rotund elderly man sitting beside her on the shoulder. "Excuse me, could we get out, please? My son's having an asthma attack."

"If you leave now, they probably won't let you back in. Court's in session, you know."

"I know. It must be the smoke. It's a medical issue. Could we please?"

"Smoke's already venting out."

Sarah paused for a moment and blinked. As if it had a mind of its own, the grey mist began to withdraw from the defendant's table, slowly but surely. Go, Amelia.

As if to underscore her point, Cory coughed so violently that other visitors around them moved away, the judge banged his gavel again, and finally, the old man rose to let them out of their row.

"Your loss if you're stuck outside."

"We'll be fine, thanks."

Sarah looked up and found herself staring into the dark, murderous eyes of Garnet. From his place at the defendant's table, he had been watching the entire scene. There was no way to tell how much he knew, or even how he knew, but his eyes marked them.

Sarah grabbed Cory's sleeve and propelled him out of the courtroom as fast as she could. The clerk at the door told her the same thing, once they left, they wouldn't be able to get back in, and Sarah nodded politely.

It didn't matter. Now that they—or, more precisely, Pixie—had the gemstone, Garnet no longer had a defense. All he could do in there was play for time, hoping that his comrades and fellow gang members would get a hold of Sarah and retrieve the sapphire.

The entire scene in the courtroom had not taken more than a few minutes, and confusion still reigned. Everybody had heard screams. Nobody could figure out where they'd come from, and a fresh plume of smoke rolled through the hall.

"Courtroom seven has been engulfed in smoke," one reporter said into his microphone, his words tumbling over one another. "I am – we are – safe – but there does not appear to be a fire."

"No smoke alarms sounded, and whatever that smoke was, it was gone as fast as it had appeared; no way to test what it, in fact, was. Whether they will continue with court proceedings today is anyone's guess. I will keep you updated."

"Excuse me, did you come out of that courtroom," another person called out to Sarah, and immediately two others turned her way.

"Sorry, I'm in a hurry, everybody's fine. I've just got to get to my – babysitter."

She and Cory all but ran from the plaza around the courthouse as other news crews arrived. Originally, they were there to get updates on Garnet's trial hearing, but now they were there to see what the fuss and the fireless smoke were all about.

∞

A block away, Sarah finally stopped and put her hands on her thighs.

"I didn't want to hang around for anyone to question us," she said to Cory, grabbing huge lungfuls of air.

"I'm fine. But you look like you're going to pass out any second. Do much sports, Mom?"

"Watch yourself," Sarah forced a smile. "We're not out of the woods yet."

"Was that really Pixie grabbing the sapphire?"

"Sure looked like it. She told me Amelia couldn't materialize, so they must have come up with a plan. Amelia would cause enough of a disturbance for Pixie to run in and grab it."

"Nice timing," Cory said and grinned. "I told you it was dumb to hold the sapphire in his hands. I think Pixie bit the guy too."

"Not that violence is an answer…"

"I know that, Mom," Cory rolled his eyes. "Kept him from snatching it back, though."

Sarah straightened up and looked around.

"I have no idea where Lily, Matthew, and Emma are. I thought they were going to wait for us around the courthouse."

"They probably tried." Cory nodded at the crunch of traffic suddenly rolling toward the courthouse. "Everybody is a news reporter nowadays. People are heading there in droves to get a good Instagrammable picture if the courthouse burns down."

"You're pretty sarcastic for your age," Sarah chuckled. "Now help me out here. We need to find Pixie first of all before she gets hurt, and we need to find the rest of our group, and then we need to lay low and make an actual plan."

Cory mock saluted and took his mother's arm. "Act old. It'll look like I'm helping you, and nobody will bug us."

"If we were not in public…"

Sarah tried to scowl, but she let Cory take her arm, and they ambled around the edges of the courthouse parkette.

"Any sign of Pixie?" Cory asked.

Sarah listened into the great ether of a world she was barely getting to know. She could feel Amelia's regal presence and clung to it.

Pixie? she asked in her mind and only heard static.

Amelia?

Nothing.

"I can't hear anything," she said desperately. "I don't know…"

"Easy." Cory squeezed her arm. "They're busy getting away. If Pixie has the sapphire, she has to run with that thing in her mouth. Ick."

The image made her smile, but her mind scanned for Pixie. Thoughts, emotions, impressions—it all gathered into a massive background hum that threatened to take her breath away.

"I see Aunt Lily," Cory suddenly said and pointed across the courthouse plaza.

Using their elbows and holding on to one another's coat sleeves, they fought the crowd across the plaza, pushing and shoving until they had caught up with her.

"Lily," Sarah said, out of breath again. "Where are the others?"

"Looking for you. What's up with you? You look like you ran a marathon."

"All but," Sarah admitted, brushing the hair out of her face. "And Pixie?"

"Don't know. All of a sudden, she tore away from Matthew's arms and ran into the courthouse."

"I saw her grab the sapphire – but did you see her come out?"

"No."

Panic grew inside Sarah now. Raw, sharp panic. Pixie was tiny and so fragile, running through a crowd of booted feet. Anything could happen. Anything. A kick, even an accidental one, could quite possibly...

Oh, relax. This darn sapphire in my mouth is gross.

"Pixie," Sarah called out, and Lily, Emma, and Cory stopped in their tracks.

Where are you?

Don't know. But I'll find you.

More people were streaming into the courthouse plaza now, attracted by the news coverage, pressing in from behind the already unruly crowd. Sarah tore Lily's hat off her head without asking and stuffed her blonde hair under it.

"I know Garnet saw me and knew this was somehow our doing," she said by way of explanation. "They're going to come after us first chance they get. We have to get out of here."

Lily only nodded, scanning the crowd.

"Where's Matthew?"

"Gone to find Pixie," Emma said, her eyes huge and shiny. "What if—"

"No what if, Emma. Pixie is fine, and she has the sapphire. We just need to find them and get out of here."

The crowd pressed in closer, surging toward the courthouse. A huge, burly man ran right into Sarah, making her stumble and almost fall. He barely turned in his headlong rush to the court building.

"Why don't you look where you're going," Sarah yelled after him, barely cutting off the cussword at the end of the sentence. "We have to get off this plaza, find something a little more protected. Matt and Pixie will find us wherever we are."

She brought her children in close, a hand on each of their shoulders, and pushed on against the surging crowd, always scanning for Pixie.

Pixie, I could use some help here. This crowd is insane. Where are you?

I'm running – it is difficult. Head east, Sarah, toward Cheryl's Inn. There's a little wooded park. I'll find you there.

"Let's go," she nodded at Lily. "I've got her, but we have to move."

As she checked her surroundings to see which way Cheryl's old inn would be, she realized that the man who had almost run her down had stopped. He turned and looked away when his eyes met Sarah's. She hardened her grip on Emma's shoulder.

"Move. Now."

Deliberately, she steered in the wrong direction, away, always away from that man, just as her phone rang.

"Matthew," she snatched it up when she recognized the ringtone. "Where are you?"

"I lost Pixie," Matthew said, his voice pained. "I don't know what happened, she just tore out of my arms."

"It's all right, Matt – I know where..." Sarah looked up, trying to spot the man in the leather jacket in the crowd. "I'll text you," she finally said and shoved the phone in her pocket.

"Let's go, Lily. I have a creepy feeling there are a few other gang members in this crowd. Push backward toward the parking lot and then run. East. Toward the old inn. There's a little wooded park."

To her credit, Lily only nodded. She took Emma's hand, knowing Cory would be able to keep up with Sarah, and started to push through the crowd hard. Lily and Emma would be fine.

Almost running, Sarah texted Matthew their destination and nodded at Cory.

"Fast as you can, Cory. I think—"

"They're here already," Cory said. "I know. How are you doing?"

"I can manage." She pulled Cory closer and whispered in his ear. "There's a wooded park east of here on the way to the inn where we were staying. If we get separated, we meet up there. With Pixie."

Cory nodded. He moved in front of her and started to move forward as if he were a football player heading for the goal line. For the moment, she was content to move in his wake.

We are on the way, Pixie.

This time she didn't get an answer. She had lost sight of Lily and Emma, and after a few anxious minutes, they finally reached the edge of the crowd. More transmission vans with TV logos appeared, and she and Cory ducked down a side street.

"We've made a bit of a detour," he admitted and checked the compass on his phone. "East is that way." He pointed directly across the crowd.

"Okay, we'll go around. Hurry."

They ran through alleys and side streets, and finally, Sarah started to recognize the road they had walked down a few days ago on their first night in Claremont.

"I think I see it."

Cory pointed, and just before them,, they sought shelter behind a copse of oak trees, a little green space with old trees and snow-laden bushes opened. Together they sought shelter behind a copse of oak trees and Sarah finally allowed herself to exhale.

Breathing hard, she rested with a gloved hand against the rough, cold bark of the nearest tree. Lily and Emma! She had lost track of Lily and Emma.

"Do you see Aunt Lily anywhere? Emma was with her," she said, and Cory shook his head.

"No. Not Pixie, either. Are you sure this is right?"

"She said east. In the direction of the old inn."

"Maybe there's another..."

"Cory, let's just wait, and not split up any further." She blew out a breath and shook her head. "Sorry. That crowd was scary."

"No worries. I just..."

"There's Matthew." She'd spotted his dark blue coat at the edge of the park and stepped out of the trees to wave. Matthew pulled her into his arms and squeezed hard.

"God, I was worried about you," he whispered into her ear and held her a foot away again to check her head to toe. "What the heck happened there in that courthouse? The news says anything from a bomb attack to a knife-wielding assailant, and somebody got killed."

"Amelia and Pixie causing a bit of mayhem, nothing more."

Matthew looked around, then back at Sarah.

"Where are Lily and Emma? I left them in front of the courthouse," Matthew said

"We saw them, told them to come here. I think the Canvas Collective knows that it was us who orchestrated all of this to get the sapphire. I'm pretty sure one of them bumped up against me on the plaza. We used the crowd to get away, but we split up then."

Matthew paced away a few steps and wiped his hands over his face.

"Okay, they are on their way here, then. Now what?"

"I don't know. We need Pixie, Lily, and Emma first. I'm not leaving here."

"I know, but we're out in the open – unprotected."

I'm on my way. Almost there. I can see you from the hill.

Sarah automatically swung around and pointed. The other side of the park rose into a gentle hill carved up by the tracks of kids' sleds and skis. Owing to the overcast sky and soft drizzle, it was deserted today, but there, skirting just at the edge of the vegetation that bordered the park, something tiny sped toward them, a flash of familiar fur bounding down the hillside. Sarah's breath hitched, her pulse quickened, and for a moment, time itself seemed to stand still. It was Pixie! Running towards them with an exuberance that defied the frosty landscape

"There." Sarah grinned broadly. "It's Pixie."

Her eyes welled up with tears of relief and joy, her lips quivering as she called out Pixie's name. The sound of her own voice was drowned out by the rush of blood in her ears, but she didn't care. With each bounding step, Pixie kicked up plumes of snow. Sarah's hands trembled as she reached out, her heart soaring as Pixie leaped into her arms, a flurry of wagging tails and wet kisses.

The world around Sarah faded into insignificance as she held Pixie close, feeling the warmth of her furry body against her own. In that moment, fear melted away, replaced by an overwhelming sense of gratitude and love. The snow beneath them seemed softer, the air sweeter, as Sarah whispered words of reassurance and thanks into Pixie's fluffy ears.

"Pixie," she said again, and Matthew and Cory crowded in close, caressing the silky soft ears, brushing dirt and twigs out of her fur.

Matthew held out his hand, and finally, Pixie opened her mouth. With a little plop, the sapphire dropped into Matthew's open hand.

The gem nestled in Matthew's hand gleamed with an otherworldly brilliance, its deep blue hue shimmering like a captive fragment of the midnight sky. Sarah couldn't believe her eyes as she gently touched it with a fingertip.

The sapphire was larger than she had expected, its facets catching the light, despite the dreary day, in a dazzling display of color and clarity. Each surface seemed to hold a universe of secrets as if the gem itself held power to unlock hidden realms beyond imagination.

Despite its journey through a mad crowd, snow, city streets, and a papillon's mouth, the sapphire remained unblemished, its surface smooth and flawless to the touch.

But more than its monetary worth, this sapphire held a deeper significance for Sarah. It was a symbol of hope, of resilience, and of the unbreakable bond between her and Pixie. Pixie had carried this precious gem in her mouth, guarding it with a loyalty that transcended words.

"Why is there blood on her fur," Cory finally asked, and Sarah's fingers probed Pixie's side.

It's just a scratch. I had to – avoid a speeding car back there.

Sarah closed her eyes and fought the panic inside her. The thought of her precious sweet dog being injured cut her to her core.

"My sweet girl." Automatically, her fingers caressed the scratch on Pixie's side, and her eyes drifted shut.

Mmmm

"Mom. Pixie — look." Cory's said, bringing her back to reality instantly, and she looked at Pixie. The spot where the scratch had been now glowed with a faint golden sheen, and then it faded away. Nothing remained of the injury, save for a darkish stain on the pristine white fur.

Thank you.

I – how did you do this?

I didn't, you did.

Pixie seemingly winked, and Sarah pulled her hand back hard, staring at her finger. It was just that – a finger.

'*Sarah is one of the strongest women I have ever met.*' Katelyn's words from last year. At the time, she had dismissed them. Now a cold shiver clawed its way past her warm coat and scarf and made her tremble. What else was hidden inside her mind? As Sarah shivered in the cold park, her body trembling with a mixture of fear and uncertainty, Matthew's hand on her shoulder brought her back to the present.

"Are you okay?" he asked, concern evident in his voice. "You're as white as a sheet."

"Yes, yes, I am," Sarah replied, hugging Pixie closer to her body as if seeking comfort.

What's going on with me, Pixie? she asked silently, her thoughts reaching out to her furry companion.

Your... power is growing. I felt it in my first mom, but nowhere near as strong as with you, Pixie replied, her words adding another layer of complexity to Sarah's already turbulent emotions.

Matthew, oblivious to Sarah and Pixie's silent conversation, grinned and tried to lighten the mood. "Ask me a question; see if I can lie," he suggested, but Sarah couldn't muster a smile.

"Not now, Matthew," she pleaded, her voice barely above a whisper.

"Oh, come on, let's try it," he continued, but Pixie intervened her voice firm and commanding.

Don't. The sapphire has its own power, Sarah. Do not use it - ever, Pixie warned, her words echoing in Sarah's mind.

"I need you to trust me and not ask again. When we get to the car, I want you to put that thing into a box or bag and hide it. Promise," Sarah insisted, her tone hard.

"Matthew, please, I don't want us to even think about using it," Sarah said, her voice tinged with desperation.

"Cory, could you please run up that tobogganing hill and see if you can spot Lily and Emma?" Sarah requested, turning her attention to her son.

Cory gave her a thumbs up and sprinted in the direction she pointed. God, he was so visible and so vulnerable with his red jacket against the white snow, she thought.

Watching him run up the hill, Sarah pulled out her cell phone and texted Lily.

We are together in the park. Where are you? she typed, her heart pounding with each passing second.

The screen remained blank for what felt like an eternity, until finally, Lily's response came through.

On our way. We got lost and ended up on the plaza again, Lily replied.

Hurry!!!! Sarah responded, her desperation evident in her message.

??? Lily replied, confused by Sarah's urgency.

Please hurry, Sarah pleaded silently, her fingers crossed in hope.

The next twenty minutes passed in agonizing slowness, with Cory scanning the surrounding streets, Matthew pacing, and Sarah refusing to let go of Pixie.

"We've almost got it done," Sarah whispered, her words a mantra of hope and determination. "We're almost there."

Matthew, meanwhile, had found a broken branch on the snowy ground and swung it at the trees, adopting a batter's stance.

"Why do you think Amelia couldn't manifest?" he asked suddenly, breaking the tense silence.

"It's the distance, I think," Sarah replied, her mind racing with possibilities. "Maybe the farther she gets away from Rosewood Hollow, the weaker her powers get. I'm not entirely sure why."

"I see something," Cory suddenly yelled, waving his arms. He stormed down the tobogganing hill, and it was all Sarah could do not to run out and push him into the relative protection of the nearby brush.

"Down that side road," Cory called out, pointing past the trees where a small fence separated the park from a quiet residential street.

"Hurry, we'll have to jump the fence," Sarah called, striding hard through the deep snow toward the fence. Out past the trees, she could already see the snow-white van with the rental car emblem, and Lily motioning through an open window. A shadowy figure in the back waved, Emma.

"Let's go," Lily yelled. "Over that fence, hurry."

"Hang tight, Pixie."

Sarah ran. She hadn't climbed a fence for years, and never with a precious dog in her arms, but today she did what she had to do. Her hands found support, and her feet found little ledges to cling to while Pixie snuggled inside her coat, holding on for dear life. Finally, she straddled the top of the fence and let herself drop to the other side, hard.

She stumbled and tripped, twisting her ankle painfully, but a moment later, she slipped into the passenger seat of the van, followed by Cory. Only Matthew took his time, ambling, looking up at the trees and the fence, standing there for a long moment, looking around as if he had just now discovered they were gone.

"Matthew, hurry, over the fence – now, ' Sarah yelled, and their eyes met through the wire mesh. "Now, Matthew."

His eyes were unfocused, and his head tilted for a moment as if he were wondering, but slowly and deliberately, he began to climb the fence.

"Should I hold the sapphire for a while, Mom?" Cory asked, seeing the blank confusion in Matthew.

"Oh no, you won't. Matt is strong, he'll be fine. We just have to get out of here, now rather than later."

As Sarah held the door and watched Matthew, a sense of unease crept over her like a chill wind. Glancing into the rearview mirror, she spotted a sleek black Chevy Tahoe behind them up the hill, waiting at a red light. Its imposing presence seemed to swallow the road, its tinted windows hiding whatever secrets lay within. The rumble of its engine sent shivers down her spine, an ominous growl that echoed in her bones.

With each passing second, her heart quickened its pace, a primal instinct urging her to flee. She looked at Lily and motioned her head up toward the mirror. Lily clenched her fingers around the steering wheel and shifted into drive.

Matthew was making slow and steady progress over the fence, and Sarah felt a feeling of dread throughout her entire body. It was as if the Tahoe itself harbored some dark intent, a silent predator biding its time. Sarah's palms grew clammy against the door, her breaths shallow and quick.

Finally, Matthew dropped on the other side of the fence. Before she could stop him, Cory streaked out of the car, across the sidewalk, grabbed Matthew's elbow, and forcibly dragged him inside the van.

The door had barely closed, as Sarah yelled, "Now!" and Lily floored the gas pedal. Their sedate family vehicle shot forward and careened around the corner on two wheels as the light turned green for the Tahoe behind them.

Lily shot through the residential streets aimlessly, left, right, left again, breaking every speed limit and a few other rules just for good measure.

After five minutes, she finally slowed down. She and Sarah hadn't taken their eyes off the rearview mirror, but the Tahoe was gone; only its presence lingered in their minds like a shadow.

Sarah turned around and found Emma sitting in the back seat like a statue. Cory all but bounced up and down, cheering.

"Rad driving, Aunt Lily! You can teach me when I get my learner's."

"Not hardly, Cory. You all okay?"

"Fine."

Pixie peeked her nose out of Sarah's coat, indicating she was fine too. Only Matthew hadn't spoken since Cory dragged him into the van. He stared ahead at the back of Lily's headrest, moving his head back and forth gently.

"I-95," Sarah said automatically, pointing at the wayfinding signs around them. "Let's get out of here."

"Sure you want to head back to Rosewood Hollow?"

Sarah dragged her hands through her hair and caressed Pixie's face. Pixie licked her hand with soft, gentle licks, and Sarah could feel her heartbeat coming down from the anxious drumbeat it had been.

"Go a few exits, as fast as you can, then pull into a rest stop some-where. I need to get the..." She looked over at Matthew, who was still staring ahead as if nothing in this van related to him in the slightest. "That thing out of his pocket and into a box or container. Then we'll make a plan."

Lily nodded, set her turn signal, and pulled straight across two lanes of traffic to catch the entry to the interstate at the last possible minute. Cory cheered at the honking drivers behind them.

"Go, Aunt Lily."

"You know, you could have used the next exit too."

"I know." She winked at Cory in the mirror.

Sarah scanned the side mirror every few minutes, fearful that the Tahoe would appear again, but it continued to be clear.

Finally, she released her deadlock hold on Pixie just a little and al-lowed herself to relax.

"Mom, what's wrong with Matthew," Cory asked, eyeing his mentor and friend closely. "He looks – weird."

"I think it's the sapphire, Cory. Can you find something there in the back that we could put it in, where nobody has to touch it? Lily will pull over as soon as she can."

She heard Cory rummaging in the back, and finally, Emma spoke up in her soft, gentle voice that made you lean in close so you wouldn't miss anything.

"I think I can feel it too, Mom."

"You can?"

"It's like a pull. I know it's in Matthew's pocket, and I really want to reach in and hold it."

"Don't." Sarah's hard response startled even Lily. "Whatever you do," she said a little softer. "Do not touch the sapphire."

She felt that cold shiver again and automatically cradled Pixie.

What do I do, Pixie? Now that we have it – how do I get rid of it? I can't just – chuck it out the window, can I?

That would not be advisable, no.

So what do we do?

Pixie gave her a long look from those deep brown eyes and blinked a few times rapidly. She shook the tangles out of her fur and finally settled back comfortably on Sarah's lap.

Most enchanted items have a spell or some way that will neutralize their power.

What is it?

That's the problem. It's different depending on the item, and without knowing its history and the origin of the enchantment, there's no way to know.

"That's just great," Sarah said out loud, forcing herself to ignore the loud rumbling from her stomach. None of them had eaten since the morning. They were running on fumes and determination—and out of time.

Lily kept the accelerator floored for what seemed like an eternity until she finally slowed down, just in time for the kids to start asking about food and a break.

"There's a rest stop ahead," Sarah said, checking the maps app on her phone. "We'll take a break, deal with the sapphire, and make a plan. Cory, did you find anything?"

He handed her one of those plastic fast food shell containers. Inside it was a drink cup with a lid and several napkins.

"Not ideal, but it will do, I hope," she said, taking the container, just as Lily set the turn signal and pulled into a parking lane at the rest stop.

Sarah thought they all looked and felt deflated as she watched Lily and the kids climb out of the car and stare at the cars and trucks around them and the never-ending stream of cars passing on the interstate.

"Cory, here's some money. Take Emma and get some food, would you?"

"Okay," Cory swiped the twenty into his pocket.

"I don't have to tell you to be careful, do I?"

"Don't talk to strangers, and don't go with anybody, got it."

"Cory, this is not—"

"Mom, I got it, okay? You don't think I saw the Tahoe? You don't think I can figure out who was in it?"

"Thank you," Sarah said softly and ruffled his hair despite his grimace.

Matthew still had not come out of the van.

Sarah wasn't even sure whether he had moved in the time since their helter-skelter flight from Claremont. He simply stared straight ahead at the back of the driver's side headrest.

She slid open the van's door on his side and reached out a hand to him.

"All right, cowboy, let's go get some food then," she said, forcing as much cheer as she could into her voice.

With agonizing slowness, Matthew turned his head to look at her and blinked a few times. His eyes were huge, shiny orbs, blank inside his face, and Sarah shivered. He cocked his head slightly as if he were trying to remember who he was and what he was doing here, and why this blonde woman was calling him cowboy.

Help him, Sarah heard inside her head.

Never taking her eyes off Matthew, she held her hand out to steady him without wavering and forced as much power and energy as she could down her arm, into her hand, and into her fingers.

Leave him be, she thought. *Leave him be.*

Over and over.

"Sarah," Lily whispered behind her, and Sarah didn't even turn her head. She saw it too. The tips of her fingers had taken on a shimmering blue light.

Leave him be.

Finally, Matthew shook his head as if he were waking from a nap.

"Sarah?" he asked. "What the..."

"Take my hand, now."

Still confused and dazed, Matthew did, and Sarah all but pulled him out of the van. With one quick swipe, she pulled the sapphire out of Matthew's pocket and dropped it into the soda cup, stuffed all of the napkins on top of it, and locked the whole mess into the plastic shell container.

Not until she had shoved the container into a grocery bag, under a blanket, and a number of their bags did she allow herself to let out the breath she'd been holding.

She had felt it.

The sapphire had been in her hand like liquid fire, burning, tempting, teasing, offering all of the things it could do for her.

Matthew shoved a hand into his pocket and stared at his palm when it came up empty.

"Where did it go?"

"Safekeeping," Sarah snapped. "We'll all go inside and have something to eat now. And make a plan, okay?"

Matthew shook his head as if he had water in his ear.

"What happened," he muttered a few times. "What happened? We were at the courthouse..."

Sarah hooked her arm through his and leaned against him for a moment, feeling his warmth and his nearness, his heartbeat.

"I'm not really sure yet," she whispered. "We just have to fix this first."

Matthew stopped and looked her in the eyes. His expression was normal again now, his eyes lively and alert, but there was a deep groove between them. Finally, he nodded.

"Okay, I trust you," he said softly and walked as close as he could beside her toward the snack shop and diner. Sarah scooped up Pixie in her arms and, for a moment, simply relished the feeling of having Matthew so close.

How come the sapphire didn't affect you when you were carrying it? she asked Pixie, and the little dog licked her hand.

Can't you guess?

No, or I wouldn't ask.

I'm still a dog, Sarah. We don't lie, we always speak the truth. What power would that sapphire have to offer someone like me?

Sarah had no answer for that one and only gave her little girl a hard squeeze.

Matthew kept wiping his hands over his face.

"It was the weirdest thing," he said as they walked into the gas station diner. "Now I realize I could see and hear you all, but it felt like something thick and heavy was squeezing out my thoughts and giving me all of these new ideas, things I could say or do..." He shivered for a moment and rubbed his hands together. "I know that doesn't make sense, but..."

"That's because you were not looking for the power to lie to anyone," Sarah said, spotting the kids in the far corner of the restaurant. "I'm sure Garnet welcomed those ideas and thoughts."

The diner nestled within the station appeared sterile, modern, and oddly cold, its fluorescent lights casting harsh shadows on the polished linoleum floors. As snowflakes danced outside, Sarah noticed only a handful of truckers huddled together at a corner booth, their weary faces illuminated by the glow of their smartphones. The atmosphere felt oddly disconnected, lacking the warmth and charm typical of such eateries. Despite the inviting scent of coffee lingering in the air, Sarah couldn't shake off the feeling of starkness that permeated the place. Automatically she checked all of their faces. No one paid them any mind. The kids already had burgers and fries in front of them and dug in heartily.

"Garnet..." Matthew slipped into the booth across from them and blew out a hard breath.

"Are you okay?" Cory asked. "You were pretty out of it."

A waitress appeared with coffee and menus but despite Cory's assurance of how tasty the burgers were, Sarah, Lily, and Matthew ordered sandwiches and ate in silence when their food appeared. With a polite smile, the waitress set down a few biscuits on a saucer for Pixie, nestled under the table by Sarah's feet. Pixie's tail wagged appreciatively, a brief moment of warmth amidst the sterile surroundings.

"Well," Lily finally asked. "If no one will say anything, I have to start. What are we going to do about that – thing?"

"Throw it out the window," Cory muttered into his fries and gave Matthew a sidelong glance. "You're sure you're okay?"

"Thanks to you and Lily's driving, yes."

"Legendary. Aunt Lily has mad skills."

"Scary was more like it, Cory, but we needed to get out of there. That's why we can't just throw it out the window."

"They'll keep coming?"

Matthew nodded slowly, folding his napkin over and over to keep his hands busy.

"I don't want you and the kids to go home, Sarah. We have to assume those people know where you live."

"What do you suggest then?" Sarah reached down and scratched Pixie between the ears. "Pixie thought..." She paused and looked up, but no one in the diner paid them any mind. "Pixie thought every enchanted object comes with a method and a way to undo the enchantment," she continued in almost a whisper.

"Cool, let's do that then."

"The problem is, Cory, that we don't know enough about the sapphire to figure out what that might be, and we don't have the time to do a lot of research or travel to Ireland, where I gather it was originally found."

One of the truckers turned on the TV, and without sound, the news station showed the scene in front of the courthouse.

"Courthouse Chaos in Claremont," the headline read, and Sarah shuddered to see the crowd, quite obviously yelling, pushing, and shoving, several TV news vans, and a thin column of dark smoke rising from the area where courtroom seven probably lay.

They'd be scratching their heads for days when they finally got to the origin of the smoke and found – nothing.

The final scene showed Garnet being led away in handcuffs and shackles again, with a scrolling notice that his hearing had been postponed for two weeks.

"Great," Lily said, reading the screen along with Sarah. "That gives them two weeks to find us, force the sapphire out of us, and do – whatever."

"We have to move on. In here, we're sitting ducks." Matthew shook out his napkin and began folding it again, over and over and over, until Sarah put a stilling hand over his.

"What about Aunt Lily's friend?" Emma finally piped up. "Was he not the one who wrote a book on all of this?"

"True," Sarah leaned back and imagined the old man, in his robes in the creaking old antique store, a tiny little relic in the center of all the modern developments. "His manuscript was stolen, but do you think he might still talk to us?"

She looked at Lily, not encouraged by the face her friend made. "I doubt it."

"These guys totally trashed his store – wouldn't it be in his own interest to make sure they are caught and imprisoned?"

"Sarah, you don't know Robbie."

"No, I don't really, but what I do know is that we need help with this sapphire, and he's the only one who can give it to us at the moment."

"He may have gone away somewhere too."

"Then we will just have to follow. But I doubt it. Last time I was there, some old lady told me he had gone south for the winter, but there he was, just sitting inside his old store like a fat spider."

Cory giggled at her little outburst, and Sarah forked her hand through her hair.

"Emma is right, he's the only one who can help. I say we go to Rosewood Hollow, and try to find him. If he's not there, we follow him to Florida or wherever he goes when he feels a shiver coming on," Sarah said.

Matthew smiled at her behind his hand and finally shrugged. "You kids heard her. Let's go finish your food and get ready then."

Their waitress approached the table again. With a practiced smile, she collected the money and set down another treat for Pixie, who wagged her tail eagerly.

"So, where are you folks headed?" she asked, her voice devoid of genuine curiosity. Matthew opened his mouth, almost saying "Rosewood," but before he could speak, Sarah put her hand on his.

"New York City," she said, her voice confident and decisive. The waitress nodded, her expression neutral, before pivoting to attend to another table, leaving Sarah and Matthew to exchange a glance laden with unspoken tension.

"That almost went sideways."

"Yeah, I guess none of us is used to being chased down for a magical blue stone."

Matthew grinned and raised an eyebrow. "A magical blue stone that is worth several million dollars, my dear."

Sarah almost spit out her coffee. "That thing?" she asked. "Pixie carried it in her mouth, and it is right now..." She looked around and lowered her voice again. "Inside an old soda cup in the trash pile in the car, probably covered in dog hair and dried cola."

Matthew pushed his glasses up on his head and wiped his eyes with both hands for a moment.

"That's another thing we'll have to work out," he said. "When this is all over, the museum is going to come looking for the stone or the value of the thing."

"Oh, brother."

Chapter Twenty-Three

Matthew suggested he should drive when they got outside again. Acknowledging Lily's driving skills, which had gotten them out of an extremely tight spot, but he'd rather not try that again.

He looked like the old Matthew after letting go of the sapphire, Sarah thought, so she merely nodded and slipped into the passenger seat. Automatically, her eyes checked the cars in the parking lot. Her heart skipped when she spotted a black SUV, but it turned out to be a different make, and Matthew pulled out onto the interstate again.

The dreariness of the late afternoon and the rumble of the tires on the asphalt put the kids to sleep. Lily sat staring out the side window at nothing, and Sarah kept scanning her side mirror.

"You think it was them," Matthew finally asked. No need to specify whom he meant by "them". Sarah shook her head.

"Maybe, or maybe not. All I know is it shook me when I saw them on the hill behind us. What if...?"

Matthew took her hand. "Don't go there. Everything is fine, for now."

Pixie climbed into her lap then and cuddled close.

Don't fret. Amelia, Simon, and I are always close. We'll never let you down.

Sarah scoffed and was about to answer when she felt the car slow down. Matthew set the turn signal and lined up for the exit ramp. Even Lily perked up in the back.

"Where are you going, Matthew?"

"Going to find a rental agency and change this out for something else," Matthew said, staring straight ahead, and she felt that fist clenching around her gut again.

She wasn't the only one who thought they were being followed.

∞

Getting a new van, slightly larger and a different color this time, took a few minutes. The daylight was fading fast as they transferred their luggage into the new van. Everybody seemed subdued.

Pixie sat staring at everyone. Then she suddenly barked once, and Sarah realized the helpful attendant had almost thrown out their trash bag.

"I'll take that," she snapped and pulled the bag so hard he almost tripped.

"Easy there. I can just throw that—"

"Never mind, we might still need that."

He looked a little disgusted but nodded and shoved the last of their bags into the back.

Sarah carefully stowed the trash bag under a towel when he wasn't looking, cursing herself all the way. He'd remember, she thought. Dammit, if anyone came around asking about a family in a rental car...

"Ready to go?" Matthew slipped into the driver's seat again, and moments later, they were back on the interstate.

Sarah realized she had nodded off, despite her anxiety and nerves. When she looked up, she could see the signs for Rosewood Hollow.

"Where to," Matthew asked softly. "Home first or the old antique store."

"If somebody is following us, I don't want to lead them to the house," Sarah said, with a hint of apprehension in her voice now.

"If somebody is following us," Lily said, "they already know where you live, or they wouldn't have located you in Claremont so fast."

"Still," Sarah shook her head. "Robert's store. I want to get this over with and get rid of this sapphire."

She could feel it. All the way in the front seat, she could feel the pull it was having on her.

"Sure?"

"Absolutely sure. But perhaps the kids and you..."

"No way, Mom." Cory folded his arms in that way he had of ending every further discussion. So much like his father, she thought with a pang. So much like Michael.

"Cory..."

"I'm with you. If Emma wants to go home, that's her deal. But I'm staying."

Sarah nodded and dragged her hands over her face until she felt the gentle touch of Pixie's paws on her arm.

Stay alert. It's the sapphire. It's pulling you into its spell, and you can't let it.

What?

It wants you to pick it up. It feeds on the desires and wishes of those who hold it.

With an effort, she sat up straight, realizing she had slumped down far in the passenger seat.

"Robbie's store," she said again, and Matthew picked an exit off the highway.

Chapter Twenty-Four

The air hummed with anticipation as Sarah, Matthew, Cory, Lily, and Emma approached the ancient antique store that stood nestled between two towering buildings. Daylight had almost entirely faded, and the evening chill reached for them with cold fingers, urging them to get inside.

To their dismay, the entrance was locked up tight, the windows dark and uninviting.

Sarah held the bag with the plastic shell container in one hand and used the other to rattle the door handle.

"It's closed?" she muttered, trying once again, just for good measure. They had come so far in their quest for answers, only to be met with a seemingly impenetrable barrier.

"You knew there was a chance," Matthew said, scanning the side of the building. Barely a couple of feet remained between the old clapboard and the neighboring condo towers, and the alleyways were choked with refuse, old buckets, and other discarded items.

"We have to get inside," Sarah insisted. "If he won't open, we'll just have to break in."

"Are you serious? And have somebody call the cops?" Matthew clamped an iron hand on her shoulder. "We definitely don't want to get caught out here with a stolen sapphire in a trash bag."

Before she could respond, a small bark caught their attention. Pixie danced around her feet, jumping up against her knee now and then, her keen senses picking up on something the others couldn't. With a curious tilt of her head, she darted towards the alleyway on the left, her tail wagging excitedly.

Following Pixie's lead, the group found themselves at a back entrance obscured by overgrown ivy. Very little light penetrated this far, and Sarah used her phone's screen to guide them, stepping over broken wooden pieces that could have been an old dresser at some point.

With a mix of skepticism and hope, they watched as Pixie furiously pawed at the door, her instincts guiding her with uncanny precision.

Before Matthew could stop her, Sarah put her hand on the handle and pushed. Slowly, the door creaked open, revealing a dimly lit hallway bathed in shadows.

As they stepped inside, a hushed silence enveloped them, broken only by the faint sound of their footsteps echoing off the bare walls.

Again, Sarah turned on the screen of her phone to light the way forward. For a moment, she hesitated, trying to get her bearings in the narrow hall. Was the store room to her right? And what about the hidden room of enchanted items?

A strange sensation, like a guiding hand, nudged her forward as she felt Pixie brush against her foot. A small, closet-sized room beckoned to their right, possibly an office. Turning back, she pressed a finger to her lips, urging the others forward in silent unison.

It was then that they caught sight of Robbie, cowering behind a dusty old accountant's desk, a sturdy thing of oak with a gleaming polished top, worn to a smooth finish over years of use. On its surface, she could see various compartments and drawers, each meticulously crafted to hold different accounting tools and documents, with slots for ledgers, inkwells, quills or pens, and compartments for storing important papers or seals. Robert Murtaugh's eyes widened with fear as he watched them coming in, a mix of apprehension and suspicion etched across his weathered features.

"I knew it!" Robbie exclaimed, his voice trembling with disbelief. "I knew you would come back. You'll bring misery to all of us. And it's right there, in your bag. It's too late."

His words hung in the air, casting a further pall over the already tense atmosphere. Sarah exchanged a worried glance with the others, feeling the chilling weight of those words.

"Robbie," Lilly stepped forward, raising her hands to ease his anger. "It's not like that. All we need—"

"All you need, Lily Morrison? All you need? These men who are after the stone and its powers – you know they broke in here. They stole the sapphire. If you feel there is anything else I need to give, you are wrong."

"Robert – Mr. Murtaugh..." Sarah tried. She stepped forward and stood there, moving her hands as if trying to grasp something, looking for the words that could move him to help her and her family. Words she didn't have, unfortunately.

We can't give up now, Sarah thought. Not when they were this close to negating the sapphire's power. Too much rested on their success.

Just then, Pixie streaked forward through all of their legs and jumped gracefully onto Robert's lap and, from there, onto the desk in front of him.

"What in the…" He tried to grab her, shove her off the desk and away from him, but the nimble little papillon evaded each one of his moves, anticipating and leaping this way and that she stayed just out of reach.

"Get down from there," he said, rising from his chair. Sarah could see that his erstwhile pristine midnight blue robe was stained and torn in a couple of places, his hands were dirty, and he still had not replaced the amulet around his neck. Things had seemingly not gone well for Robbie Murtaugh in the past few weeks.

"Get that dog out of here."

He was reaching for Pixie again when his hand suddenly froze in mid-air.

"What? What?"

He dropped heavily into his chair again and stared at Pixie.

He was silent then, staring at Pixie and she at him. She had ceased her constant movements and sat up straight on his desktop, her big fluffy ears moving this way and that like little antennae.

"Pixie," Sarah asked softly, but for once, she couldn't sense or hear her little companion. Pixie's attention was one hundred percent focused on Robbie. After a while, she relaxed, slipping down a little, and rested her head on her front paws.

She looked at Sarah and winked.

What did you do?

You humans talk too much. I merely gave him the thirty-second download on what happened and why we need him.

But…

He's coming around, don't worry.

Robbie leaned back in his chair and brought his hands flat together and to his face.

"You are indeed a most unusual family, what with this high spirit in the form of a dog you have."

High spirit? Sarah thought, and Pixie winked again.

Just a label.

"Well, can you help us or not," Matthew asked, confused and fed up with the silent exchanges going on. "Because we need to neutralize this darn stone. You see, there are—"

"Matthew Turner, do you really think there is anything your words can add to the information this high spirit has already imparted to me?"

Matthew stopped, looked at Pixie and then Sarah, and spread his hands.

"What?" he whispered to Sarah, who put a finger to her mouth. Robbie, meanwhile, rose awkwardly from the old chair and brushed ineffectively at the robe he wore.

"I've seen better days," he muttered and stepped out from behind the ancient desk.

"Come on then." He held out his hands to Pixie who gracefully jumped into them and allowed him to carry her through the public area of the antique store and the far back, where the door to the backroom was closed and locked once again.

He had only given the place a perfunctory cleanup, tidying broken glass and porcelain, removing the ruined furniture pieces, and sweeping away the dirt. The broken front window and glass door still featured emergency plywood paneling, and Sarah began to wonder if he had been sitting back there in that tiny office space since the night of the attack.

He carried Pixie like a precious ceremonial object, and the little papillon did not seem to mind at all.

When they reached the rear wall, she gracefully hopped out of his arms and sat in front of the locked door to the back room.

Robbie dug the key out of his pocket, muttered a few words that no one caught, and finally unlocked the door.

They were familiar with this room of enchanted objects, but today a different energy crackled in the air. Unseen lights still brightened their path, and the pull of the magical artifacts remained, yet the atmosphere hummed with unsettling tension. Pixie, bathed in the invisible light, stood still: ears perked, tail high, eyes squeezed shut.

"What you would need," Robbie said awkwardly, leaning on an old piece of wooden shelving. "What you need is the text on ancient enchanted gemstones. The very one those criminals stole when they followed you here in the first place."

"I don't think they needed to follow us," Cory muttered. "A simple Google search would have pointed them in the right direction."

Robbie glared at him and chose to say nothing. He raised an arm to indicate the expanse of the back room – a room that seemed somehow larger than the relatively small building should have allowed.

"If you can find something here to help your cause, you are welcome to it," he said as if it didn't matter to him whatsoever.

"That's where a backup would have come in handy," Cory said with an eye roll. "But no, old people never think they will need a backup. Jeez."

Scanning the cramped back room, Matthew, Lily, and Emma dispersed at Sarah's direction, each tasked with finding something useful—anything. Robbie, however, remained a fount of negativity, muttering under his breath.

Sarah, attempting to tune him out, closed her eyes and reached out with her senses.

The room pulsed with an otherworldly energy. Sarah felt a pull towards specific artifacts as if they held secrets waiting to be discovered.

Glancing sideways, she noticed a change in Robbie after a while. Gone was the mocking; his eyes now burned with focused determination as he moved purposefully among the shelves, scrutinizing objects and muttering to himself in hushed tones.

Despite Sarah's strained efforts, frustration gnawed at her. No answer materialized.

"Everyone alright?" she called out, flashing back to the memory of Matthew's vacant stare in the van.

"I'm good," that was Cory.

"Fine," Lily.

"Just peachy with all of this dust." That was Matthew.

"What about Emma? Emma, are you all right?"

No answer.

"Emma? Say something."

Still nothing. Sarah reached down and put her hand on Pixie's head.

Pixie, can you feel Emma?

She's – fine, Pixie responded. *But odd, somehow.*

Odd, odd how?

Sarah came out of the aisle between two shelves and looked around, left and right. Where was her daughter?

"Emma?"

"Here." The voice seemed faint, muffled even, but not frightened.

Sarah hurried over to the far wall, where she saw Emma standing by a tiny, blind window, covered in cobwebs and shreds of old newspapers.

"Emma, for crying out loud. I was afraid you were hurt."

"Look," her daughter pointed. On the other side of the old window sat a raven, its glossy black feathers shimmering in the light. Its beady eyes fixed on the transparent barrier separating it from the store room and the group inside.

"No. Hush, go away." That was Robbie behind her, waving his arms, trying to shoo the bird. Sarah cocked her head and slowly took a few steps toward the window.

With a swift and precise motion, the raven extended its sleek beak, tapping against the glass surface. Each peck echoed softly, a rhythmic percussion amidst the stillness of the surroundings. The raven's movements were deliberate yet filled with an unmistakable urgency as if it sought entrance or attention from those within. With each successive peck, the window reverberated, as if acknowledging the persistent visitor's presence.

"Go, go away."

"Leave him alone," Sarah said and took a few more steps.

Be careful; that is no ordinary bird.

Her eyes locked with the raven's, and Sarah felt something electric course through her entire body.

"The truth lies within," she heard herself say. They were her words, and it was her voice making those sounds, but somehow—not. It was as if it were coming to her from somewhere far, far away.

The electric feeling ran through her body once again, then it was gone. Sarah gasped, and would have fallen if it hadn't been for Matthew catching her by the arm.

"The truth lies within. What does that mean, Sarah?"

"I don't know."

"But you said it."

"Yes, but I still don't know. I'm trying to figure all this out, like all of you. To find a solution to the problem." Sarah covered her mouth after her outburst.

"I know," Emma said quietly.

"Mom, Matthew," Emma took their hands each into one of hers. "Stop. This is not you, it's the sapphire. I can feel it too."

"We have got to get out of here," Matthew said, forking his fingers through his short brown hair. "It's starting to affect everybody, even at this distance."

Sarah had left the bag with the sapphire in the old office, shoving it inside one of the cubbyholes of Robbie's desk, but she could feel its pull all the way into the back of the store room. Goosebumps erupted on her skin as she hugged herself, each deep breath a struggle against the cold fear gripping her.

"Giving up isn't my style," she admitted, exhaling a long breath. "But I'm at the end. Robbie, are you sure you can't recall anything else about the sapphire?"

The old man shook his head. In the dim light of the store room, he looked like just another old shopkeeper hanging on to a past long gone.

"Let's get out of here then. We'll figure out something else," she said and took Matthew's hand to anchor herself in the here and now. She could feel Cory, Emma, and Lily behind her, and as always, Pixie darting around her feet.

As Sarah walked past the end of a shelf, and past an ornate mirror, a chill crept down her spine, sending a shiver rippling through her body. Out of the corner of her eye, she caught a glimpse of her reflection, but it was not the familiar image she expected to see. Instead, she saw herself cloaked in a haze of darkness, her eyes gleaming with an unsettling intensity. The sapphire's blue shimmer of power seemed to wrap around her like tendrils of shadow, whispering promises of wealth and temptation. She held out a hand, and instantly in the reflection in that mirror, her hand was filled with gold and diamonds overflowing.

Beside her, Cory and Matthew approached the mirror, their steps hesitant as they, too, caught sight of their distorted reflections. Cory's usually warm gaze was clouded with uncertainty, his features drawn tight with the weight of the enchantment's hold. Matthew, normally steadfast and sure, looked haunted as he met his own gaze in the mirror, the realization of their predicament dawning upon him with chilling clarity.

Every wish could be fulfilled.

In the eerie reflection of the mirror, the enchantment's grip on her and the others materialized into dark, shadowy figures, their sinister presence looming over them like a gathering storm. Sarah watched in horror as her reflection succumbed to the allure of the sapphire, manipulating events for personal gain, oblivious to the devastation left in her wake. Cory, Matthew, Lily, and Emma were similarly ensnared by the enchantment, their distorted reflections painting a grim picture of the consequences of their actions. It was a chilling realization: the sapphire's power was a double-edged sword, capable of inflicting as much harm as it promised good.

"The truth lies within," her own voice echoed in her ears.

Pixie crowded closer to her, but the connection she felt with the little papillon suddenly became weaker and more tenuous. Just out of the corner of her eyes, she saw Emma break away from the group.

She shouldn't be alone.

Stop her, we have to stay together and get out of here.

Sarah couldn't move. As if transfixed she stared at the dark figure of Sarah in the mirror.

Robbie laughed suddenly, a loud, shrill noise that felt completely out of place. And then – Emma was back.

"Emma."

Sarah screamed silently. Emma cupped her hands in front of her, and the sapphire lay nestled between her fingers.

"No."

"Don't be afraid, Mom. We are going to take its power away."

"Put it down—quick—before..." Sarah fought against the pull from the mirror. She wanted to reach out and slap the sapphire out of her precious daughter's hands and hurl it as far as possible. Something held her strangely immobile as Emma raised her hands with the gem.

"This is how we do it," she said. "We forsake its power, all of us. Then it won't have any hold and turn into a simple stone."

"Emma, don't. Its power..."

"Its power can't touch me. The truth is in us, not in here."

She raised the sapphire a little higher, and a flash of the unseen light glinted off its many facets.

"I, Emma Anderson, pledge never to use the power of this sapphire for any reason. My truth lies within."

A flash of silver lit up the sapphire, and somewhere thunder rumbled.

She handed the sapphire to Sarah, who held it just as she had seen her daughter do.

Her voice echoed through the room; her words laced with a haunting melody.

"I, Sarah Anderson, pledge to forsake the power of this sapphire for the greater good. My truth lies within," she declared, her voice carrying a hint of unearthly wisdom that hinted at ancient secrets.

She gently offered her cupped hands to Cory, who received the sapphire and stared at it.

Again, a soft rumble of thunder rolled.

"Mom, I can't."

"Yes, you can. Think of Katelyn in her prison cell."

Cory pressed his lips together and straightened his back.

"I, Cory Anderson, solemnly swear to never succumb to the temptations of this sapphire. My truth lies within," he whispered, his words tinged with an eerie intensity that sent shivers down her spine.

One by one, they spoke the words, waiting for the flash of silver and growing clap of thunder before passing it on and watching their reflections in the mirror turn back to normal.

Robbie stood at the end of the line.

"You too," Sarah said, nodding.

"No."

"Yes. Unless you want those thugs who visited you before, or others just like them, to come back again and again seeking this sapphire. It will only become worthless to them when its power is broken."

Robbie spat a curse and finally received the sapphire in his cupped hands. Resenting every word, he declared his freedom from the sapphire's power. This time, the clap of thunder shook the tiny building and made the shelving around them wobble precariously.

Somewhere in the back, something fell and shattered with a crash, and all at once, the light that had traveled with them through the store room went out, plunging them into darkness.

"Sarah?"

"Mom."

She felt Matthew, Cory, and Emma. Pixie automatically jumped into her arms and hung on.

"Cory, your phone," Sarah called out, her voice echoing strangely in the store room.

A small rectangular light blazed right where her son stood, and the beam traveled over them one by one.

"Where's Robbie."

"Here."

The old man had been standing off to the side, and he stepped into the tiny beam of light. He still held the sapphire, nothing more than a pretty blue stone now, and Matthew quickly took it out of his hand. Emotions crossed his face like thunderclouds in a storm.

"It has lost its power," he said softly.

"Yes." Emma took his hand. "It's just a beautiful stone now, what it was always meant to be."

Robbie grumbled to himself and moved his hands, ushering them out of his precious store room.

"Out, out of my place, out of my store, out of my life. You people have brought nothing but misery to me, ever since you crossed my threshold. And you..." He glowered at Lily. "You brought them here. Go now. All of you."

Sarah walked out into the main store and stopped so suddenly the others almost walked into her from behind.

"What?"

"What's the matter?"

Sarah blinked and looked around. Bright sunlight flooded in through the gaps in the panels covering the broken windows.

"Sunlight!"

"That can't—it was..." Matthew started. "But it was night when I parked the car," he protested. "We were barely in there..."

"No way," Cory said, staring at the screen of his phone. "Mom, look at this."

"Let me see."

She took Cory's phone and stared at the screen just as uncomprehendingly as he had.

She then reached into her back pocket and checked her own, but the data didn't change.

"Three days," she said, feeling dread curling up inside her stomach. "We've been in here three days."

"That can't be right." Lily checked her phone and paled when it confirmed just that.

"Out." Robbie pointed at the door. "Out – now. I never want to see any of you again. And that includes you, Lily Morrison."

"But we need to…"

Robert Murtaugh put his hands firmly on their backs and ushered them out the front door without any further ado.

Chapter Twenty-Five

Sarah squinted in the late afternoon sun. The pale white February sunlight glinted off the salt residue left behind by the snowplows. A cold wind tore at their sweaters, clawing its way down to chilled skin.

Lily wrapped her decorative scarf tighter around her shoulders and shivered.

"Any idea where we left our coats?" she asked Sarah softly. Sarah shook her head.

"Maybe in Robert's back room? I don't remember, and I surely don't want to go back there."

She hooked one arm through Lily's and the other around Emma and Cory and began walking slowly toward where she thought they had left the rental car.

"Three days," she said, trying to make herself believe the words she was hearing. "Three days? All in that back room?"

"Time moved differently because of the sapphire," Emma said, and Sarah stopped.

"And you, Emma," Sarah's said. "Suddenly, you're an artifact expert? And what were you doing picking it up anyway?"

Emma shrugged. "It was fine. You were caught between the sapphire and the mirror."

"You could've gotten hurt, or worse," Sarah said, her voice laced with concern.

"No," Emma replied softly, "I could feel Amelia. All along."

Sarah's brow furrowed. "Amelia?"

Emma nodded. "She feels awful she couldn't help us in Claremont."

"She did pretty well, I'd say," Cory scoffed. "That courthouse smoke? Awesome."

Sarah gave her son's shoulder a little squeeze. "That's right. And your research, we couldn't have done it without you."

Matthew, who had been walking behind them, scrolling through the messages on his phone, caught up with them again.

"Anybody asks, I've been sick with laryngitis the past week," he said and grinned. "I haven't had to make excuses for missing work in a long time."

He felt in his pocket for the sapphire. "And I still have a problem to solve."

"One thing at a time. First, we need to find out what happened with Garnet and the Canvas Collective," Sarah said. "I need to know if we can go back home."

"I can help you with that." Matthew turned the screen of his phone to show her the headlines from the national news app he consulted daily. At least when he wasn't caught in a time loop with an enchanted gemstone.

"Took a minute to update itself, but…"

"Garnet confesses, Major blow against the Canvas Collective," Sarah read and scanned over the article. "Says here most of them were caught."

"Can we go home now then?" Cory complained. "It's cold out here."

They finally reached the car, and Matthew peeled several police tags off it.

"I guess I shouldn't have parked in a quick-stop area," he grumbled and shoved the tickets into his pocket.

"I think we can handle that." Sarah gently elbowed him in the side. "Are you okay?"

"Why shouldn't I be?"

Sarah nodded at his jeans pocket again, where he had put the stone again. "Last time..."

Matthew winked and patted his pocket. "Nope, it's just an ordinary gemstone now. Great job, Emma."

Emma glowed at the compliment, and Sarah squeezed Cory's shoulder again.

When they had all piled into the car, Pixie chose Cory's lap to sit, and she buried her little paws under his arm.

"You cold little girl? Here, let me warm you up."

Sarah turned around to hide her smile. Pixie certainly had her ways.

∞

Lily decided to stay with them for dinner, and the house on Maple Street was once more filled with the sounds of laughter, barks, footsteps, and harmless jokes flying back and forth.

Sarah directed them with the efficiency of a troop coordinator, making sure bags and overnight cases were emptied, laundry put away, and clothes aired. She sent Matthew to pick up some food for them and finally opened a bottle of wine for herself and Lily.

"Turn on the news," Lily urged.

"Can't. I promised Matthew I would wait until he got back."

"But couldn't we..."

"I promised him I would wait." Sarah tucked her legs under her on the plump, comfortable couch, pulled a blanket into her lap, and snuggled Pixie close. "I thought I would freeze out there. I really wish I knew what we'd done with our coats."

Lily only shrugged. They were both pretty sure they knew where they had left them.

Finally, Matthew returned with the one thing he knew everybody would enjoy — pizza — and turned on the television. He zapped around until he found the local news, and Alexander Williams, the news anchor who looked as if he really should be a surfer.

"Good evening. Our top story tonight revolves around developments following the strange incident at Claremont Courthouse. The cause of the rapidly developing smoke still has not been identified. 'Garnet,' Spencer Gates, the primary suspect in the theft of a valuable gemstone from the Rosewood Hollow museum, has confessed to his involvement and named several accomplices. Four of these individuals have been apprehended, while two remain at large at this time."

Sarah and Matthew exchanged a look, and Matthew took her hand.

"Gates, in exchange for his cooperation, may receive a reduced sentence," Williams continued. "However, crucially, he has not disclosed the whereabouts of the stolen sapphire. His claim of a magical entity absconding with the artifact can, at this point, not be substantiated."

Williams cleared his throat and looked straight at the camera for a moment. Kudos for not grinning, Sarah thought. Most of the involved

authorities probably felt Gates had either been on drugs or hallucinat-
ed.

"The final determination of his sentence reportedly hinges on his willingness to provide complete and honest information, as well as the eventual recovery of the stolen gem. Law enforcement agencies contin-ue to investigate leads and pursue all avenues in the case. We urge anyone with information regarding the remaining accomplices or the location of the sapphire to come forward and assist in the ongoing investigation. Stay tuned for further updates on this developing story."

Matthew bit into his pizza with gusto, and Sarah leaned in a bit closer.

"Where is the stone?" Sarah whispered, so Cory and Emma wouldn't hear.

"Empty salt jar in the kitchen," Matthew shrugged. "Best thing I could think of."

Sarah had opened her mouth to protest when, out of the corner of her eye, she saw the by-now-familiar cloud of white mist forming in the corner of the room, right where the raw stone fireplace edged against the wooden wall panels.

"Amelia," Emma called out and jumped to her feet.

Lily put a hand on the girl's shoulder. "Hold on for a second."

Matthew turned off the TV, and a sense of stillness hung in the air, broken only by the gentle crackle of burning wood in the fireplace. A soft whisper of wind stirred, swirling in the corner of the room like a delicate ballet.

From the midst of the swirling mist emerged the ethereal figure of Amelia, draped in the elegant fashions of the early 1900s. Her gown, a vision in white, cascaded around her slender form like wisps of silk, adorned with delicate lace and intricate embroidery that shimmered in the firelight. A high-necked collar framed her graceful neck while billowing sleeves trailed behind her as if caught in an eternal breeze.

Eyes, pools of liquid moonlight, gazed out from beneath long lashes with a haunting intensity. Lips, seemingly painted the softest shade of rose, curved into a gentle smile that held a hint of melancholy.

As she drifted closer, the scent of vintage perfume lingered in her wake, a sweet and heady aroma that filled the room with a sense of nostalgia. Each movement was fluid and graceful as if she were gliding effortlessly on unseen currents of air.

She stopped, and her eyes met with Sarah's.

"Pray, forgive my absence in Claremont. The distance from this house proved too great for my spectral form to materialize. I trust you managed alright."

"We did," Sarah said, her tongue suddenly working around a mouth dry as the desert. "You and Pixie..."

"Yes, the little sprite." Amelia smiled at Pixie, a sight that was just the slightest bit disconcerting. "She is quite a character and enormously resourceful."

"That she is, thank you."

"The girl, Katelyn," Amelia continued. "I trust she will be released in due time. It was but for her that I made this effort to return."

"Hopefully," Matthew said. "It's too soon to say. Mostly the authorities are worried about the whereabouts of the Royal Veritas sapphire, which..."

Sarah added, "Which at this moment is in the kitchen of my – of this very house in an entirely unsuitable container."

Amelia advanced on Matthew, and he paled a bit, shrinking back into the pillows of the couch as far as humanly possible.

"I see." Amelia pulled back a bit, and Matthew exhaled visibly.

"I will return." As if someone had switched off the lights, Amelia disappeared. Just — gone.

"Well, that was," Matthew said, pausing as he reached for Sarah's wine glass. "Something."

"You okay?"

"The way she – looked at me..."

"She just wants to help," Emma said

"Emma, there are moments when I'm wondering if your preoccupation with this ghost is entirely healthy." Matthew took another sip from Sarah's wine glass and shook his head. "And I can't believe I actually just said something like that."

Sarah took his hand and squeezed.

"Thank you for not running at the first sight of her," she whispered and took back her glass. The thought of her ex, Michael hearing about ghosts, talking Papillons, and enchanted gemstones made her grin and slide a bit closer into Matthew's embrace. She'd been so lucky since moving to Rosewood.

As if he could read her thoughts, Matthew blushed just a tiny bit and looked down at his hands.

"That still leaves the problem of the sapphire," she said with a sigh. "We can hardly just pick it up and wander into the museum with it. Here – I think you might be missing this."

"Jail time," Cory said and snagged another piece of pizza. "You could just mail it."

"Mail...? No, I don't think that would work either. Not secure."

"Besides, it's too easy to track," Cory said, wrinkling his nose. "We need a guaranteed undetectable way to get into the museum and leave it somewhere."

"Could you just bring it in and casually leave it in — I don't know — a room somewhere," Lily suggested.

"You know how many cameras there are in the museum?"

"FedEx?"

"Traceable."

"Drop it at the front door?"

"Cameras."

Back and forth they went for the better part of an hour. At one point, Matthew got up and checked the salt jar in the kitchen, just to make sure it was still there. Then he spiraled about law enforcement coming to the door, discovering the stone, and arresting Sarah.

She barely managed to stop him from taking the sapphire and burying it in the backyard in the middle of the night.

"Why can't we just turn it in?"

"Emma, do you want to be the one to try explaining how we suddenly got to have it? Mom and Matthew would likely be arrested for something, and who knows what they would do with us. Be smart about this – okay?"

"Cory, I don't think—"

"Easy, everybody." Sarah raised her hands. "For now, we're not going to do anything. I'm going to find a better hiding spot for the thing tomorrow, and we'll all give it more thought."

"No. Isn't Katelyn going to rot in jail while we hold on to the stone?"

"Do you want your mother to go there instead?"

More back-and-forth and another hour passed without a workable idea. Sarah went to put the dishes and empty pizza cartons away, Lily gave Pixie a break outside, and Matthew rebuilt the fire.

They sat staring at it, each lost in their own thoughts in the dimly lit confines of the den.

With each proposed solution, the air grew thicker, a tangible weight settling on their shoulders. Hope flickered and died as their ideas unraveled under the harsh light of reality, leaving them tangled in a web of frustration.

"How do real criminals do it," Lily suddenly said, jumped to her feet, and began pacing. Sarah only shook her head.

The flickering flames cast dancing shadows on the walls, mirroring the tumult within their hearts. As the night wore on, they became more silent and more desperate.

"All right, kids, bedtime," Sarah finally said and rose to her feet. Even Cory, usually the first one to insist on staying up only a little while longer, gathered his tablet and phone with a weary nod.

Just as he, too, got up, a cold draft swept through the room, chilling them to the bone, as if nature itself mourned their plight. And then, amidst the oppressive silence, a familiar spectral figure materialized. Amelia was back.

As Sarah watched the shimmering form materialize in the dimly lit den, a mixture of apprehension and hope stirred within her. Amelia's sudden appearance, though always unsettling, brought with it a glimmer of hope. While she couldn't interact with their world in the same way humans did, perhaps, just perhaps, within the ethereal wisdom she possessed lay the elusive solution. Clinging to this fragile hope, Sarah's gaze locked onto Amelia, silently pleading for guidance.

Matthew slid a little closer again, but this time, Amelia ignored all of them. Without disturbing anything in the room, the ghost glided to stand in front of the fire, where Pixie napped on a pillow, her form flickering slightly in the dancing flames.

Pixie raised her little head and blinked.

"You are able to manipulate objects on this plane, correct?"

Pixie blinked again and sat, draping her tail regally around her hind paws.

To an extent, Sarah heard.

Matthew was half out of his seat, but she held him back.

"Don't," she whispered. "Let's see where this is going."

"But Pixie..."

"Pixie is fine."

"They're communicating, right?" Cory asked, his voice barely above a whisper, and Sarah nodded.

"Then you will help me."

Pixie raised a dainty paw and began cleaning it as if none of what Amelia said concerned her the slightest.

"Much akin to our endeavors in Claremont. I shall conjure a diversion, while you may drop the sapphire wherever you see fit, provided these good folk be elsewhere."

"I think they are planning to return the sapphire together," Sarah said for the benefit of everyone else who simply saw a ghost and a dog staring at one another.

Claremont Courthouse was not alarmed.

"Oh, please." Amelia's translucent form shimmered and reformed for a second. "These electronics are no match for my energy."

Pixie lowered her head and went into a deep stretch that brought her forehead down to her paws and her rear end and fluffy tail high into the air.

Amelia glowed a light orange for a moment. Surely not a sign of patience, Sarah thought, but she had already disappeared.

"Well?"

"What? What just happened?" Everyone was asking at once.

Sarah raised her hands again. "I don't know. I'm not sure exactly what this is all about, but one thing is certain…" She looked into a circle of excited faces and shook her head. "Whatever they are planning — it won't happen tonight. Let's all get a good night's sleep."

Lily borrowed a coat to go home, the children said their good night's and disappeared upstairs and Matthew went to make sure the house was locked up safely.

For a long moment, Sarah sat staring into the flames, until she felt Pixie by her side.

She's right. The two of us are the only ones who can return the stone.

She's a ghost Pixie. Nothing can happen to her. You, though. I worry about you. And guards, people with guns and… other weapons. I don't want to lose you.

You won't. Pixie hopped into her arms and snuggled hard against her. *I will come back to you. I always come back to you.*

Chapter Twenty-Six

I *always come back to you.*

Sarah woke up with that thought in her head, feeling Pixie snuggled tight against her side.

She reached out with one finger and ran it gently down Pixie's soft white snout, hearing a little groan from the tiny dog.

Pixie looked up and pawed at the air with her front paws. For that, they did not have to speak to understand.

Sarah cuddled the little Papillon close.

Amelia will be there.

I know that's some comfort. But remember, you only weigh five pounds.

Pixie pawed at her again, gently, and fitted her tiny body tight against Sarah.

Don't worry. Your power has kept me safe before.

Sarah finally got out of bed to find Matthew in the kitchen handling all manner of foodstuffs and utensils. Normally he was an accomplished cook. Today the sharp tang of burned food hung in the air.

"Couldn't sleep in?" he asked and hugged her close.

Sarah only shook her head and poured coffee.

"I keep worrying..."

"As do I."

"She's..." Her fingers kneaded restlessly, and her eyes stung with tears. "Sending her in there...it worries me."

Pixie finally came downstairs, and together they went for a long walk through the outskirts of Rosewood Hollow and played a fierce game of fetch in the yard. All day long, Sarah pretended not to notice that everyone in the family snuck her favorite treats to the little Papillon whenever they thought no one was looking. As if by agreement, they didn't talk about the dangers of the mission Pixie and Amelia had set for themselves. It had to be done, and there was no other way.

Your power has kept me safe before.

All too soon, the harsh February day began waning again, the sun set in a fiery ball of red, and Sarah sat by the fireplace, staring into the dancing flames, her arms wrapped tight around Pixie.

Over at the games table, Matthew, Cory, and Emma played a board game they'd neglected for months, and Lily texted she would be by after the store closed.

Sarah rocked slowly back and forth when suddenly, a wispy figure materialized beside her, the translucent form shimmering like moon-light on water.

It was, of course, Amelia, sporting a mischievous glint in those non-existent eyes.

"Leave everything to me, dear Sarah," she declared, her voice a gentle echo. "Being incorporeal has its perks, you know."

She locked eyes with Pixie, comfortable in Sarah's embrace, and nodded.

Are you prepared then?

Pixie stretched, shook her coat, and gave Sarah a little lick on the cheek.

I cannot hold the sapphire, Amelia continued.

I know. But I was able to carry it halfway through Claremont. I'll manage.

Amelia turned back to Sarah and spread her wispy, shimmering arms.

"Should you not be somewhere else when we are at the museum? In a restaurant, perhaps?"

"She's actually right," Matthew said. "A nice public place – the whole family – and Lily should be there too."

Amelia shimmered brightly for a moment, enjoying the compliment.

"Well then..."

"Well then."

Pixie hopped down and ran into the kitchen, sitting in front of the cupboard where Matthew had stuffed the antique salt jar containing the sapphire all the way in the back.

The air crackled with nervous energy as Sarah clutched the sapphire in her hand.

"This is crazy," she muttered, but a glint of determination shone in her eyes.

Here we go.

Gently, Pixie took the sapphire from Sarah's hand, and for a moment, Sarah thought she saw her wink.

She touched Pixie's head and felt the uncanny, unbound strength she had felt before radiating out of her fingers and into the little dog.

The doggie door flapped softly as the little Papillon jumped outside, and before Sarah knew it, Amelia had melted through the walls and was gone.

"Is she going to be okay," Emma asked, and Sarah put her arm around the girl and lifted the kitchen curtains just a bit.

"Look."

Out in the yard stood Pixie, bathed in the soft glow of a full moon. She was emitting a faint, shimmering trail. The light, invisible to the naked eye, pulsed subtly, tracing a winding path towards the street and eventually the museum.

"She's showing Amelia the way."

The shimmering trail, visible only to Amelia's spectral sight, would act as a map, guiding her through the city and the museum's intricate layout and bypassing any security cameras or tripwires that might stand in her way.

"Here, you can watch."

Cory handed her his precious tablet, where a tiny red dot sped down the street on a map.

"Is that..."

"Pixie. I put a transmitter on her collar when she was taken last time."

Sarah put her fingers to the little dot.

Matthew finally took their coats and hats and walked them down the street to a small restaurant that promised to be both a diversion and an alibi.

Chapter Twenty-Seven

"Anything?" Cory asked for about the tenth time and Sarah chanced another look at the tablet.

"I don't know. She stopped moving. Oh my…"

Quite suddenly, the red dot on her screen careened this way and that, bouncing from one end of the display to the other.

"Cory! What's happening."

Cory tore the tablet from his mother's hand and reloaded the display again and again.

"I don't know."

"Is she in danger?"

"It could be just a transmission failure," Cory tried. "Maybe Amelia messing with electronics…"

"But?"

Cory never got to answer. Just then, Matthew's phone shrilled with an insistent tone, and he checked the screen.

"It's the museum," he said softly.

He took a few steps away from the table to take the call. When he returned, his face was ashen, and the line between his eyes deepened.

"The museum," he said, his voice toneless. "My presence is requested."

"Pixie, where's Pixie, have you – did they say…?"

Matthew put a finger to his lips.

"I'll head over there. You guys get back to the house. Lily – go with them. I'll let you know as soon as I can."

"But didn't they say…"

"Not much. But I gather – it seems they may have caught something. I'm not sure if they mean on camera, or what."

Sarah took back the tablet from her son. The tiny red dot had stopped moving, which could mean a lot of things, amongst others…

"Can I not come with you?"

"I think it's better that I go alone for now."

On the way home, Sarah stared out the window, a litany of what-ifs swirling in her silent mind.

At the house, Sarah stood staring at the corner of the fireplace trying to will Amelia to appear.

"Where were you," she said out loud. "You were supposed to take care of the alarm. You were supposed to…" She made a hard fist and struck the side of the armchair. "You were supposed to keep her safe."

Amelia didn't appear.

An agonizing hour later, she could hear the sound of Matthew's car again in the driveway and ran to meet him.

"Where is she, is she safe?"

Matthew shook his head.

"I don't know."

"What do you mean you don't know? Was she there? Is she... is she okay?"

"Sit down for a second." Matthew took her shoulders and led her back into the den. "Where are the kids."

"Upstairs. Cory is obsessively checking his tracker, it's gone offline."

"Let him keep at it. We might still need it."

"Please, tell me something."

With a sigh, Matthew sat down, elbows on his thighs, head buried in his hands. "This is what I heard. Something tripped the alarm at the museum tonight."

"Amelia was supposed to..."

"I know. The alarm went off. The security guards deployed, and one of them thought he saw...something. Out of the corner of his eye."

"Was it...?" Lily handed Matthew a cup of tea.

"I really don't think so. The guard thought it might have been a small robot thing or a small animal of some type. He tried to get closer to it, but couldn't. And in the resulting security sweep of the grounds, guess what they did find?"

He let a few seconds pass, then leaned back, his eyes closed, his hand over the lower portion of his face.

"They didn't find a sapphire, but out in the museum's park, they caught the two remaining members of the Canvas Collective."

Sarah dropped her wine glass where it shattered against the edge of the stone fireplace.

"I'm guessing they were watching the museum, figuring we would try to bring the sapphire back," Matthew finished. "And they were going to get it, one way or another."

Sarah was very still. Images of sweet afternoons on the sun porch with Pixie in her lap danced through her head, opening the Christmas stockings with Pixie tearing at the ribbons impatiently, holding the little Papillon in her arms.

Lily cleaned up the glass and put a hand on Sarah's shoulder. Sarah closed her eyes and listened into the void.

Where are you, my girl – and you, Amelia?

The silence that greeted her was perhaps more frightening than any answer she might have received.

❧

Amelia didn't show up that night, or the next one. Sarah went through the motions of life, attempting to do everything the way she usually did, but every few moments she stopped and listened into the void, calling Pixie's name.

She spent some time in a café across from the museum doing the same thing, ignoring the staff giving her odd sideways glances.

She went for a long walk in the park around the museum, casually looking under the shrubbery, until a guard asked her if she had lost something.

On the third day, she was sitting motionless in the kitchen, cradling a long cold cup of coffee, staring into Pixie's empty little dog bed, when she finally felt the familiar tingle of energy building in the corner of the room.

She let the chill that presaged Amelia's appearance envelop her.

"You were supposed to take care of her," she hissed before Amelia could say anything. "Keep her safe."

Their...electronics were more than we could handle easily. They must have strengthened their alarm systems.

"Where is Pixie?"

Sarah raised her hands a little higher, showing Amelia the shimmering power that emanated from her fingers, reaching for the ghost.

Amelia hissed softly. A faint and inhuman sound.

"Where's Pixie?" Sarah lowered her arms momentarily, and Amelia closed the gap.

In my attempt to overcome the alarm systems, the constables arrived unexpectedly. Unfortunately, the little sprite chose her escape poorly and now finds herself in a precarious situation. Amelia wavered slightly. *She was inside the room of perplexity, where the contraptions of this modern age held her captive.*

"The room of... you mean the security office?" Sarah sputtered.

I cannot open doors, remember? Amelia's form flickered faintly.

"You should have come to me sooner." Sarah jumped up and paced back and forth in her bright, spacious kitchen. "If she's trapped in that room, we need to get her out now. One of the guards thought he may have seen a small animal the night of the break-in, and some of the museum staff know Pixie."

Amelia didn't respond, her form wavering slightly. She stood glowering, ever mindful of Sarah's hands. She vividly remembered that when Sarah focused, she could strike out with enough power to immobilize the ghost—for days.

"She hasn't had any food or water in days," Sarah continued, hugging her arms as much to ward off Amelia's chill as to imagine Pixie's plight. "What about that cursed sapphire then? Why hasn't it been found?"

It's not truly cursed, rather it's—

"Amelia!" Sarah raised her hands a fraction, making the ghost recoil ever so slightly.

She bears it with her.

"We have to get her out of there, right now. Jesus." Sarah pressed a hand to her forehead. "Matthew's going to kill me," she muttered. "I am so dead."

And how do you plan to enter the museum and free the little sprite undetected?

"Let me think." Sarah paced with quick strides, drumming her fingers against her thighs. "I'll take Lily," she muttered. "One of us can pretend to bring something to Matthew, the other one will let Pixie out. That could work."

"That chamber is under constant surveillance."

"That's why I'll have a ghost with me," Sarah snapped. She pressed her fingertips together, fixing Amelia with a withering glare.

Amelia shimmered, the dark orbs of her eyes still following Sarah's hands until she lowered her head. *So be it.*

"I'll pick up Lily and meet you there. I don't know—just make yourself known when you see us at the museum. Preferably in a way that won't get us arrested."

Amelia hissed softly and faded away.

For the first time in days, a small smile touched Sarah's lips as she bundled up in a coat and scarf to visit the town historian at the museum. She was carrying a folder of paperwork he definitely did not need.

Chapter Twenty-Eight

At the Rosewood Hollow Book Nook, she encountered her first problem. The young lady manning the sales counter informed her that Lily had driven to the next town to pick up a book delivery. Sarah smiled and politely said thank you. Inside, she seethed.

For a moment, she stood staring out into the road, where soft February snow had begun to fall and finally slipped her hands into her gloves again.

"Thanks again," she said to the young clerk. "Would you ask Lily to ring Sarah the moment she gets back?"

Out in the car, Sarah squeezed the steering wheel, knuckles white. Taking a deep breath, she rallied herself. "You've got this, Sarah. You've faced down criminals and fought a ghost. Rescuing Pixie shouldn't be that hard, right?" A tremor of unease ran through her.

Resolutely, she pushed the start button and turned toward the museum.

Matthew, as the town historian, split his time between the local historical society, sometimes teaching at a nearby university, and advising the Rosewood Hollow Museum when required. Since the theft of the sapphire, he'd been spending a lot more time there.

Sarah could have called him and warned him about what she was planning to do, but she knew he would only try to talk her out of her it.

As if she didn't have a care in the world, she walked up to the entrance and gave the young man at admission her broadest, most charming smile.

"Excuse me? Hi. I'm Dr. Matthew Turner's partner, Sarah. He seems to have forgotten this at home this morning". She held up the folder and waggled it slightly. "He was a bit...flustered when he left." A small smile played on her lips. "I'd like to get this to him. Perhaps before his meeting?"

The young man looked up and gave her an equally charming smile.

"Of course. Go on in. Just be mindful that a few of the exhibits are still closed."

No need to mention why they would be closed.

Sarah rushed inside, turned a corner, and stood for a moment at the directory, hoping Matthew wouldn't choose that very moment to show up and question her.

"Amelia," she said under her breath. "Could use a hand here. Where is that security office?"

"Sarah, what are you doing here?"

Busted.

Sarah turned around to find a young, raven-haired girl of about twenty-five, wearing big, heavy boots, in a loose white sweater, her right leg sporting a walking cast.

"Katelyn!"

The folder was forgotten as she enveloped the girl in a massive hug.

"You're ... out. And here already?"

"Yeah. You know, after they nabbed those guys from the Canvas Collective, there was really no reason to keep me."

Sarah looked left and right, but no one paid them any mind.

"No worries," Katelyn said. "Everybody in here has been super nice, and I really just had a few meetings today to – to figure out if I want my job back."

"I am so sorry for all you had to go through."

"Don't be." Katelyn waved a hand and began walking, and Sarah automatically kept up. "I heard that it was mostly you, Lily, and Matthew, along with Emma and Cory, who made sure that this day would actually come. I've been wanting to see you, but your phone..."

Her phone had gone unanswered as Sarah tore herself up worrying over Pixie's fate. Somewhere at the end of the hall, a light fixture flickered, and Sarah wondered if that was Amelia.

"What are you doing here then? Did you come to see Matthew?"

Sarah stopped. The light fixture flickered again. Definitely Amelia. Sarah crowded a bit closer and took Katelyn's arm. The young woman cocked her head and gave Sarah a questioning look.

"Sarah?"

"I need your help," she finally said, deciding on the spur of the moment to put everything on the table.

"You're not—Sarah, you're not here to do anything illegal, are you? I can't be involved in that right now."

"No, not at all. But—you see—Pixie is stuck in the security office."

"Pixie..." Katelyn stopped, and Sarah all but plowed into her. "Pixie... of course. That's what the security guard saw when the museum was broken into again."

"Yes, most likely."

"Sarah, what are you doing? I just got out of jail, and I don't have to tell you that that is a bad place. Whatever you did, now is the time—"

"There is no time."

The two women froze. Sarah shivered, knowing what she would encounter when she turned around.

"Amelia," Sarah said with a sigh. "She's here to help."

"I—just—can't."

"You won't have to." Amelia swept a shimmering white cloud of mist around the two women, and for a moment, Sarah thought she enjoyed the panic in Katelyn's eyes. "There is a problem with something called the sensors in the basement. Just keep the constables busy there."

"She means the security guards," Sarah clarified. "And I swear to you, nothing illegal is going on here."

Katelyn wavered, and Amelia closed in a little more. Katelyn gasped for breath and reached for her throat.

"Leave it be, Amelia," Sarah commanded, running a hand through her hair. Alarms blared from somewhere deep within the museum, followed by the sound of approaching footsteps.

Amelia yielded, drifting back to the shadows. Katelyn, catching her breath, coughed harshly.

"The alarms," Katelyn stammered, eyes wide. "I'll go... check."

Sarah hesitated, then jerked her head toward the end of the hall. "Thank you, Katelyn."

Katelyn turned to head down a side passage, her back rigid, her shoulders set. She took a few steps down then stopped.

"Security office is down this hall," she said over her shoulder. "In the rush to get downstairs, I hope no one leaves the door open."

Sarah stood and leaned against the wall for a second. Katelyn had just spent months in jail. She was possibly the last person in this entire museum who should come to her aid. She only hoped she could make it up to the young girl.

This way. Amelia glided toward the hall Katelyn had indicated, leaving a shimmering trail of mist and golden glitter.

"We're going to have to talk about you choking my friends," Sarah said, slightly out of breath as she rushed after the ghost. "It is not done. And just what did you do to the alarm in the basement?"

Amelia hovered for a moment and made a sound that in her world might pass for a laugh.

An old-fashioned oak door was a thing of substance, dear Sarah. These modern things... I am beginning to understand these... electronics. It is fun to play with.

"Great," Sarah muttered, putting her hand on her forehead.

A ghost in the electronics was more than she could handle right then. She peeked around a corner to make sure everyone had rushed off to take care of the basement situation and approached the door that carried a stainless-steel designation plate, Security Office.

"Here we are." She put her hand on the handle, said a silent prayer, and pushed.

Katelyn had come through. The door opened silently to a room full of monitors, keyboards, and panels of security lights. Almost instantly, one of the panels lit up with bright red lights and an urgent beep, something Amelia swiped away with a simple brush of her translucent arm.

"Pixie," Sarah hissed. "Pixie – are you in here? It's me."

For a heart-stopping moment that felt like an eternity to her, she heard nothing; then, from somewhere under and behind a small rolling file cabinet, a fierce rustling and scrabbling began.

Sarah dropped to her knees and reached a hand under the cabinet.

"Pixie? Hurry."

What do you think I am doing? I've been under here for so long that I think I'm stuck.

More rustling and scrabbling ensued, and the cabinet wobbled precariously until Sarah finally lifted one end of it. A dusty, dirt-streaked Pixie appeared from underneath, shook quickly, and bounced into Sarah's arms.

Let's get out of here. I've had just about enough of this place.

"Amelia – what is the status of the security people?" Amelia did not answer. "The constables, Amelia?"

"They are busy. Pray tell, how are you going to take her out of here?"

Sarah opened her tote of a purse and held it out to Pixie, who hopped inside and ducked down.

"She's only five pounds."

Less now. Let's get a move on. I'm hungry and tired, and worst of all, I need to pee.

Sarah grinned despite their precarious situation.

"Got it. Amelia, what's the hallway like?"

She expected to turn and leave, but Amelia shook her head.

Bad idea. Amelia melted through the wall for a moment and back into the room almost instantly.

There are four constables coming down the hall, and they are headed for this room.

"Dammit," Sarah swore and clutched her tote to her side. "Can you not create a diversion?"

Too late.

"Think of something," Sarah muttered to herself, squeezing behind the inward swinging door, one hand inside the tote caressing Pixie slightly. Then her fingers hit something hard and round, and she almost gasped out loud—the sapphire. Of course, Pixie had brought the stolen sapphire along.

The door opened slowly as she stood behind it, and three security men talking in excited voices entered the room. This is how it was going to end then, Sarah thought. In the security office of a museum with a stolen million-dollar gemstone in her pocket.

Cory, Emma, I am so sorry. And Matthew...

She pressed a fist to her mouth to keep from crying out loud as the three men checked the alarm panels across the room. If only one of them turned around... Her heart pounded, her vision tunneled, and then everything went black.

Now, move.

It wasn't the fear that had blacked out her sight, it was Amelia, fooling with the lights in the entire south wing of the museum.

Sarah cautiously inched out from behind the door, ever mindful of the three guards, fumbling for flashlights and cell phones in the windowless room. She had almost made it when she bumped into one of them.

"Hey, who, what, wait a minute." The man's hand reached for her, grasped the sleeve of her coat, just as she tore free, and took off down the hall, running in blindly following a white-hot dot of light she hoped was Amelia.

They turned a corner and then another in pitch darkness, and finally, the dot slowed down and disappeared entirely. Sarah stood motionless, orienting herself.

Atrium, straight ahead, she heard and was alone in the hall a second later.

The bright glow of the lit atrium guided her onward. Security guards still ran this way and that, but in the main atrium, amongst a smattering of museum guests who were rushing to leave, no one paid her any mind.

Pixie, what are we going to do about the Sapphire?

Ask me later, I have to go – now.'

Sarah barely waved at the attendant who had so graciously let her in earlier and took massive ground-eating strides toward the exit. They were almost there.

"Ms. Anderson, Ms. Anderson, wait."

Sarah wanted to ignore the man. If she pretended not to hear him, perhaps...

"Wait, Ms. Anderson..." A hand clamped around her upper arm, and Sarah cried out. She tore around, ready to call Amelia, or confess or throw the sapphire — whatever it might take to get out of there. But the attendant waved her file folder at her.

"Glad I caught you. You must have dropped this earlier. I didn't want you to get home and have to come back. It's crazy today."

Sarah felt her knees buckle.

"Are you all right, Ms. Anderson?"

"Yes, no worries," she said, moving her tongue around her dry mouth with monumental effort. "You have – a lot going on here to-day."

"Our electronics keep going on the fritz. Did you see Dr. Turner?"

"Yes, all good. Thanks again."

Sarah all but fled. Out through the massive double doors and down the stairs, almost running down a group of elderly museum visitors in her rush.

She walked around the side of the museum and let Pixie jump out of her tote bag to relieve herself under a bush. The groans of satisfaction and relief she heard told their own story. Finally, Pixie appeared again, tongue lolling out of her mouth, eyes bright and shiny despite the grime that covered her entire body.

I am not proud of it, but I drank out of a puddle. Thankfully there were cookies at the bottom of your bag.

Pixie, I am so sorry.

Don't be, they were delicious. But I need to eat.

I'll take you home right now, baby, I was so worried.

Stop worrying and start trusting your own power—and me when I tell you I will always come back to you.

Pixie winked and stared at Sarah's tote until she lowered it to the ground, and the little Papillon jumped back in.

Wait. What did you do with the sapphire?

Don't worry, it's all taken care of.

Matthew arrived home later, just as Lily was stepping out of her orange Volkswagen Beetle.

"Have you seen Sarah?" he asked.

"No. She came to the store, but I was out picking up books. It sounded urgent, so I headed right here. Got any idea what's going on?"

"None."

Sarah stepped onto the front porch, and Matthew did a little double-take. He'd left Sarah behind, staring depressed and silent at the walls of the house, and suddenly, here she was, bubbling with happiness once again.

"Hey guys, good you're here. Come on in. We can all sit down to dinner."

"Sarah?"

"Are you okay?"

Lily and Matthew stepped onto the porch. The doggie door opened, and Pixie shot out, greeting first Matthew and then Lily.

Once again, she was fluffy, white, and clean. She bounced around all of her favorite humans, barking with glee.

"Oh my God, Pixie is back. Where did she come from?"

"Just showed up," Sarah said, crossing her fingers behind her back, but Matthew wasn't fooled. He took a few steps to stand directly before her.

"Would this have anything to do with the paperwork you were supposedly bringing me today?"

Sarah lowered her eyes.

"Mmmm... The museum was a bit of a madhouse today. For some odd reason, the electronics kept going on the fritz."

Oh yes? The power was off... and then?"

"And then..." Matthew sighed. "I was hoping you would tell me. Because when they did a sweep of the grounds to make absolutely sure everything was okay again, they found the sapphire. Right where they caught the two remaining members of the Canvas Collective."

Sarah dropped into a chair, exhaled hard, and rested her forehead on her knees.

Pixie came to nuzzle her hands and pressed her little body close.

"So the police came," Matthew continued. "The two remaining art thieves got arrested, the sapphire is back, and all the electronics are functional again—life is good, right?"

"Looks like it," Sarah said, accepting a glass of wine from Lily.

"Sure, on the face of it," Matthew nodded. "Except... I seem to recall those two were watching us and the museum, hoping we would be... uh, bringing back the sapphire, so they could nab it again. But they were sitting outside the museum with it?"

"Well..." Sarah shrugged, took a sip, and winked at Lily. "Change of heart maybe? It happens, right?"

Matthew stood up to stretch.

"No," he finally said. "I don't think I want to know. "I'm happy Pixie is back, and the sapphire is where it belongs, and the rest—the rest is just..."

"Magic," Sarah finished with a grin. "We're not supposed to understand everything. It's just magic."

Also by Sabine

Cozy Mysteries: The Magical Papillon Mystery Series
Whispers in the Attic
The Mirror and the Matrix

Financial Thrillers: The Cannabis Preacher Series
Sermon One
Sermon Two
Sermon Three
Sermon Four
Box Set

Romance Novels (Pen Name, Sabine Keevil):
SoundMaster Romance Series:
Guitars & Cadillacs
Foolish Pride

Coming Soon

Pinch of Peril (Magical Papillon Mysteries)

Joyce AI (Financial Thrillers)

Ghost Mountain Gold (Financial Thrillers)

This Time (SoundMaster Romance)

Coming Soon

Thanks for reading! Please leave a review and watch for **Pinch of Peril,** the next Magical Papillon Mystery novel featuring Pixie.

For more fun and updates follow Pixie on TikTok, @papillon_pixie

∞

Want early access to Pinch of Peril?   Email me here to get on the list for release updates – **sabine-author@pm.me**. Or use the link below to sign up to get notifications of the release date Pixie's next adventure.

https://docs.google.com/forms/d/e/1FAIpQLSf6wLjWBuZqqJJg uR-_mtBVCHYE1UtbqxHE1uxpKWOPnlY8hA/

Scan to Sign Up

Spotify Playlists

Enjoy the following Spotify playlists with music mentioned or inspired by my novels.

Guitars & Cadillacs:

https://open.spotify.com/playlist/71ymCTx5YJPzroWBg4g WHF?si=fcf531d7a84b46cc

Foolish Pride:

https://open.spotify.com/playlist/1lR5rhB840RyeecFLvb1pG

The Cannabis Preacher:

https://open.spotify.com/playlist/4P90ZeynKOI7gyGUcVF HJE?si=484f28ffa7fb4b2a

Magical Papillon Mysteries

https://open.spotify.com/playlist/46FQGJn3T7qnAnoau63 BxU?si=379b6a6be4874ef3